OUTLAW'S PROMISE

Center Point
Large Print

Also by Ray Hogan
and available from Center Point Large Print:

The Searching Guns
The Cuchillo Plains
The Scorpion Killers

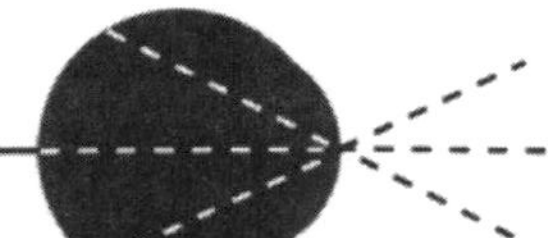

This Large Print Book carries the
Seal of Approval of N.A.V.H.

OUTLAW'S PROMISE

A Western Duo

RAY HOGAN

CENTER POINT PUBLISHING
THORNDIKE, MAINE

This Center Point Large Print edition
is published in the year 2011 by arrangement with
Golden West Literary Agency.

The text of this Large Print edition is unabridged.
In other aspects, this book may vary
from the original edition.
Printed in the United States of America
on permanent paper.
Set in 16-point Times New Roman type.

ISBN: 978-1-61173-105-7

Library of Congress Cataloging-in-Publication Data

Hogan, Ray, 1908–1998.
[Tenkiller Flats]
Outlaw's promise : a western duo / Ray Hogan.
p. cm.
ISBN 978-1-61173-105-7 (library binding : alk. paper)
1. Large type books. I. Hogan, Ray, 1908–1998 Outlaw's promise. II. Title.
PS3558.O3473T46 2011
813′.54—dc22

2011004815

TABLE OF CONTENTS

Tenkiller Flats

I

The old diamond-stack labored up the final grade, chuffing industriously, wheels clanking noisily as it belched smoke into the afternoon air. There were only two coaches, one for passengers, the other for freight, but the locomotive was worn and weary and the climb to the rim overlooking Tenkiller Flats was steep.

When they reached the summit, Dave Keegan would be able to see the settlement, Cabezon, with its collection of weathered buildings, low-roofed houses, and single, dusty street. He wondered if it had grown during the ten years he had been away, then decided such was unlikely. Towns like Cabezon changed little during the passage of time.

From the rim he would be able to see other things, too—the towering Tenkiller Mountains, lifting in shadowed majesty beyond the valley; the broad, sage green flats that flowed from them in seemingly limitless undulations; Wolf River, a bright, jagged slash cutting diagonally across the land on its way to join the Río Grande.

A hard-jawed man with quiet eyes, his features softened as he had that thought. There he had been born, had grown, attended school, and finally at fifteen, unable further to abide his father after the death of his mother, had taken his leave. But there were good memories, as well as bitter ones, and often at night as he lay near the fire in some lonely cow camp, Dave Keegan thought back over the years and wondered if he had done right.

He guessed there was no way of really knowing. He had taken to the trails; Sam Keegan had stayed to run his ranch in the manner he thought best. Therein had lain the bone of contention. Pride Seevert, owner of the vast Seven Diamond spread, had proposed a combine of ranches on the Flats—a syndicate in which he, by virtue of size and power, would be the head. Outwardly it was a voluntary organization, but those who opposed Pride and his two brothers soon found themselves under brutal persuasion.

To Dave's young mind it had appeared only a variation of peonage and he'd taken no pains to hide his opinions; Sam Keegan, however, saw it otherwise. Influenced, perhaps, by factors overlooked by Dave and possibly tired of the everlasting battle to survive in a hostile world, he had signed with Pride Seevert.

After that had come the quarrels, bitter and deep-scarring, in which Sam had reminded the boy that he was the father, Dave the son, and as such he would make the decisions concerning the future of the Lazy K. It was at the end of one of those heated conversations that Dave had climbed onto his horse and ridden off.

He had never seen his father again, or heard from him until a letter, written by Hannah

Bradford, daughter of a neighboring rancher, had caught up with him on the Mexico/New Mexico border where he was working. Hannah had informed him of his father's death. She further stated that the Lazy K was steadily going to ruin, that he should return as soon as possible and take over. Fed up with drifting, Dave had replied at once, telling Hannah he was leaving within the week and giving her the approximate date of his arrival in Cabezon.

The engine topped the rise, started down the grade for the depot. *Almost there.* Keegan stared through the streaky glass of the window, wondered what to expect. Did Pride Seevert, along with his brothers Gabe and Chancy, still rule the Flats? Were they still imposing their combine on the ranchers? And what of the Lazy K? Hannah Bradford's letter had been two months running him down—had been written four months after the death of his father. Six months was a long time for a ranch to go untended.

Regardless, it was his, and, if it had fallen into ruin, as Hannah's note indicated, he'd simply have to start and rebuild. Rebuild? With what? He had something less than $50 to his name, and he'd sold his horse and gear to raise that, but he'd make out. The Lazy K couldn't have decayed completely, and for cash he'd sell off a few head of beef. As to the Seeverts—his ideas concerning them hadn't changed; he'd run his ranch to suit himself, and, if it meant trouble, he reckoned he could handle it. He was no fifteen-year-old boy now.

He watched the building that served as a depot rush forward to meet the train. It still needed paint, he saw, probably would continue to for another ten years while the cracks in the boards widened gradually and the yellow color faded steadily to an eventual dead white.

The stationmaster waited patiently on the built-up platform, and beyond him half a dozen loafers squatted in the shade. Farther along, near the hitch rack, three riders slouched on their saddles, eyeing the approaching engine expectantly.

Dave Keegan's jaw tightened. The one in the center astride a tall white horse was Chancy Seevert, the youngest brother—the one Dave had gone to school with. Chancy was waiting for him, he realized, waiting to talk, to find out where he stood, what his intentions were.

Keegan sighed quietly, settled back on the seat as the brakes of the coach clashed, began to screech. Absently he reached for the pistol strapped to his hip, examined it briefly, allowed it to drop again into its oiled holster.

Welcome home . . . to trouble, he thought bitterly.

II

The train jolted to a halt. Dave Keegan got to his feet, walked the length of the car, and stepped out into the bright sunlight. He nodded to the stationmaster, glanced curiously at the loafers, some of whom looked vaguely familiar, and then swung his attention to the men on horses, now moving up to the platform.

Chancy had changed considerably. He had filled out, was thicker through the chest, and his shoulders had widened. He had a cigar stuck in a corner of his mouth, and, as he spoke, it bobbed up and down. Whatever it was that he said apparently was intended to be humorous, for the two cowpunchers with him laughed dutifully.

They halted at the edge of the platform. Chancy brushed back his hat and grinned broadly.

"Howdy, stranger. Heard you was comin' back. We figured you ought to have a welcomin' committee."

Keegan moved his head slightly. He hadn't given it any thought but he guessed now he should have written his reply to Hannah Bradford in a sealed envelope rather than on a postal card. Likely everyone on the Flats knew he was returning.

Chancy shifted the cigar to the opposite side of his mouth. "Just wanted you to know the deal we had with your pa'll still stand for you. Be nothin' changed."

So the Seeverts were still at it. Dave Keegan shook his head slowly. "No. The deal died with him. I'll handle my own stock."

Chancy Seevert's eyes narrowed. He ceased chewing on his weed. "Maybe," he murmured, and looked around. Then: "What's wrong with the set-up? Everybody else in the country's agreeable."

"Only because they don't want to fight you," Dave replied evenly, and paused. Behind him the train had begun to creak and groan as it again got under way.

"And you aim to," Seevert said when the racket had dwindled.

"If need be. I'm not paying the Seeverts or anybody else ten percent of my herd to market it . . . and standing trail losses and expenses, too. Cheaper to handle it myself."

Chancy shrugged. "There's been them who figured the same way, only they found out it was more expensive. A lot more."

One of the riders with Seevert laughed. Several of the loafers had risen and eased in nearer as if to hear better. The stationmaster lounged in the doorway of the depot, his expression intent.

"Be my problem," Keegan said coolly.

"And a powerful big one. What's the use of bein' mule-headed about it? Ain't nobody big enough to buck Seven Diamond."

"Don't intend to. If there's any trouble, it'll come from your outfit."

Seevert sighed audibly. "Seems you had your mind made up before you ever got here," he said dryly. "I . . ."

"Made up my mind ten years ago," Dave cut in. "Nothing's changed it . . . nothing will."

Chancy flung away his cigar. "Reckon we'll just see about that," he said, and swung off the saddle.

Keegan waited quietly. Knowing Chancy Seevert, he figured the second he stepped off the train that this moment had to come; Chancy always was one to settle things with his fists.

On the platform Seevert paused, unbuckled his gun belt, and let it fall. He waited until Dave had followed suit.

"Be a right good time to change your mind," he said.

"Not now . . . not ever," Dave said, and, taking three swift steps, drove his balled fist into Seevert's jaw.

Chancy yelled, staggered back, and sat down. One of the onlookers shouted and the two Seven Diamond cowpunchers started to climb off their horses, both scowling. Seevert waved them away and scrambled to his feet.

"I ain't needin' no help!" he rasped, and lunged at Keegan.

Dave leaped aside, smashed a blow into Chancy's ribs as he stumbled by. The momentum of it drove Seevert to his knees, but he was up instantly and wheeling. Curses rumbled from his lips and a wild light filled his eyes.

"You god-damn' saddle bum!" he raged as he surged in. "I'll break you into pieces!"

"Got to hit him first!" someone in the crowd yelled.

Chancy seemed not to hear. Bent low, he moved toward Dave, thick arms poised. Abruptly Keegan rushed. His churning fists met Seevert head on. There were half a dozen dry slapping sounds as they made contact. Chancy stalled, fell back. Dave bore in relentlessly, arms working like pistons. Seevert went to his knees.

From the corner of an eye Keegan saw the two cowpunchers coming onto the platform. He pulled back, prepared to meet attack from that quarter.

"Now, you boys just hold on," a dry, cracked voice sounded above the gusty breathing of Chancy Seevert. "Reckon this here shindig's betwixt them two. Let's keep it that way."

Dave cast a glance over his shoulder. It was one of the loafers—a tall, hawk-faced old man who looked familiar. Weems—Pete Weems. Recognition came to Dave in a flash. Weems owned, or had owned, a ranch to the west of the Lazy K. He had stepped in when the two Seven Diamond men had made their move, snatched up Keegan's pistol, was now pointing it carelessly in the direction of the pair. Keegan gave the old rancher a tight grin, brought his attention back to Seevert.

Chancy was upright but his eyes no longer held a brightness. His mouth hung open. He shook his head, shuffled forward. Dave eyed the man narrowly. Seevert was cunning; he appeared to be out on his feet but it could be a trick. Keegan retreated a step, another, keeping his guard up. Suddenly Chancy yelled and lunged. Dave, half expecting it, was still taken unexpectedly.

Pain flared through him as Seevert landed two solid blows to his head, followed with a third to the belly. One of the cowpunchers shouted his encouragement. Chancy pressed his advantage, nailed Dave cleanly with another sharp blow to the ear. Keegan went to one knee, fighting to throw off the haze that was closing in.

He got back to his feet, lashed out blindly. His arm blocked the roundhouse swing Seevert had loosed and gave him another moment's respite. He moved off, back-pedaling slowly while his mind cleared. Suddenly Chancy was before him again, head low, crushed, bleeding lips split into a grin.

Keegan feinted, spun, and came in fast from the side. Seevert, off balance, tried to wheel. Dave caught him with a left to the belly, a right that crackled when it connected with the man's jaw. Chancy yelled, threw himself forward, and caught Keegan around the waist.

Locked together, they began to wrestle about on

the platform, Dave hammering at Chancy's head and shoulders with his free hand while the squat rider struggled to tighten his grip around Keegan's waist. And then suddenly they were on the edge and going over.

Chancy was on the bottom, so took the brunt of the three-foot drop. The throttling hand around Dave loosened. He wrenched free and bounded to his feet, dragging deeply for wind. Seevert was up almost as quickly, that fixed grin still on his face. He rushed in, anxious to finish the fight.

Keegan set himself squarely, brought a right from his heels. The blow met Chancy straight on, popped like a whip when it landed. Seevert halted in his tracks. His arms fell. He stared at Dave through wide, glazed eyes, and then dropped heavily into the dust.

Cheers went up from the platform. Dave stepped back, still heaving for breath. A hand clapped him on the shoulder and Pete Weems's voice shouted in his ear.

"Boy . . . you done it! Town's been waitin' years to see this!"

Keegan nodded woodenly. His body ached and there were places on his face where Chancy's knuckles had removed the skin and set up a sharp stinging. After a moment he turned away. Weems dropped off the platform, thrust his belt and gun into his hands.

"Expect you ought to be strappin' this on,

Dave," the old cowman said. He paused, lifted his brows. "You are Sam Keegan's boy, ain't you?"

Dave nodded, buckled on his weapon.

"Figured as much from what was bein' said. You're back to take over your pa's place, I'm guessin'."

Again Keegan nodded. "That's what this was all about."

"Way I understood it. Just wanted to be sure."

The two Seven Diamond cowpunchers moved up, looked questioningly at Dave, and then at Chancy, still flat on the ground. Keegan nodded curtly, reached back onto the platform, and retrieved his hat.

"You'll be needin' some help. I'm askin' for a job right now."

Dave frowned, glanced at the older man. "What about your own place?"

"Ain't mine no more," Weems said, his lips pulling tight. "Got euchred outta it by the Seeverts . . . same as a lot of other folks did. Am I hired?"

"We'll talk about it later," Keegan replied. "Right now I need a drink . . . bad."

The two cowpunchers had Chancy on his feet, but he was still out. The taller of the pair paused, faced Dave.

"You're goin' to be needin' more'n a drink, once he comes to," he said in a promising voice.

Dave shrugged, pointed to the Fan-Tan saloon down the street.

"That's where he'll find me," he said, and, trailed by Pete Weems, moved off through the ankle-deep dust.

III

Simmering, Dave Keegan allowed his glance to swing from side to side as he strode toward the saloon. Weems said something but he did not hear; he was seeing the town just as it had been ten years ago. The Gem Café, Cabezon Bank & Trust Co., Dollarhide's Hotel, Herman's Livery Stable, R. Raskob, General Merchandise, Miss Pringle's Ladies Shop. Nothing had changed. Cabezon had stagnated under the rule of Pride Seevert and his brothers—and those who lived there were aware of it. But they would do nothing about it just as surely as they would resent his return, for they knew he would never accept the Seven Diamond yoke, and that meant trouble. But it would be his problem, not theirs, and he would keep it so.

They reached the Fan-Tan and turned into the open doorway. The place was cool, shadowy, and almost deserted. Dave crossed to a table in the back corner, sat down, facing the street, and signaled to the bartender for a bottle and glasses. Pete Weems, mopping at the sweat on his beet-red cheeks, dropped into the chair at Keegan's left.

"From the looks some of them folks was givin' us, I'd reckon you ain't goin' to be real popular here on the Flats."

"Had the feeling myself," Dave replied, filling the glasses. After a moment he added: "Guess I expected it."

The old rancher downed his liquor in a single gulp and blinked. "You right sure it's worth it . . . takin' on the Seeverts, I mean?"

"I didn't come here just to fight Pride and the others. I came back to run my ranch."

Weems nodded slowly. "The two go together . . . unless you do it Pride's way."

Dave started to speak, then paused, eyes on the street. The two Seven Diamond riders, with Chancy Seevert between them, were passing in front of the doorway. None of the three glanced toward the saloon; they simply continued on down the street.

Pete Weems grinned, rubbed at the stubble on his chin. " 'Pears Chancy's had enough for one day."

Keegan smiled briefly, sipped at his drink. "You see much of my pa before he died?"

"Two, maybe three times a year. Mostly while I still had my place. Toward the last he just sort of give up, let Pride and his bunch do what they liked." Weems hesitated, then added: "You ain't goin' to find much left of the ranch, son. Went to hell mighty fast."

"The Seeverts?"

"Well, maybe partly. Sam just sort of quit, like I said. Didn't take no interest in anythin'."

"Any stock left?"

"Not that I know of. You'll have to build up a herd from scratch."

"Be hard to do unless I can get the bank to go along with me."

Weems wagged his head. "Don't go pinnin' much hope on Tom Gower. He's Pride's man."

"Who isn't?" Dave said with a short laugh.

The rancher looked down at his glass, began to twirl it between his fingers. "Me . . . for one. And Herman Gooch at the livery stable. Maybe a couple more."

"Cass Bradford . . . where does he stand? Was his little girl who wrote me about Pa."

"With the others. Ain't much else a man can do unless he's honin' for a right smart of trouble. Man has to think about his family, but I always had a feelin' Cass'd kick over the traces was ever he to get a chance." Pete checked his words, cocked his head to one side. "And that little girl you're talking about . . . she ain't no girl no longer, she's quite a woman. You forgettin' she's growed some in ten years?"

He had, Dave realized with a start. Hannah Bradford would be twenty or so—and he was still picturing her in his mind as a spindly little kid with pigtails and freckles across her nose.

"Pretty as a moonflower, too," Weems went on. "Got most of the young bucks around here gettin' their hair cut regular like. Even Chancy Seevert."

"He have any luck?"

"Not with her. She's a spunky one. He tried shining up to her for a spell, finally give up." Pete chuckled. "One time the Seevert name didn't mean nothin'. You say it was her that wrote you?"

Dave nodded, refilled the glasses. "Reckon I'd better drop by and pay my respects, first chance I get. Anybody new on the Flats?"

"Folks don't ever move in here . . . they move out. Little man ain't got a chance under Seevert's deal. Goes broke quick."

"That what happened to you?"

"Along with the hard winter we had in 'Seventy-Eight. Never did have much of a herd, as you'll recollect, and what with payin' the Seeverts ten percent and what I lost in the freeze, I was down to nothin'. I'd 'a' made it, howsomever, if it hadn't been for that ten percent."

"You just walk off?"

"Sold out to Pride. Was real generous to me. Give me about ten cents on the dollar for my holdin's. Knew I was in a squeeze with the bank breathin' down my neck, and that I'd take whatever he offered. Always will believe he went to Tom Gower and found out how much I owed, then made that his price."

That would be the way Pride Seevert would handle it, Dave thought. There had been a time, when old Horace Seevert was alive, that Seven Diamond stood for honesty and fairness. All changed when Pride, eldest of the three sons, took over. The freshly turned earth was scarcely dry on his father's grave when Pride had called a meeting of all ranchers on the Flats and served up what amounted to little less than an ultimatum. Matters had not been the same since, and Pride, using his brothers Gabe and Chancy as iron-fisted persuaders, was still riding high.

Dave stared with unseeing eyes through the doorway. What chance did he have against the Seeverts? Broke, inheritor of a neglected, run-down ranch, and with the hand of almost everyone on the Flats turned against him—how could he hope to survive? He didn't know the answer to that but he knew he must—somehow. A man had a right to what was his, along with the privilege of living his life as he saw fit—and that all added up to running the Lazy K according to his own ideas. And that's what he intended to do, or at least attempt to do. If he didn't at least try, he knew he'd never be able to live with himself.

"About that there job . . . ?"

Dave roused at the gentle prodding of Pete Weems.

"You never give me no answer. Am I hired?"

"You are," Keegan said, pushing back his chair. "We're going to work right now."

The old cowpuncher grinned broadly. "Sounds mighty good to me. What's first off?"

Dave rose, dug into his pocket for a coin to pay for the drinks, and dropped it on the table.

"Have a talk with Gower at the bank, see if I've got any credit there."

"Can give you the answer to that right now," Weems said morosely. "Tom ain't doin' nothin' that'll cross him up with the Seeverts."

"Want him to tell me that," Keegan said, starting for the door. "If that's the how of it, then we'll figure something else. One way or another we're putting the Lazy K back on its feet."

IV

Tom Gower was sitting at his huge roll-top desk when they entered the bank. He was alone except for the teller behind his wire cage, and the expression on his lean features was guarded as he looked up.

"How are you, Keegan?"

"Good," Dave replied, and came right to the point. "You interested in my business?"

Gower toyed with a paper-cluttered spindle. "Be glad to have your account, of course. You want to make a deposit now?"

"Not what I had in mind. Was thinking of a loan. Intend to start working my ranch . . . will be needing a little cash to buy cattle with."

Gower shook his head slowly. "Times are a bit hard. . . ."

"I'm willing to put up the property and the cattle as security. Not much of a risk for you."

"Realize that . . . but money's tight. I'm having to watch our loans. . . ."

Anger pushed through Dave Keegan. He took a half step forward. "Why don't you lay it on the line? What you mean is that Pride Seevert wouldn't like it."

The banker's face darkened. "I run this place," he said stiffly. "I decide who . . ."

"You decide . . . as long as it's all right with him!"

"Not the way of it . . ."

"Forget it! Don't even bother to talk it over with him. I'll make other arrangements."

Dave spun about, shouldering up against Pete Weems, who had been standing behind him, and came to a full stop. The squat figure of Dewey Dalton, owner of one of the larger ranches on the Flats, came through the doorway. Dalton halted, staring at Dave.

"Keegan!" he said in a surprised voice. "Heard you were coming back . . . hoped it wasn't so. You ain't changed much in looks . . . how about otherwise?"

Again anger burned through Dave. "If you mean Pride Seevert, there's no change there, either."

"You aim to take over your pa's place, start ranchin'?"

"It's my place now," Keegan said quietly, "and I intend to rebuild it and run it my way."

Dalton's eyes squinted. "And to hell with everybody else, that it? Country's a powder keg now, just waiting for somebody to strike a spark. That could be you."

"Then the smart thing for you to do is pass the word to the Seeverts to leave me alone."

"Which they won't . . . you know damned well!" Dalton shouted. "All right. When Pride starts clamping down, don't come running to the rest of us for help. Maybe we don't exactly like the way things go, but we've got sense enough to ride along when we've got no other choice."

Keegan shifted his shoulders. "Just another way of admitting Pride Seevert's got you by the throat and you don't have guts enough to shake him off."

Pete Weems laughed softly.

Dalton flushed. "We're doing all right," he murmured defensively. "Making a little money, and having no trouble. Smarten up, Keegan. String along with the rest of us. Things'll change."

"Seems they haven't in the last ten years. Way it looks, they won't in the next ten."

"And you figure you can do something about that."

"Not even going to try, far as you and the rest are concerned. I'm just aiming to run the Lazy K to suit myself."

Abruptly Dave moved forward, pushed by Dalton, and returned to the street. Pete Weems was chuckling at his shoulder.

"You sure hit old Dewey where it hurt," he said, and then suddenly he was sober. "You got yourself an idea now how the rest of the ranchers'll be feelin' about it. They just plain won't want you around. You're pickin' a hard row to hoe."

Dave grinned at the old cowman. "If you think that, why're you so anxious to line up with me?"

Weems scratched at his chin, laughed. "Well, now, I ain't right sure, but I reckon I seen Pride Seevert's comeuppance standin' there on the depot platform beatin' the hell out of Chancy and figured I wanted to be in on it."

"Pride's not going to think it's funny. And he plays for keeps."

"So what? I ain't a-scared of bullets. Way I feel I could die happy was I to see him crawlin' around, eatin' dirt. What's next?"

"Raskob. We'll be needing supplies."

Weems spat. "Wastin' your time again. You'll get the same runaround Tom Gower handed you."

"There another general store in town?"

"Nope."

"Then we'll have to try Raskob," Dave said, and stepped off the boardwalk into the street.

They crossed, mounted the two steps to the porch, and entered the low-roofed building. The thin, spare figure of the merchant, wearing an apron and a green eye shade, emerged from a room off the back, halted. Keegan, trailed by Weems, threaded his way through the piles of harness, tables of house wares, and racks of clothing, and pulled up at the counter. Raskob greeted him warily.

"You want my trade?" Dave asked bluntly.

The merchant's eyes flickered briefly, and then he shrugged. "You know the situation around here. Ought to answer that for you."

"In other words, if I'm a friend of the Seeverts, you're interested."

"But you're not. I seen that little fracas down at the depot. No use claiming . . ."

"Don't intend to. Point is . . . you willing to sell me what I need or not? Say it straight out."

"I . . . I can't, Keegan. You've got to see my . . ."

"All I wanted to know," Dave said, and, holding tightly to his temper, wheeled and moved back through the clutter of merchandise to the street.

Almost immediately a voice from down the way hailed him. "Dave Keegan . . . it iss you, eh? Sam's boy, eh?"

"It's Dutch . . . Herman Gooch," Weems said.

Dave nodded. He remembered the livery stable owner. He lifted his hand in salutation, headed for the sprawling structure.

Gooch, a ponderous man with a moon-like face, gave him a firm handclasp, slapped him on the shoulder. "It iss good you have come back. A man you are now."

"Good to see you again," Dave said.

The stableman sank back into his chair, leaned against the wall. "You move onto the old place, yes?"

"What I figure to do. Outside of Pete here, I'm not getting much encouragement, however. Seems I'm plenty unpopular. Talking to me's not going to do you any good, Dutch."

Gooch's round face sobered. He wagged his head dolefully. "It iss sad. I come to this country because it has no kings, no barons who can say if you live or die. America iss a free land, I tell myself. There I should be. Now it iss here. It follows me. It should not be so."

"Outside of Pete, you're the only one feeling that way."

Gooch shifted his massive bulk. "They are fools. They do not understand what it iss to be a free man. Slavery they do not believe in, yet they give it roots to grow. It iss like a disease . . . will grow . . . spread, and soon it cannot be stopped. I tell them this . . . Gower, Dollarhide, Raskob, but they will not believe."

"Ain't the only ones," Pete Weems said. "Dutch, Dave's needin' help to get started on his pa's place. You reckon you could do him any good?"

"What I can do, I will. You only ask, boy."

Keegan shook his head. Herman Gooch was a businessman and he could suffer for his actions. "Don't want to get you in trouble with the Seeverts and some of the others around."

Gooch shook a fat finger at him. "You leave the Seeverts to me. And the others. Before you were born, I learn to deal with their kind in the old country. What will you need?"

Keegan studied the man, smiled. "You're not afraid of getting hurt?"

"I am too old for fear. And always there iss a way to skin cats, even the mean ones. What do you want?"

"Horses and tack for Pete and me . . . for one thing. Don't know for certain what's left at the ranch. Have to take a look, make out a list."

"Grub," Weems said.

Herman Gooch bobbed his head. "It iss easy. Horses and tools I can give you from here. Grub I will buy from Raskob. He will sell to me even though he knows it iss for you."

"They're all scared, Dutch. Can't blame him too much."

"Such makes no difference. A man cannot be a rabbit. A man must fight for what iss right, or soon he will have no rights." Gooch paused, motioned to Weems. "Pete . . . the horses in the back corral. Pick what iss needed. Saddles and bridles you will find in the harness shed."

The old cowman nodded, moved off into the stable.

Dave said: "I'll have to ask you for credit, Dutch. Soon as I get things going, I'll pay you. . . ."

"Pay! What iss pay? Sam was to me a kind friend. This much I owe him, and more."

"I've got a few dollars. I can take care of the stuff you get from Raskob."

"The few dollars you will keep for other things. Someday, when all goes well for you at your ranch, we will make a settlement."

"I don't like . . ."

"What iss it you don't like . . . that I would be a good friend to the son of my good friend, Sam? There iss no need for more talk of it. All is arranged. Understood?"

"Understood," Dave said slowly. "And thanks. Means a lot to me."

Gooch waved off the expression of appreciation. "You ride to the ranch today?"

"Soon as we can saddle up."

"Good. Bring your list to me and all the rest I will do." The stableman thrust forth his hand. "Good luck, boy."

"Thanks again," Keegan replied. "Expect I'll be needing it."

V

Half an hour later Keegan was on the road leading west from Cabezon. He was alone. Pete Weems had decided to take that opportunity for dropping by the cabin where he had set up residence and pick up his belongings. He was to rejoin Dave later at the Lazy K.

The morning sun was at his back and it felt good to be in the saddle again, to have a horse under him. Weems had chosen a tough little buckskin gelding for him, one not much for looks but barrel-chested and sturdy and built for hard work. Mentally he again thanked Dutch Gooch for his help and hoped it would not lead to trouble for the stableman.

A short distance from the settlement the road forked, the trail to the left continuing westward, the other angling toward the towering crags of Tenkiller Mountain and the ranches that lay against it. Here, for a brief expanse, was a narrow strip of country commonly called the Roughs. Its rocky, sandy soil supported little other than snakeweed and small desert flowers that managed to grow despite adverse conditions. Now, as in the past, Keegan hastened to cross this intervening slice of wasteland that separated the lower flats from the mountain lushness, and soon was loping into the more desirable area of trees and grass-covered ground. Things looked good. It must have been a fine spring, he thought, and hoped he would find the Lazy K range in equally excellent condition.

He reached Wolf River with its wild cherry and plum-lined banks, forded the knee-deep stream while a hundred memories of the past—of the times he had swum in the icy water, hunted cottontails in the brush, picked fruit and berries—crowded into his mind. Those were the good days before the Seeverts had risen to heights of ruthless power; he wondered if it would ever change, if the Flats could ever be as they had been.

He followed the banks of the river, keeping to a well-marked trail running close to the water's edge, and thus avoided the road. He had no particular reason for taking such measures other than it was cool and pleasant along the Wolf and it made him think of the days when he was growing up.

The slopes of Tenkiller began to take substance as he drew nearer, and he could make out the long cañons filled with brush and rock, the higher ledges and hogbacks that linked the peaks. Far to the right he could see the Flats proper, looking like a gray-green sea with their coverlet of grass.

He came to the point where the river entered the eastern boundary of Dewey Dalton's spread and he paused there. He was in no mood to encounter the squat, hard-talking rancher again, and considered the advisability of swinging away from the stream. But Dalton likely was still in Cabezon and after a few moments Keegan rode on, keeping to the banks of the Wolf.

He crossed Double-D range without interruption and shortly was riding into Box C territory, owned by Ed Corrigan—or at least it had been Corrigan's ten years ago. Almost immediately he saw two horsemen break out of timber half a mile to his left and lope toward him. Dave pushed on, having no reason to fear interception; Ed Corrigan had been a friend of his father's and there was no cause to be disturbed.

He watched the two men halt, wait for him at a bend in the trail. One was a stranger of about his own age; the other, much older, he recognized from the past. The younger man rode forward to meet him, his face hard and set under his broad-brimmed hat.

"Mister, you know where you are?" he demanded.

Keegan pulled the buckskin to a stop, smiled amiably. "Reckon I do."

"This here's Box C range. Didn't you see the markers when you come to them?"

Dave looked beyond the cowpuncher to his companion. The older man was studying him thoughtfully.

"I saw them," Keegan said. "Fact is, I helped put them there."

"Well, Mister Corrigan don't care much for drifters traipsin' across his land, so I . . . ," the rider said, and then caught at his words. He frowned, started to say more but the older man spoke first.

"Say . . . you wouldn't be Sam Keegan's boy . . . ?"

Dave grinned. "I would. And you're Asa Bowersox. I remember you now."

The old rider's mouth broke into a crooked smile. He kneed his horse forward, shook Dave's hand.

"Right glad to see you again. What're you doin' around here . . . passin' through?"

Keegan glanced at the young cowpuncher, scowling in quiet suspicion. Bowersox nodded.

"That's Billy Joe Hinkle . . . we call him Primo. Primo, meet Dave Keegan. His pa's place's over there t'other side of the short hills."

Hinkle took Dave's hand soberly. His eyes had brightened with narrow interest, but he said nothing.

"You just ridin' through?" Asa asked once more.

"No, figure to start up the Lazy K, get it going again."

Bowersox looked down. "Fear you won't find much left."

"Been hearing that. Doesn't matter. Land's still there, and that's what counts."

"Mister Corrigan know about this?" Billy Joe asked suddenly.

Temper moved through Keegan. He faced the cowpuncher. "Some reason he should?"

Asa Bowersox bridged the abrupt quiet. "Primo don't mean nothin'. Just takes his job real serious like. Your ranch . . . reckon you can do what you want with it."

"Intend to," Dave said bluntly. He shifted his attention to Bowersox. "If you're up my way, drop in. Be glad to see you."

"I'll do that," the old cowpuncher said. "*Adiós*."

"*Adiós*," Keegan answered, and rode on.

A short time later he reached the end of Box C range and entered his own range. Following the trail across a flat meadow, he climbed a small rise, dropped again to level ground. There he halted, his eyes on the almost obscured road that he and his father, by dint of much sweat and back-breaking toil, had hacked through the brush. The ruts had filled with grass but their course was still evident; the rocks they had rolled aside, the trees they had felled—all were still apparent. He studied it all briefly, having his moments of recollection, and then moved on, anxious now for a glimpse of the house itself.

He entered the clearing and pulled up. The building was before him—old and sagging, its windows gaping, empty eyes. The porch had collapsed at one end, the slanting roof providing a playground for two striped ground squirrels that scurried off at his appearance. The well house had been toppled, and fire had all but consumed the shed where he had once stabled, in favored, solitary majesty, his first pony. The remaining outbuildings were graying shells, some upright, some canted drunkenly, others simply prone. The Lazy K had not died six months ago when Sam Keegan passed on; it appeared to have been dead for years.

Heavy with despair, Dave rode in closer, halted at the remains of the hitch rack. It was worse than he had expected; he had spoken of rebuilding—there was little to rebuild from other than the land itself. But he could make out—he would. He'd begin . . .

The sudden, sharp *crack* of a rifle, the dull *thunk* of a bullet smashing into the wooden planks of the wall beyond him, scattered Dave Keegan's thoughts. Instinctively he went off the saddle in a long dive, plunged through the open doorway into the house.

The rifle slapped again. Dust spurted at Keegan's heels. He dragged out his pistol, crawled to a window, and peered over the sill. There was no one in sight. Cocking the .45, he waited for the next shot, hoping for a smoke puff that would allow him to target the marksman in ambush.

There was only the hot silence, and then, faintly, he heard the rapid tattoo of a horse beating a retreat eastward. Whoever had thrown the shots at him was pulling out.

Dave rose slowly, slid his pistol back into its holster. The meaning of the incident was clear; the rifleman had not meant to hit him—only to warn. In strong language he had been told to forget the Lazy K, to move on.

Grim-faced, Keegan moved back into the open. It would have been one of Pride Seevert's men looking down that rifle barrel at him. Or would it? Seevert, ordinarily, was not the kind to serve warnings. Then who? He shook off the question angrily. It didn't matter. Nobody was going to drive him off his ranch.

VI

He began work at once. The rails of the corral were down, and, after picketing the buckskin nearby, he rummaged around until he located a few tools and with those he set to putting the kitchen and one room of the house in passable order. Such would afford temporary shelter for him and Pete Weems; later, when funds and time permitted, he would build a new house.

He had just finished with the second of the slat bunks when Weems rode into the yard and dismounted. The old cowman looked around slowly, shook his head.

"Sure in bad shape. Worse'n I figured."

"It'll do," Dave replied. "We'll have a place to sleep and a stove to cook on. Improvements'll come later." He reached into his shirt pocket, drew forth a slip of paper. "Here's the list for Gooch. Been making it as I went along."

Pete studied the items, whistled softly. "Powerful lot of stuff."

Keegan nodded. "We won't have time to go running into town every few days. Expect that to hold us for a month or so."

"Sure ought to. You want me to take it to Dutch now?"

"Hate to ask you to make that ride again, but I guess you'll have to. We'll be needing grub for supper tonight."

"Don't mind," Weems said, tossing his bundle of spare clothing onto one of the bunks. " 'Spect I can make it back by dark."

Dave said: "Be fine." He pointed at the pistol on the cowman's hip. "Keep that handy. Had me a visitor right after I got here."

Weems frowned. "Somebody shootin' at you?"

"Twice. From the brush."

"You get a look at whoever it was?"

"No. He pulled out without showing himself."

Weems swore deeply. "The Seeverts. Had to be them."

"Maybe. Could've been somebody from town . . . or one of the ranchers wanting me to keep moving so's I wouldn't stir up any trouble. Doesn't matter."

"Not scarin' you off any, eh?"

"Take more'n that."

Pete grinned. "Good. They want a scrap, we'll give it to 'em," he said, and turned for his horse. "Be a right smart idea for you to keep your eyes peeled, too."

"Aim to do that," Dave said, and watched the man ride out of the yard.

By the middle of the afternoon he had accomplished all he could until the supplies arrived and, needing a drink to quench his thirst, crossed to the well. He found the pulley broken and the bucket shot full of bullet holes, but a rock dropped into the shaft told him water was still available.

He walked then to a small spring 100 yards or so below the yard, satisfied his needs, mentally noting that he and Weems would have to use that source until the well was put back in shape.

After that he visited the small hill where his mother was buried, found the townspeople had also placed his father there. He spent a little time replacing the rocks that had washed aside and cleaning up the weeds, then returned finally to the house to await Pete Weems's arrival. He hadn't noticed it earlier but he was beginning to feel hunger.

Shortly after dark he heard the *thud* of horses' hoofs and the grate of iron tires cutting into the soil. He rose quickly from his bunk and, hand resting on the butt of his pistol, moved to the window where he could have a full view of the yard. A minute later Herman Gooch, driving a spring wagon, with Weems on the seat beside him, came into view. Keegan relaxed, stepped out into the yard.

The livery stable owner drew to a stop in front of the door.

Pete stood up. "Was so much stuff Dutch figured he'd better haul it in a wagon," he explained, climbing down.

Gooch smiled widely. "Also, I want to see your place. I have not been this far from town in many years. A man gets old and fat." He paused, glanced around. "It iss a big job you have here."

Dave shrugged. "You run into any trouble?"

Gooch said: "No . . . no trouble. With Raskob business iss business so long as his nose is kept clean."

Pete, already beginning to unload, said: "I didn't see nobody neither."

Keegan moved up to help the old cowman. Gooch crawled off the wagon, grunting and groaning at the effort. Sitting down on the edge of the porch, he mopped at his face.

"Weems has told me of the shooting. He did not come again?"

"Just that one time. Guess they're giving me time to think it over."

"But you do not change, eh? Good . . . good."

He watched in silence after that while the two

men transferred the load of supplies into the house and alongside, and then rose to take his leave. Keegan waved him back.

"Stay for a bite of supper. Won't be much but it'll keep you going until you can get to town."

Gooch agreed readily and all moved into the kitchen. Together Dave and Pete Weems prepared a meal of fried potatoes, meat, cornbread, and coffee. For dessert they opened a can of peaches. Finished, they went back into the coolness of the yard, and, using some of the wooden boxes the supplies had come in as chairs, they settled back for a smoke.

"Expect it was you who looked after Pa when he died," Dave said after a few moments had passed. "Want to thank you for it."

"Was several of us," the stableman said. "Bradford, Ed Corrigan, Pete . . . even Raskob. We put Sam next to his wife. We think he would want it so."

"Where he should be. I'll thank the others, too. If there was any expense . . ."

"There was nothing," Dutch cut in. He stared at the glowing coal in his curved-stem pipe. "You have made a start here. Now what will you do for cattle?"

"Thought I'd talk to Cass Bradford, see if he'd sell me enough to start a herd. Always was friendly enough."

Gooch nodded slowly. "Bradford iss a fine man,

but help you I am not sure. He iss obligated to the bank . . . to Tom Gower. And Gower . . ."

"He's under Pride Seevert's thumb," Pete Weems completed. "Reckon Cass'd like to help but he won't take no chances."

"Means I'll take a ride to Junction City then, have a talk with the banker up there. Figure this place ought to be good enough for a small loan."

Keegan looked questioningly at the stableman, seeking verification. Gooch bobbed his head.

"It iss so . . . and, if recommendation by me iss needed, I will give it. You tell the banker."

"Be obliged," Keegan said. "But already you have done too much."

"Too much!" Gooch echoed, pulling himself laboriously to his feet. "It iss very little compared to what you have in mind to do. Now I must go."

Dave and Weems followed the man to his wagon, aided him to the seat. When he had settled his ponderous bulk, he took up the reins and looked down at Keegan.

"There will be things you forgot. Send for them. And for the meal, you have my thanks."

"You have mine," Keegan said as Gooch wheeled the vehicle about and cut back to the road. "So long."

"So long," the stable owner called back, waving his thick hand.

Keegan and Weems returned to the kitchen,

untouched after the meal. Pete began to stack the tin plates.

"Let it go till morning," Dave said, reaching for the lantern. "We both need a night's sleep."

Weems signified his agreement, followed Dave into the room where bunks had been constructed. "Was just thinkin', we're goin' to be right busy, you and me. Be a good idea was we to get us a cook."

Keegan kicked off his boots, lay back on his blankets. "Have to raise some money before we can do much of anything . . . much less hire help."

"Feller I'm thinkin' about won't need no wages. Be glad to work for found and keep."

"Kind of hands we're needing," Keegan muttered. "We'll talk about it in the morning."

His eyes were heavy and his muscles ached from the unaccustomed labor. He was too beat even to undress. Vaguely he heard Weems stirring about, and then it was dark as the lantern was turned down. Pete said something but Dave only half heard.

In the next moment he was sitting on the edge of the bunk. Daylight brightened the room and he realized what had seemed but short minutes actually were hours during which he had slept soundly. Weems, snoring gently, had not awakened.

Dave frowned. What had roused him? A noise—a sound of some sort? Tension suddenly building within him, he slipped quietly from the bunk and made his way to the window in the next room. Keeping well back, he peered through the glassless opening.

Chancy Seevert, flanked by half a dozen Seven Diamond riders, was pulling to a halt in the yard.

VII

Dave wheeled instantly, silently returned to his bunk. Pulling on his boots and strapping on his gun, he shook Weems roughly. The old cowman rolled over.

"On your feet," Keegan said in a hoarse whisper.

Pete sat up, rubbed at his jaw. "What's wrong?"

"Chancy . . . and a bunch of his hardcases. Out front."

Weems was on his feet instantly, pulling on his clothing.

From the yard Seevert's harsh voice issued a summons. "Keegan . . . come out here!"

"Probably figures I'm alone," Dave said hurriedly. "Take your rifle . . . go out the back . . . but don't let them see you. I'll signal if I need help."

"Keegan! You hear me?"

Dave turned, crossed the room, and stepped lazily into the open. A hard grin cracked Chancy Seevert's lips.

"Well, now . . . here's our squatter, boys. Reckon we got him outta bed."

The rider beside him laughed. "Looks like he's gone and fixed hisself a reg'lar roost in that there shack."

"And all for nothin'," another said.

Keegan leaned against the wall of the house. Folding his arms, he studied Seevert coldly. "What's on your mind?"

"You," Chancy replied bluntly. "Ain't very smart, comin' out here. Thought I made that plain yesterday."

"Other way around. Was me made it clear I intended to do what I want. One look at you proves it."

Chancy's swollen and skinned face darkened. He shifted his weight, glared angrily.

"And taking potshots at me's not going to work, either."

Seevert frowned. "What's that mean?"

"That bushwhacker you sent out here yesterday to scare me off. . . ."

"You're loco . . . I never sent nobody."

Chancy was genuinely surprised. Evidently it had been someone from town, or perhaps a rancher hoping to head off trouble.

"Doesn't matter. Point is you and your friends might as well get it straight . . . I'm here to stay."

"You are like hell! You ain't stayin' unless you

line up with the rest of the Flats. We're runnin' things around here, Keegan."

Dave smiled quietly. "Not me . . . not the Lazy K, you're not," he said, deliberately baiting the man.

Seevert's eyes narrowed as his flush mounted. "You're sure askin' for it, mister. I rode over here this mornin', friendly like, to give you another chance. But if you think I'm goin' to let you smart-mouth me . . ."

"I'm just telling you what's what. I'm having nothing to do with the Seeverts."

"We'll see about that!" Chancy yelled, and piled off his horse. "When I get through with you, you'll be wishin' you'd never even heard of this country. Couple of you boys . . . grab him, hold him for me!"

Dave stepped quickly off the porch into the yard as the riders next to Chancy dropped to the ground, began to move in.

"You ever try doing something without help?" Keegan asked acidly.

Chancy grinned. "Nice thing about bein' the top dog. Can do things the easy way."

"Could be you've got a little mush in your backbone, too," Keegan said, and then turning his head, called: "All right, Pete . . . let 'em know where you are!"

The loud *click* of a Winchester's being levered broke through the hush. The two men siding

Chancy froze. Weems stepped from behind a clump of brush at the side of the house, rifle leveled.

"Reckon we'll keep this argument same as it was yesterday . . . just between them two," the old cowman said. "I'm servin' notice right now . . . first one of you that tries to take a hand gets a bullet in his belly."

Keegan beckoned to Seevert. "You were in a big hurry a minute ago. Come on . . . let's get on with it."

Chancy did not move. He glanced at Weems, then at the men behind him. He shook his head. "You ain't gettin' away with this!" he yelled suddenly. "You ain't pushin' me around . . . !"

Keegan lunged forward, grabbed Seevert by the shirt front. Swinging him half about, he slapped the man smartly across the face.

"You god-damn' four-flusher . . . I do what I please on my own place!" he shouted, abruptly angry. "You tell that to Pride and Gabe . . . and anybody else that's interested!"

Shoving hard, he sent Seevert stumbling back to his horse.

"Now get on that saddle and pull out! I ever see you or any Seven Diamond man on my property again, I'll start shooting. Hear?"

Chancy, off balance and clinging to his horse, managed to recover his feet. Without looking up, he slid his foot into the stirrup and swung aboard.

Face tipped down, he wheeled about and started for the road. Silently the others filed in behind him.

Pistol in hand, Dave watched them leave. He heard Pete Weems move up to stand beside him. The old cowman was chuckling in a low, throaty rumble. But there was no humor in the moment for Keegan. All the bars were down now and the matter was far from being finished.

"Made him eat dirt . . . that you sure did," Weems murmured. "Was a sight for sore eyes."

Chancy and his men had halted at the edge of the yard. Dave, alert, took a step forward, gun half lifted. Seevert stared, shook his head, and rode on.

"They've always been the ones to play rough," Pete continued. "Now, buckin' up against somebody that hands it right back sure has stopped old Chancy cold. He jus' don't know how to figure it."

Dave Keegan's attention was still on the brush beyond which the Seven Diamond men had disappeared. After a moment he heard the steady drum of running horses, knew they had gone on. Only then did he holster his weapon.

"Let's get something to eat," he said, turning for the door. "Then I'm taking a run over to Bradford about some stock. Got a chore for you while I'm gone."

Weems let off the hammer of his rifle. "What's that?"

"Want you to string a wire through the brush around the yard, knee high or so. Then hang some tin cans on it. Anybody tries sneaking in on us, we'll know it."

"Mostly Chancy . . . I take it."

"Chancy . . . and maybe whoever it was that took those shots at me yesterday."

VIII

An hour later Dave Keegan was on the buckskin and moving north through the fetlock-deep grass of his upper range. His final words to Pete Weems had been to keep an eye open for trouble and not to attempt a defense should the Seeverts return; if they came, they'd come in numbers, and one man would have no chance against them.

"Reckon you're the one that'd better do some watchin'," the old cowman had countered. "Chancy ain't goin' to draw a long breath till he's squared up for what you done to him this mornin'."

There was no doubt in the truth of that statement. "I'll keep a sharp look-out," he had assured Pete. "You do the same."

Keegan felt it was unlikely, however, that they would see any more of Seven Diamond that day. There would be repercussions. He wasn't fooling himself on that—he had been fully aware of the possibilities when he roughed up Chancy. But it would be the Seeverts' way to bide their time, wait for the moment when they could move in unexpectedly, and catch the opposition off guard.

The bushwhacker was something else. Whoever he was, he could try again—and perhaps this time not purposely miss with his shots. Aware of this possibility, Dave took closer note of the country through which he was passing, but when he finally reached the rise from which he could look down on Cass Bradford's Quarter-Circle B spread, he guessed that the mysterious marksman, too, was holding off.

He started down the long, gradual slope. Far below he could see the scatter of buildings and trees that made up the Bradford place. Beyond those, Wolf River cut a silver slash through the green carpet, and to the south numerous dots on the hazy landscape marked the location of part of the herd.

Reaching level ground, he loped across a flinty meadow, entered the yard, and pulled to a halt at the hitch rack. Bradford, apparently having heard Dave's approach, stepped out onto his porch, a smile on his lips.

"Light a spell," the rancher said. "Got coffee on the stove."

Keegan dismounted, and moved up onto the long gallery that fronted the house, took the rancher's extended hand. His clasp was firm and his greeting cordial. Dave felt his hopes rise.

"Can't see as you've changed much," Bradford said, motioning to one of the several chairs. "Bigger, filled out." He looked toward the door. "Hannah . . . how about that coffee?"

Dave made himself comfortable in a cowhide rocker. "Seems nothing much has changed on the Flats, either."

Cass Bradford gave him a keen look. "Meaning Pride Seevert?"

Keegan nodded. He started to say more when the door opened and Hannah appeared with a tray on which were cups, sugar and cream, and a pot of coffee. Dave got to his feet. Pete Weems had not done Hannah justice; she was a beautiful girl.

"Hello, Dave," she said, placing the tray on a table. "It's good to see you again."

"Good to be back," he mumbled, and then, finding himself, added: "Want to say I'm obliged to you . . . again . . . for writing me about Pa."

"Thought you ought to know," Hannah said. "Have you moved back onto your place yet?"

Dave nodded. "Yesterday. Got Pete Weems working for me. Ranch's run down plenty bad."

Cass Bradford leaned forward. "Pride Seevert know that . . . that you're back on your place, I mean?"

Temper lifted within Keegan. "Expect he does. Had Chancy waiting at the depot for me yesterday morning," he said stiffly. "Paid me another call a few hours ago."

The rancher's face was sober. "I take it you've not changed your thinking about Pride's deal."

"Not a bit."

Bradford shook his head, settled back with a sigh. "Hate to think of all hell breaking loose around here again."

"It won't, long as they leave me alone."

"Pride's in no position to do that. He lets you get away with it, then there'll be others. It'll be like a dam . . . if you don't repair the first crack, the whole works goes."

"Be the best thing that could happen to this country," Dave said. "You can't deny that."

"Maybe, but a man pays a price for everything he gets. Stringing along with Pride Seevert is the cost of peace here on the Flats."

Hannah, standing to one side, had been listening quietly. After a moment she said: "I'm glad . . . glad somebody's finally going to stand up to the Seeverts."

Bradford looked up at her, shook his head. "Sounds simple when you say it, and it'd be fine to have everything all laid out, neat and straight, but that's not the way it works. You give and you take."

"But mostly it's take where Pride's concerned."

The rancher sighed. "We haven't done so bad. We've all made a little money . . . and there's been no trouble." He paused, stared directly at Dave. "You didn't see things when they were at their worst around here. You'd already pulled out. We had a year or so of pure hell . . . barns burned, beef slaughtered on the range . . . shootings. Nobody was safe, and a man with a family . . ."

Hannah moved forward, placed her hand on her father's shoulder. "I'm sorry, Papa. I know what you went through . . . and I guess I didn't mean that the way it sounded. But I still think Pride Seevert's had his way long enough . . . and I'm still glad somebody's going to fight him."

Dave shifted in his chair. "I didn't come back to start a row with the Seeverts. I'm here to get my ranch started. Don't want anybody thinking wrong about that."

Hannah glanced at him, and then looked down. Disappointment sobered her features.

"I'm not saying I won't fight, if it's forced on me. I can't knuckle under to any man . . . but I'm not looking for trouble."

Dave felt the girl's eyes on him searching, assessing, as she considered his words, sought to understand them fully. Cass Bradford, too, was silent as he gazed out across the land.

"Had two reasons for riding over here this morning," Keegan continued. "Wanted to pay my respects . . . and ask for your help."

The rancher leaned back, placed his empty cup on the table. Resignation settled over his face.

"Except for the land and the shacks left on it, I'm broke. To get back in the cattle business, I need cattle. I don't like to ask for credit, but is there a chance you'd stake me to a starter herd . . . a hundred head or so? Probably be at least three years before I could pay you off, if I have no bad luck."

Very carefully and with great deliberation Cass Bradford placed his fingertips together, studied the pyramid thus formed.

"Dave . . . I'd like to," he said slowly. "Want you to believe that, but I reckon you know what it would mean."

"Pride Seevert?"

Bradford nodded. "Exactly. Any man who turns a hand to help you will find Seven Diamond on his back. And I . . . or any other rancher in the country . . . can't afford that. I hate it, but that's the way things are."

Dave Keegan shrugged, masking his disappointment. He got to his feet. "Was just an idea. Expect I can get some backing from . . ."

"I'll stake you to a herd," Hannah Bradford said abruptly.

The rancher sat up straight, alarm filling his eyes. "Now, hold on, girl . . . you can't . . ."

"Why can't I? It'll be my cattle . . . you gave them to me. I can do what I like with them."

"But you don't know what you'll be starting. . . ."

"Obliged to you, Hannah," Keegan broke in. "And I appreciate the offer, but I couldn't let you do that."

The girl bristled. "Why? Are you too proud to take help from a woman? That it?"

Dave stirred. "Your pa's right. Could be the cause of big trouble."

She flashed him an angry look. "So I ought to be afraid! Well, I'm not!" she snapped, and, wheeling about, stalked into the house.

Keegan watched the door close behind her. When she was gone, he picked up his hat, moved to the edge of the porch, hesitated.

"Obliged for the hospitality. Appreciate it if you'll tell Hannah so for me."

Bradford rose, leaned against one of the roof supports. "Be glad to. Dave, hope you understand my position. Chances are you'd do the same was you standing in my boots."

"Maybe," Keegan said indifferently, and turned toward the hitch rack. "So long."

The rancher lifted his hand. "Drop by again."

Dave nodded, but he thought: *It's not likely, knowing how you feel about the Seeverts.*

IX

Keegan pushed the buckskin to gain the crest of the rise, temper and impatience crowding him hard. He should have expected Cass Bradford to take the stand he did; Pride Seevert had everyone on the Flats buffaloed, it seemed—everyone except Pete Weems, Dutch Gooch, and Hannah.

He grinned wryly as he allowed the sweaty horse to pick his way at will toward the Lazy K: a broken-down cowman, a livery stable owner—and a girl. When and if it came to a showdown with the Seeverts, he'd really have some strong backing! There'd be no *if* about it, he realized. As Cass Bradford had said, Pride Seevert could not afford a show of independence on the part of any one man; it could result in a full rebellion and the ultimate collapse of his empire. Thus he could expect Seven Diamond to act quickly. And he would have to face them alone. Weems and Gooch, while perhaps willing, could do little. Hannah Bradford was out entirely—he would not permit her to become involved and endanger her life. What he needed was half a dozen good men, all expert with guns and imbued with the natural dislike ordinary riders have for big ranchers who have set themselves up as kings. He knew many such men but they were far away and he'd never be able to get them to the Flats in time.

Might as well face it, he told himself. *You're on your own. Is it worth it?* That question, placed to him by others, again claimed his mind. The Lazy K was a shambles. He had no cattle, and the prospects for obtaining a starter herd appeared slim. Then—why? Dave Keegan was unsure, but it had to do with the resentment born within him long ago—ten years or so, in fact. The belief that no one man should rightfully impose his will upon another by force, the conviction that a man possessed the privilege of living, deciding, and doing in accordance with his own wishes. Those were the factors shaping his determination, and, while it was all slightly hazy when he tried to sort out his reasoning, he was subconsciously committed to them.

He looked ahead. The sagging buildings of the Lazy K were just beyond a knoll. Touching the buckskin with spurs, he urged him to a lope, anxious now to get home. And then, as he topped the rise, he pulled in the horse. Pete Weems was not alone. He could see others in the yard.

Drawing his gun, Keegan began to curve in from the left, walking the buckskin slowly to minimize the sound of his approach. Moments later, through a break in the bush, he caught sight of a rig—a two-seated affair hitched to a span of matched grays, standing in front of the house.

Five men hunkered in the shade. One was Weems; the others he recognized after a few moments study: Ed Corrigan, Gower, Raskob, and Dewey Dalton. Dave holstered his pistol and rode on in, his mind filled with wonder and suspicion.

The men came to their feet when they saw him. Weems moved up to take Dave's horse, lead him back to the corral. Ed Corrigan, a thin, dark man, extended his hand.

"Good to see you, Dave."

Keegan nodded, swept the quartet with his glance. "What's this all about?"

Dalton, eyes snapping, spat impatiently. "We're here to try and talk some sense into you."

Ed Corrigan gave the rancher an angry look. "No call for that, Dewey." He shifted his eyes to the banker. "All right, Tom."

Gower cleared his throat. "Keegan, several of us got together, held a meeting. Think maybe we've come up with a solution . . . one that'll be good for everybody."

"Solution to what?" Dave asked softly.

"To your coming back . . . wanting to start up this place again!" Dalton shouted.

"There some reason why I shouldn't run my own ranch?"

"No, naturally not," Tom Gower said hurriedly. "Only, well, let's say that maybe it's not the wisest thing for you to do."

Keegan said nothing, simply waited. Gower toyed with the gold nugget hanging from a chain looped across his vest. After a moment he continued.

"Be the best thing for you and the country. Now, we know how you feel, so we've put our heads together and come up with a proposition."

Dave remained silent. Pete Weems, his chore completed, returned, squatted down, back to the wall of the house, and began to fill a blackened pipe with shreds of tobacco.

"There are some fine ranches over in the Marin River Valley country for sale. Good places a man can buy at the right price," Gower said. "We're willing to help you get your hands on one. Ride over, look at several, and take your pick. Then let me know what it'll take to make a deal. I'll go along with you on a loan."

Keegan nodded slowly. He touched the other men with his glance. "That all?"

"No," Corrigan replied, "there's more. Dewey and me'll sell you a starter herd . . . credit, of course. We're agreeable to settin' the payment up over a five-year stretch . . . give you plenty of time to get on your feet."

"And you?" Dave pressed, placing his attention on Raskob.

Gower answered for the storekeeper. "You'll be needing supplies . . . food, tools, wagon, and such. Raskob'll extend you all the credit you want, and you can pay him on the same basis Corrigan mentioned." The banker paused. "What do you think about it?"

"My place here . . . what happens to it?"

"The bank will take it over, allow you a fair price, and apply it to the loan."

Dave studied the faces of the four men. Dalton, as always, was angry, belligerent; Corrigan and Tom Gower were calm, hopeful; Raskob, as if he might be regretting the generosity of an offer extending unlimited credit indefinitely, appeared worried.

"Pride Seevert put this idea into your heads?" Dave asked finally.

Dewey Dalton took a hasty step forward, but Gower laid a hand on the redhead's shoulder, restrained him.

"No, he didn't," the banker said. "Matter of fact, we haven't seen or heard from Pride. None of us. This is our own proposition."

"He's behind it just the same," Keegan said doggedly. "You're thinking about him and how to keep him happy and satisfied . . . and to hell with anybody else."

"We're trying to keep this country from blowing up in our faces!" Dalton shouted.

"It's not me you ought to be worrying about!" Dave yelled back. "I'm not looking for trouble. Try working the other side of the table . . . call on Pride Seevert and tell him to leave me alone."

"He'd never listen. . . ."

"And neither will I. I've as much right here on the Flats as the Seeverts . . . and I intend to stay."

"It's hotheads like you that get people killed, that stir up a whole . . ."

"I'm not asking you or anybody else to throw in with me," Dave cut in.

"You won't have to! There's always some damned fool ready to join up at a time like this . . . and then we'll have hell again. Move on, Keegan. We don't want you around here. Ride out . . . leave us in peace!"

"The man to talk peace to," Dave replied in a barely controlled voice, "is Pride Seevert, not me."

Tom Gower stepped into the heated breach. "This is getting us nowhere. Think about it, Keegan. It's a fair and sensible proposition. Nobody wants things like they once were around here. Be reasonable."

"I am . . . and maybe I ought to appreciate your offer, but that's a mite hard to do, knowing why you've made it. I'm staying."

"And do what?" Dalton demanded. "Hatch yourself a herd? You're broke and nobody's fool enough to lend you money or stake you to cattle. How'll you get started?"

"My problem."

Dalton muttered angrily, spun, and walked to the carriage. Ed Corrigan mopped at his face.

"Your mind's made up?"

Kecgan nodded. "I'll say it once more. I don't want trouble, either. Man you need to talk to is Pride Seevert."

X

Dave watched the rig cut about and head for the road. He half turned as Pete Weems moved up to his side.

"Was quite a deal them jaspers offered you," the old cowman said.

Keegan shrugged. “This place is paid for . . . every square foot of it. I’m not about to go in over my ears for another ranch just to suit somebody else.”

“Don’t blame you . . . and it plumb tickled me to hear you tell ’em so. Was afeared there for a minute you was goin’ to give in.”

Dave looked closely at Weems. “Bringing the Seeverts to ground means a lot to you, doesn’t it?”

The older man gazed off toward the Flats. “Reckon so . . . but no more’n it does to a lot of other folks. What happened at the Bradfords’?”

“Cass was friendly enough but figured he’d better play it safe. Was different with Hannah. She offered to stake me to a starter herd.”

“That’s fine . . . mighty fine. Told you she was quite a woman. When we gettin’ the stock?”

“We’re not.”

Pete Weems stared at Dave in disbelief. “You mean you ain’t takin’ her up on it?”

“You know the Seeverts as well as I do . . . better, most likely. I won’t let her get mixed up in my troubles. Too risky.”

The old rider bobbed his head. “Reckon you’re right. Her bein’ a woman wouldn’t make no difference to the Seeverts and that bunch they got workin’ for them. They’d as soon crack down on her as they would a man. What comes next?”

Keegan wheeled, glanced about the yard.

"Looks like you got some work done while I was gone."

"Sure did. That there wire's been strung, like you wanted. Acrost every foot around the place, 'ceptin' the road comin' in. Got a piece handy there we can put up at night. And the corral's fixed."

Dave nodded his approval. "Place's starting to look like something."

"All we're needin' is cows."

"We'll get 'em. Aim to start for Junction City about dark."

"How long you be gone?"

"Three days, likely. What about that cook you mentioned?"

"Joe Henley?"

"Never told me his name. Can you get him?"

"Sure. Seen him when I went after that load of grub. Said he'd be right pleased to take the job. He ain't got no hankerin' for the Seeverts, either. Used to work for 'em, but somethin' happened and they up and give him his time. Want me to fetch him?"

"Long as he knows how things stand out here."

"That'll make him want the job more'n ever. He sure hates them Seeverts after what they done to him. Joe's kind of up in years, like me, and he ain't been able to get work nowhere."

"About all it'll amount to will be cooking chores and the like."

"He'll jump at the chance. When you want him?"

"Now . . . today. Don't think it's smart to leave one man here alone."

" 'Spect you're right. I'll be linin' out for town right away, then. Anythin' you're needin'?"

"Nothing," Dave said, and added: "Keep your eye out for that bushwhacker."

Weems, turning away for the corral, paused, seemed about to say something. He thought better of it, merely nodded, and went on.

Keegan waited until he had ridden out of the yard, and then entered the house. Going through the supplies on the shelves, he selected what he would need for the trail and placed it on the table. Obtaining his saddlebags from the buckskin in the corral where Weems had loosed him, he carried them back to the house and loaded the pockets. When that was done and he had filled his canteen with fresh water, he looked around for something to do while he waited for the return of Weems and Joe Henley.

The tool shed. They'd be needing a place to accumulate the various implements and keep them where they'd be handy. He went out into the yard behind the house, crossed to the small, square structure, fortunately still upright. The roof had blown off, lay a few steps beyond.

Hoisting it into place, Dave obtained the hammer and a handful of nails, secured it. The leather hinges on the door had rotted through. Locating another piece, a remnant of a discarded trace, he cut new lengths, reset the warped panel, and affixed the wire latch. He began then to collect the tools, those left by his father and the new ones supplied by Dutch Gooch, and stacked them inside where they would be out of the weather. The job took little more than an hour, and he looked around for something else to occupy his time. He was trying to keep busy and giving little thought to the visit paid him by Gower and the others. But now Dewey Dalton's words came back to him: *Hothead,* the rancher had called him. *Get people killed,* he had said.

Keegan considered that. Was he a hothead because he wanted to run his ranch in his own way? As for getting others hurt—he was asking no one to side in with him. Pete Weems had asked for the job—seemed anxious to get it. And Henley, he would have a clear understanding of what it was all about. As to other ranchers, so far none had made their intentions to join with him known. Of course, he could hear from some of them later; word had hardly had time to get around. If there were some who felt as he did, it would be because they wanted to make a stand against Pride Seevert, not because he asked or encouraged them to. Could he be blamed because they were fed up with paying through the nose to the Seeverts? Hardly. It would be their own decision, and, if they threw in with him, they would do so fully aware of what it meant. He'd see to that. But he doubted if there would be many who . . .

The loud rattle of loose pebbles in a tin can brought Dave Keegan's thoughts to a sudden halt. Someone had blundered into the low-strung wire. The sound came again, almost immediately—and from the opposite side of the yard.

Dave stepped back against the tool shed. His hand dropped to the pistol on his hip, froze as a sharp voice laid a warning across the quiet.

"Forget it, Keegan!"

A moment later Pride Seevert rode into view.

XI

Cursing himself for his carelessness, Dave allowed his arms to fall. He should have known better—he should have been on his guard. Motion to the left caught his eye. Chancy—moving in slowly, gun in hand. And on the right brother Gabe, husky, sullen-faced, following a like pattern. They had him pinned from three sides.

He brought his attention back to Pride, now halted a few paces in front of him. The eldest Seevert had changed little: a bit older, perhaps, but the same tight mouth, cold blue eyes, and beak-like nose. Watching intently, he settled back, waited for Chancy and Gabe to complete their chore.

Tom Gower and the others had lost no time getting word to Pride, Keegan thought, and then realized that would have been impossible. Less than two hours had elapsed since the men pulled out of the yard; likely they were still on their way to town. The banker, the merchant, and the two ranchers had been acting on their own behalf, just as they'd insisted.

"Get his gun."

Chancy's harsh voice registered on his consciousness. He drew back, preparing himself for what he was certain the next few minutes would bring. There was a lessening of weight on his hip as Gabe lifted the Colt from its holster—and then he buckled forward as Chancy drove his knotted fist deeply into his belly.

"Here . . . none of that! Don't want it looking like there was a fight around here!"

Pride Seevert's words seem to come from a far distance. Dave, gasping for breath, straightened slowly. Chancy, grinning broadly, posed before him.

"Owed me that . . . and plenty more."

"Maybe so," Pride answered, "but this ain't the place . . . or the time. Get a rope around him."

Keegan felt a loop drop around him, cinch tight, pinning his arms to his sides. He faced the elder Seevert squarely. "Roughing me up won't change anything."

"You made that plain to Chancy," Pride

answered. "Don't figure to waste any more time on you."

Understanding came to Keegan. He nodded. "Explains why you haven't got half a dozen of your hired hands along. Don't want them seeing you commit murder."

Seevert shrugged. "You had your chance . . . twice. Instead of taking it, you wanted to play it hard-nosed. All right. We'll do things your way."

"You're overshooting the mark this time. Had some visitors here less'n two hours ago. Anything happens to me they'll know you had a hand in it. Even they won't stand for cold-blooded murder."

"They'll stand for anything," Seevert said with a half smile. "Besides . . . who said anything about murder? You're just going to disappear."

"Nobody'll swallow that one, either."

"You sure of that? All I've got to do is show a bill of sale for this place and say you rode on. They'll believe it."

"There are a dozen men who know I won't sell. You try convincing them. . . ."

"Won't even bother," Pride cut in. "They know better'n to question me. Gabe, get that horse of his saddled and ready to ride."

"You're takin' a little trip," Chancy said coyly, prodding Dave sharply with his pistol. "One you won't be comin' back from. Ever hear of Hell Cañon?"

"I've heard of it," Keegan snapped angrily, "and, if you jab that god-damn' gun barrel into me once more, I'll stomp you into the ground . . . no matter what!"

Chancy fell back a step. Pride laughed quietly. Over in the corral Gabe mumbled irritably as he threw gear onto the buckskin.

"Talk mighty tough for a man about to take his last ride," Chancy said, recovering his bravado.

"Not over yet," Dave said, thinking of the cañon. It was a short, very narrow, and deep cleft in the mountains just off a wall of towering palisades. A veritable trap because of its sheer walls, it had meant doom for countless wild animals, straying stock, and an occasional unwary rider.

"Was about to take your pa on the same ride," Chancy went on, "when he up and died. Saved us the trouble."

Keegan's eyes pulled into slits. "What the hell were you picking on him for? He was going along with you and your high-binding deal."

"At first," Pride Seevert said, coming into the conversation. "Then he got lazy . . . or maybe too old to do his ranching. Just quit. Wanted to get rid of him so's I could put somebody here who'd work . . . raise cattle. Like Chancy said, he died, solved the problem."

Dave Keegan was trembling with fury. "Expect you helped things on a little."

"Guess maybe we did," Chancy said, shaking his head. "Old buzzard was sort of hard-nosed. Can see where you get it."

Temper roared through Keegan. Forgetting the rope that bound his arms, he hurled himself at Seevert. His shoulder caught the man in the chest, bowled him over. Pride yelled, spurred forward. Dave saw him coming, saw the pistol in his hand lifted as a club. He dodged to one side, took the blow high on his arm.

In the next instant Chancy was back on his feet, rushing in. Keegan whirled again, striving to protect himself. The youngest Seevert caught him flush on the chin with a hard right. Dave felt his senses waver. A second blow to the side of his head dropped him to his knees. He hung there, helpless, wavering uncertainly.

"That's enough!" Pride's voice said.

Pain shot anew through Keegan's body as Chancy drove a boot into his back. He felt himself slipping sideways.

"I'll kill him!" Chancy's words were high pitched, almost a scream. "I'll kill the bastard!"

"Grab him, Gabe!"

Prone in the dust, Dave's head began to clear. Through a faint haze he saw Gabe wrap his thick arms around his younger brother, bodily lift him off his feet, and set him aside.

"You heard Pride . . . cut it out!"

Keegan fought himself to a sitting position. Pain

was shooting through his kidneys and cobwebs still cluttered his mind.

"Throw some water on him," Pride ordered.

Gabe obtained the bucket from the kitchen, dashed its contents against Dave's sweat-coated face. The shock brought him around instantly. He shook his head, got slowly to his feet. Chancy stood in his direct line of vision.

"Damn you," Dave muttered, and lunged again.

Gabe, holding to the rope around Keegan's middle, brought him up short. Chancy laughed, swaggered forward a few paces.

"Good thing he stopped you. Was all set to knock your . . ."

"Bring that horse up here!" Pride shouted impatiently. "We ain't got time to set around here while you show off what a big man you are."

Chancy paused, threw a look at his oldest brother, and then shambled over to where the buckskin waited. Gabe, taking a couple of hitches in the rope that bound Keegan, jerked him around to where he could mount.

"I'm fixin' this," he said, "so's I can yank you right offen the saddle if you try somethin' cute. Put your foot in that there stirrup."

Leaning to one side, Dave managed to anchor his boot toe in the wooden opening. Gabe immediately seized him about the waist, swung him onto the hull. Handing the buckskin's reins to Pride, he turned to get his own mount.

"What're you waiting on?" the elder Seevert asked, glaring at Chancy. "You want Gabe to help you up, too?" Chancy swore angrily, spun, and strode to where his horse stood.

Pride glanced at Dave, wagged his head. "Reckon I ought to just turn him loose on you, let him have himself a time. Do him good, maybe."

"Better wrap another rope around me if you do," Keegan said coolly. "I get half a chance, I'll kill him."

"Expect you would at that," Pride answered, and turned to face Gabe and Chancy riding into the yard. "Everything ready?"

Gabe bobbed his head. Pride looked around the yard. "Like I said, I don't want it looking like there was a scrap here."

"Ought to burn the damned place . . . right to the ground," Chancy said sourly.

"Be a fool thing to do . . . burn our own holdings. Belongs to us now."

The youngest Seevert grinned. "Yeah, I forgot about that."

"I'll lead off," Pride continued. "Put Keegan in behind me . . . then you, Gabe. We'll head straight for the palisades."

"What about me?" Chancy asked, frowning.

"You trot along back of Gabe, keep your eyes peeled on the Flats in case somebody starts trailing us. You see somebody, sing out. Understand?"

"Sure, Pride, only I'd ruther look after Keegan, keep him humpin' along."

"Gabe'll take care of him. Need you to do the watchin'. Sooner we get this troublemaker and his horse dumped into the bottom of Hell Cañon, better I'll like it."

Chancy laughed. "Me, too," he said.

XII

They moved off, Pride leading them immediately into the dense tamarisk windbreak bordering the north side of the yard where they were quickly out of sight. Seevert veered then to the west, following a well-beaten cattle trail that pointed in a direct line for Tenkiller Mountain.

Keegan moved his arms slightly, experimentally. The rope encircled him with two loops and had been drawn tightly. Gabe was maintaining tautness by steady pressure that permitted no slack in the line. One thing was in his favor—they had not tied his hands, and that offered hope.

He looked ahead, calculating his chances. Pride was ten feet or so in front of him, leaning forward on the saddle, eyes on the distant slopes. Gabe Seevert was a like distance behind, a squat, solid, uncommunicative man with an expressionless face. Fifty yards beyond him Chancy brought up the rear of the little column.

Simply to make a break for it was out of the

question. Gabe had his end of the rope anchored firmly to the horn of his saddle, thus preventing any sudden flight. And even if he were fortunate enough to escape the rope, Pride and the others would shoot him down before he could get a dozen paces.

Grimly he raked his brain for another idea; there had to be some avenue, some means of breaking free. He just couldn't sit quietly and let them lead him off to slaughter without a fight. But he would have to come up with something soon; already they had reached the first gentle slopes of the mountain and were picking their way along a narrow path.

He glanced at the sun—mid-afternoon. Pete Weems and his friend, Henley, had likely returned to the ranch by that hour. They would wonder what had happened to him. Pete would then discover his saddlebags, loaded for the trip to Junction City, on the table, realize immediately that something was wrong. But he would do nothing for the simple reason that there was nothing he could do. Keegan swore deeply as tension built steadily within him; there was nothing anyone could do for him—he was strictly on his own.

Again he tried the rope. His arms, numbed by their bonds, moved slightly. Hope stirred as he realized the irregularity of the trail was making it hard for Gabe to keep the line taut. It was a small encouragement and opened up no specific possibilities but he worked covertly at increasing the slack, nevertheless.

Time wore on, hot and silent, and with it dragged the slow miles. The trail grew steeper and the horses began to lather and suck for wind. Pride Seevert did not pause but pressed on as if reaching their destination at the earliest moment was of prime importance.

Keegan wondered at that. Was Seevert afraid of encountering someone? It didn't seem likely, as they were now directly west of Seven Diamond range and the only persons in the area would be their own hired hands. There was some other reason, he finally concluded, but he could think of nothing logical.

They topped out a rise in the trail, swung to the left. The gray, ragged walls of the palisades reared before them. Dave's nerves tightened. Hell Cañon was less than a mile distant. Every passing moment now was putting him closer to his last breath.

He pressed harder against the rope, felt it give as the knot slipped. A little more and he'd be able to hook his thumbs under the hemp loops and throw them over his head. Then what? He studied Pride Seevert's hunched shape. His best chance lay there—digging spurs into the buckskin, sending him straight ahead. He'd try to knock Pride off his saddle as he raced by, hope Gabe would hesitate to shoot for fear of hitting his brother. Chancy was too far back to be a problem.

Keegan bowed his elbows again, pushed once more against the rope. The loops gave easily, slid downward an inch or two.

"Hey . . . what the hell you doin'?"

Gabe's raspy voice shattered the silence as he hauled back on the rope savagely. Keegan felt the coils tighten around his middle, almost jerk him from his seat. Pride stopped short, looked back, and there was a quick pound of hoofs as Chancy hurried up.

"What's goin' on?"

"Tryin' to shuck out of my lasso, that's what," Gabe said. "Real cute."

Pride said: "Watch him close. We're almost there. Chancy, you better side Gabe . . . just in case."

"He won't be tryin' nothin' again," Gabe promised as the column resumed.

Keegan rode in silence. His one chance, however slim, had vanished. There was nothing left now but wait it out, hope for a last moment opportunity.

Abruptly Pride halted. Standing in his stirrups, he stared down a gentle slope the end of which was marked by a low hedge of snakeweed, sage, and other stunted growth. The lip of the cañon, Keegan realized.

"Good a place as any," Seevert said, settling

back on the saddle. "Gabe, bring him over here, put him below us. Chancy, give your brother a hand there."

"You wantin' him on his horse?"

"Of course I want him on his horse. You think I want any boot tracks showing around here?"

Chancy muttered something, moved up to Keegan, and took a firm grip on the buckskin's bridle. Spurring his own horse, he led Dave's mount to a point halfway between Pride and the edge of the cañon.

"Right here suit you, mister?" Chancy asked, his tone sarcastic.

"Good," Pride answered, undisturbed. "Now come up here next to me while Gabe gets that rope offen him."

The plan was clear to Dave Keegan. The Seeverts were trapping him between them and the cañon. At a given signal all would rush him, haze the buckskin over the edge to certain death on the rocks far below. When—if ever—his body was found, it would appear an unfortunate accident ended his life.

Tense, he waited while Gabe, keeping at a safe distance, shook the rope free and flipped it clear. He could make a run for it, but he knew in advance that would end in failure. Pride would use a gun if forced to—and it would be easy to down the buckskin when he tried to cross in front of them. Likely they would then knock him unconscious and throw him over the rim. It would still look like an accident.

He watched Gabe move upgrade and wheel in beside Pride, coiling his rope as he did. The oldest Seevert drew his pistol, pointed it skyward.

"All right . . . you boys ready?"

Chancy and Gabe had their weapons out.

Pride said: "Now, be damn' sure you don't hit him . . . or the horse."

Gabe nodded. Chancy, his face glistening with sweat, eyes bright, simply waited. Keegan, crouched low, touched the buckskin lightly with his spurs, started him walking slowly across the grade. He had no plan, no thought as to how he might avoid the charge; he could only face it on a moment to moment basis.

"Get him!" Pride yelled, and, pressing off a shot, drove his barbs into the flanks of his horse.

All three riders, yelling and shooting, instantly swept down the short slope. At the first report Keegan brought the buckskin around sharply, started him directly upgrade. The gunshots, the yelling, and the oncoming horses brought him to his back legs. He wheeled in mid-air, came down solidly, began to stampede toward the lip of the cañon.

Keegan sawed at the reins, succeeded in turning him half around. Abruptly the Seeverts were on him, yelling, shooting, crowding him toward the rim. Dave lashed out at the nearest, Gabe, struck the man a glancing blow on the head. He had the buckskin pointed uphill again, was goading him cruelly with his spurs.

"Push him over . . . push him over!" Pride Seevert yelled.

Dave had a brief glimpse of Chancy, lips pulled back in a tight grin, rushing straight for him. He drove spurs home again, slapped the buckskin sharply on the neck. The horse wheeled, lunged away. Chancy thundered by, and collided solidly with Gabe. Both mounts went down, thrashing wildly. Keegan, fighting the buckskin, found himself behind the Seeverts, in the clear. He leaned forward and goaded the animal into a straightaway run for the trail.

Reaching it, he looked back. One of the horses had gone over the edge. Pride and Chancy were on their knees, assisting Gabe, who also had lost his footing but had managed to arrest his fall by grabbing onto the weeds that lined the brink of the cañon.

XIII

The buckskin was tired but Keegan held him to a steady lope down the trail. That there would be pursuit he was certain—just which of the Seevert brothers it would be was the only question. Most likely Chancy, Dave decided. With only two horses between the three of them, it was logical to assume Pride would take Gabe with him, riding double, back to Seven Diamond while he sent the youngest Seevert to finish the job they had started. And this time it would be no cunningly devised plan designed to leave no trace, no evidence. Pride's instructions would be to kill, employing any means and opportunity available.

A gun—he must get a gun. He considered that, concluded his best bet was to return to the Lazy K, despite the fact that the Seeverts would undoubtedly look there first for him. But he had a spare six-gun in the few belongings he had brought—an old, bone-handled .45 with a hair-trigger given to him years back by a friend. Once he had a weapon with which to defend himself, he could decide what his next move should be.

The buckskin began to heave and he pulled the horse into a trot. Turning his head, he listened into the fading day. Faintly, above the drum of his own horse, he could hear the hollow beat of an oncoming rider. He hadn't guessed wrong; one of the Seeverts was trailing him.

Dave looked ahead. He was almost to the foot of the mountain. Once off the narrow, winding path and on the wooded slopes it wouldn't be hard to shake the pursuit. He glanced at the sun. Still a couple of hours, at least, until darkness. No help there.

The end of the trail appeared abruptly. He broke out onto the barren knoll, veered hard right for a thick stand of piñon trees. The buckskin had to rest, if only for a few moments. Halting well back from the base of the mountain, he waited behind the screen of foliage. The tattoo of beating hoofs was much louder and he realized that Seevert had gained on him during the descent. If the trail had lasted for another mile or two, he would have found himself a target for gunshots.

Abruptly a rider swept around the last bend and raced into view. It was Chancy, crouched low and flogging his horse unmercifully for more speed. Dave watched him race out into the open, continue without hesitation along the main path up which they had all ridden earlier. Chancy had jumped to a conclusion; he was assuming that Keegan would ride straight to the Lazy K.

Dave allowed the buckskin to rest for a quarter hour and then moved on, taking a southerly direction until he was a full mile below the route Seevert had taken, and then swung east. Chancy would eventually discover his error and backtrack; unarmed, Dave Keegan was taking precautions to avoid an encounter.

He reached the Lazy K well after dark. There were no lights showing and he halted in the tamarisk outside the yard while he studied the weathered buildings thoughtfully. Where were Pete and Joe Henley?

After a few minutes he dismounted, secured the buckskin to a stout clump, and walked through the shadows until he was directly opposite the house. Again he paused, listened.

Somewhere, back in the direction of Tenkiller Mountain, a coyote was barking. Insects clacked in the night, and off to his right there was a dry rustling in the leaves as a field mouse, or some small creature, scurried about. And then from inside the house Keegan heard the low, muted sound of a man's voice. Weems and Henley were there, evidently on guard.

"Pete," he called softly.

There was no answer. Dave cupped his hands to his lips. "Pete . . . it's me, Keegan."

A hinge screeched faintly. Weems's high-pitched tones cautiously probed the darkness. "Dave . . . that you?"

"It's me. I'm coming in."

Keegan crossed the yard in half a dozen hurried strides and entered the house. "What's this all about?"

The old cowman closed the door, struck a match for the lantern. He waved carelessly at an elderly man sitting beneath a window, a shotgun across his knees.

"That there's Joe Henley . . . feller I was tellin' you about."

Dave nodded to the newcomer. "Why are you all forted up? Something happen?"

"Was somebody out there a while ago. Didn't hear 'em come, but heard 'em go. Wasn't takin' no chances, seein' as how you just up and disappeared sudden like. Where in tarnation you been?"

"With the Seeverts . . . at Hell Cañon," Dave replied, stepping to his bunk. Unrolling a bundle, he obtained the bone-handled .45, flipped open the loading gate, and began to insert cartridges into the cylinder.

Weems was staring at him. "What the devil you doin' up there?"

"Seems to be their private burying ground . . . for people they don't want around," Keegan said, and related what had taken place. "That probably was Chancy you heard outside, looking for me."

Pete Weems was nodding slowly. " 'Spect, was we to climb down into that cañon, we'd find some of them folks that just dropped out of sight. Could explain a whole lot of things." He paused, watched as Dave slid the pistol into his holster. "What're you aimin' to do? Pride ain't goin' to let you run loose, knowin' what you do now."

"My thinking hasn't got that far yet. One thing I'd like to ask you . . . my pa ever tell you he'd been beat up by the Seeverts?"

Pete clawed at his chin. "Don't recollect him ever sayin' so."

"He ever look like it?"

The old cowman frowned. "Well, maybe there was a couple o' times it could've been that. Rode by here once and he was all bunged up and hobblin' about. Said he'd fell offen his horse.

Remember thinkin' it was the wrong kind of bungin' up for that. Face was all swole and both eyes was black. Why?"

Keegan's voice was taut with anger. "The Seeverts were trying to force him off his land."

"You sayin' they beat him up?"

Dave nodded slowly. "Chancy dropped the word that his dying saved them from taking him up to the cañon when they couldn't make him do what they wanted."

Joe Henley swore harshly. "Day's comin' when somebody'll take care of them Seeverts."

Dave's hand dropped to the curved handle of his weapon. "The day's here," he murmured.

XIV

Henley asked: "How you goin' to do it? The Seeverts are a big outfit."

There was a thread of doubt in the man's tone. Weems, eyes bright, was grinning broadly.

"Don't you worry none about Dave, here. Seen him take on Chancy and his crowd twice now. He can handle them . . . the whole dang' push!"

"Chancy's one thing. Pride and Gabe are somethin' else."

"Don't make no difference to Dave!" Weems, glowing like fanned embers, wheeled to Keegan. "What're you figurin' to do . . . pay 'em a little visit?"

"Won't need to. They'll be looking for me."

"And you'll be settin' here . . . waitin'."

Keegan made no comment. Henley stood his shotgun against the wall, reached into his pocket for a plug of tobacco.

"Man's got a right to defend his property. You takin' them on alone? Nobody comin' to help?"

"Nobody," Dave said. "Expect you two'd better head back for town in the morning. Anybody the Seeverts see hanging around me they'll figure's against them, too."

Henley gnawed off a corner of the plug, shifted it into the hollow of his cheek. "Thought you was tryin' to stir up some help against them."

"Maybe I was, at the start, but I got to thinking about it. Wrong thing for me to do, talk people into fighting, getting themselves shot up, their places burned. I'm the one who's not satisfied. Makes it my problem."

"Well, I ain't pullin' out!" Weems declared. "I been honin' for a crack at Pride Seevert!"

Joe Henley leaned back, bobbed his head thoughtfully. "You got yourself a powerful hate for Pride 'cause of what he done to you. Reckon that goes for you both. Now take me . . . the Seeverts done me dirt in another way, and I ain't forgettin' it. Howsomever, there's still more to it. Them and their kind is ruinin' this whole country . . . and that's somethin' I can't abide. Way I see it, any man ought to rise right up and do his share when it's time to start skinnin' snakes."

Pete Weems stared at his friend. "All that windy palaver . . . that mean you're of a notion to help?"

"It does," Henley said.

"Obliged to both of you," Keegan said, "but I'm not sure you understand what you'll be up against. The Seeverts don't just plan to run me out of the country. Way it stands now, they've got to get rid of me for good. You side me, you'll be in the same wagon."

"Ain't tellin' me somethin' I don't know," Pete said.

"Me, neither," Henley added. "What the hell . . . man can't expect to keep on livin' forever. Anything special we ought to be doin'?"

Dave was silent for a long moment, and then he smiled. "We shouldn't be holed up in here, that's for damn' sure. Be a trap if the Seeverts hit us tonight."

"Where can we go?" Weems wondered.

"Out in the brush. Grab up a couple of blankets. We'll pick a place where we can keep an eye on the yard."

"How about grub? You ain't et yet, have you?"

Keegan reached for his saddlebags, still on the table.

"Can make out with what's in here. There coffee in that pot?"

Pete stepped to the stove, tested the weight of the blackened granite utensil. "Nigh half full."

“That’ll hold us until morning,” Keegan said. “Let’s move.”

They settled on a low rise just west of the yard. It was densely covered with rabbit brush, stray clumps of tamarisk brought in by the wind, scrub oak, and mountain mahogany. By parting the thick foliage, they had a good view of the house and yard—as well as the far side, which was the direction the Seeverts would most likely come in from.

He doubted very much, however, that they would see anything of the Seven Diamond crowd before morning. Chancy, failing to find Dave at his ranch, would have then returned to the Seevert place and rejoined his brothers. After that would come the planning, during which Pride would set forth what had to be done. All of this would require time.

They made themselves comfortable and Keegan, after eating from the supplies in his saddlebag and drinking two cups of the still warm coffee, lay back, suddenly aware of his weariness and the need for sleep. He dozed immediately, unmindful of the voices of Weems and Henley as they argued amiably over some trivial matter.

He awoke to find them already up and about. Henley had made a trip to the house and returned with a frying pan, a section from the side of bacon, and some potatoes he had thoughtfully put in the stove's oven that previous afternoon. Weems had a small fire going and the coffee ready.

He greeted Dave with a cup of the steaming black liquid and smiled. "You sure been poundin' your ear."

"Didn't know I was so beat," Keegan answered, thanking the old man. He glanced at the sun, commented: "Pretty late."

"Was just about to roust you out. Company ought to be comin' pretty quick. We stayin' here?"

Keegan nodded. "Good a place as any. Expect we ought to bring the horses over, have them handy." He drained his cup, set it on a rock near the fire. "We can do that while Joe's fixing breakfast."

Together he and Weems walked to the corral where their mounts had been placed and, after throwing on the gear, led them to the rear of the thicket. When they rejoined Henley, he had their plates well filled with slices of fried bacon and browned potatoes. He grinned at Dave.

"They always give a condemned man a hearty meal. Figured we was entitled to the same treatment."

There could be considerable truth in the words, Keegan thought, finding himself a place to sit. He wished it were possible to settle things with the Seeverts without bloodshed, but that was now out of the question. After what had happened that previous day there wasn't any other answer. One thing he was glad of—he hadn't dragged any other rancher into the showdown. He was in it alone, except for Pete and Joe Henley, and they had their own private reasons for taking a hand.

"Somebody comin'!"

Pete Weems's warning brought him to his feet instantly. He had heard nothing, but there was no reason to doubt the old cowman. Setting his plate aside, he felt for his pistol, and then moved to the front of the screening shrubbery. He caught the sound then—the quiet *thud* of approaching horses.

Keegan frowned. He had expected the Seeverts to appear on the opposite side of the yard. Seven Diamond lay in that direction. These riders were coming in on their left.

"Watch sharp," he said quietly. "They could be all around us."

Earlier he hadn't considered the possibility—that of finding themselves surrounded. It seemed more likely that Pride and the others would strike head-on.

"Hello, the house!"

At the summons Dave Keegan stiffened. He doubled back through the brush, looking to the source of the call.

"Ain't any of Pride's bunch," Pete Weems said. "Sounds like Cass Bradford."

"That's who it is," Keegan replied in a falling voice. "He's got Hannah with him."

XV

"Sure the wrong time for them to be showin' up," Weems muttered. "What you reckon they want?"

Dave stepped into the open. Immediately the rancher and his daughter angled toward him. Hannah was smiling faintly but Bradford, sensing something was amiss, held a straight face. They halted in front of Keegan and swung down.

"Trouble?"

Dave nodded slowly to the rancher's question.

Bradford asked: "The Seeverts?"

Again Keegan moved his head. "Had a run-in with them yesterday."

"Bad?"

"Bad enough," Dave said, skipping details. "Don't think you and Hannah ought to be found here."

Instantly the girl bristled. "Neither Pride Seevert nor anybody else can tell us what we can do . . . ," she began angrily, and then fell silent as her father lifted his hand.

"Don't guess it'll make much difference, anyway," he said resignedly. "Rode by to tell you we'd moved a hundred head of beef onto your south range. Starter herd. After you left yesterday, Hannah convinced me it was the thing to do."

"About the worst . . . far as you're concerned," Keegan said. "Pride's taken it into his head to crack down on me. Same thing'll hold for my friends."

"You mean you don't want the cattle?" Hannah demanded.

"Of course I want them, and I'm obliged to you for giving me a hand. But with the Seeverts . . ."

"The Seeverts," Hannah echoed. "I'm sick of hearing about them. Why are you all so afraid of that bunch? They're just men. If I had a gun . . ."

"Now, hold on!" Keegan broke in harshly, temper finally getting the best of him. "Being a woman, maybe you've got a right to speak out that way, but that kind of talk's going to get somebody killed . . . most likely your pa. Let me give you a little advice . . . stay out of this . . . keep your lip buttoned."

Hannah flushed hotly and looked down. Cass Bradford slanted a glance at his daughter, grinned slightly, and then brought his attention back to Keegan.

"See now I should've done some talkin' before I had the boys drive those steers over. But they're here. Ain't much we can do to change that."

"Still a way out," Dave said. "You two get off my land fast as you can. Don't let any of the Seven Diamond outfit see you."

"But the cattle . . . ?"

"If the Seeverts spot them, I'll say they drifted over the line onto my range . . . that I've sent word to you to come get them."

Bradford nodded. "Just might work."

"Feared it won't," Joe Henley said from the depths of the brush. "We got company right now."

Keegan wheeled in alarm, threw his glance to the far side of the yard. All three Seeverts, with half a dozen riders flanking them, were strung out along the windbreak. He could see more Seven Diamond hired hands moving in the brush.

"Circlin' us," Weems said. "Like a bunch of Injuns."

"Pull back," Dave said hurriedly. "Don't think they've seen . . ."

A pistol shot cracked sharply. The sound of a bullet clipping through foliage just above his head caused Keegan to duck involuntarily. Cursing, he dragged out his gun, then paused. He could make no stand there—not with Hannah Bradford with him.

"Keegan!"

It was Pride Seevert's voice. Dave motioned the others deeper into the brush where the horses waited.

"Keegan . . . I know you're holed up in there. We've got you cold . . . but I'm willing to give you one more chance. Come out with your hands up and we'll talk sense."

Dave looked over his shoulder. The Bradfords and Henley had reached the horses. Pete Weems had halted, was staring at him.

"You ain't swallerin' that, are you? Only talkin'

Pride'll do will be with that gun he's holdin'. He just plain can't afford to let you keep on livin'."

Keegan said: "Know that. Go on with the others. Take my horse . . . lead them all straight back. I'll follow. Got to get out of here before we're surrounded."

Weems was staring beyond him at the men on the far side of the yard. His lean, hawk-like face was set and his eyes burned fiercely. "Could easy blast that god-damn' Pride offen his saddle from here," he murmured.

"And have them open up on us with every gun they've got? We've got Hannah to think about . . . and her pa."

The old cowman's shoulders slumped. "Reckon you're right. Wouldn't make no difference to the Seeverts. What're you figurin' to do?"

"Move out of here before it turns into a trap. Lead the others, like I told you, straight back. Brush runs for a couple hundred yards . . . ends at a dry wash. Once we've reached that, we can make a run for the mountains."

"Keegan!"

Dave turned, hopeful that Pete Weems had understood; he could ignore Pride Seevert no longer.

"I hear you!" he shouted.

"You comin' out?"

It was Chancy this time. Dave cast a quick look over his shoulder. Weems, followed by Hannah and her father, and with Henley bringing up the rear, were disappearing into the thick growth.

"Thinking it over," he replied, glancing to the sides. He could see nothing to his left, but to the right he caught sight of a rider winding in and out of the brush. They were closing the circle. Dave smiled grimly. Both he and Pride Seevert were playing a game of delay: he holding back until Weems and the others were out of danger, Pride striving to occupy him while his men slipped in and formed a ring.

"Thinkin' over what?" Chancy yelled. "One way or another you're comin' out of there!"

Keegan once again turned away. Weems and his party were out of sight—and beyond the approaching rider. "Guess you're right," he answered.

Removing his hat, he perched it on a low stump in front of a thick clump of oak brush. Then, crouched low, he wheeled and began to make his way toward the point where he had last seen Weems and the others. He had taken no more than a dozen steps when a sound to his left brought him to a dead stop. Peering through the shrubbery, he saw another of Seevert's men, the one he had failed to locate earlier, working in. The Seven Diamond rider was on foot, leading his mount. Keegan grinned. The man would pass within a long stride; it would be easy to move swiftly, club him to the ground with no one being the wiser.

Dave throttled the impulse. The second rider would see the unattended horse, immediately suspect something was wrong, and set up an alarm. His scheme for an escape depended on keeping the Seeverts and their men concentrating on the brush where he supposedly was hiding. The planted hat, he felt, should prolong that belief.

Scarcely breathing, he watched the man walk by, and then, quiet as smoke, he hurried to overtake the others.

XVI

The trail was dim, all but wiped out by ten years of encroaching underbrush, yet he followed it with no difficulty. Countless times as a boy he had made his way along the path as part of a short cut leading eventually to the mountains, and now he was taking it again. But on this day it was for a different reason and under desperate circumstances.

He reached the arroyo, dropped to its sandy floor where the others awaited him, went straight to his buckskin, and vaulted to the saddle.

"Stay close to me," he said, and spurred forward.

Stilled by the tautness of his manner, the rest of the party swung in behind him and in a close, compact column headed up the wash.

Almost immediately a shout lifted from the brush where they had hidden.

"He ain't here!"

Pride Seevert's voice bellowed a reply. "What do you mean he ain't there?"

"Tricked us . . . with his damned hat!"

Dave swore quietly. He had hoped to gain more time, and thus a better start, but his ruse had been discovered quickly. He glanced back at those following him. Hannah's features were strained; the faces of the men were set, grim. He wondered if the girl realized, as did the men, the seriousness of their position. If so, she betrayed no fear at the prospects.

"Keep up," he called over his shoulder, and dug his spurs into the buckskin.

The horse broke into a lope. It was punishment for the animals, he knew, laboring upgrade in the loose sand of the wash, but they could not afford to let the Seeverts get within gunshot. He looked again to the rear. The Seven Diamond men had not yet found the trail to enter the arroyo. *Luck's with us so far,* Keegan thought.

The buckskin began to heave, his wind going fast on the tough climb. Dave stared ahead, calculating distance. Still a good quarter mile to the bend in the wash where they could climb out and be on firm ground. He eased up on the horse, allowed him to drop into a trot.

"Good thing," he heard Pete Weems say in a grumbling voice. "Nag o' mine's about done for."

Keegan made no reply, simply held the buckskin

to the pace. He could see the slope leading up from the arroyo. Snakeweed had found purchase in the hard clay and it was almost covered. Erosion, too, had left its scarring mark but it appeared ascendable.

He drew abreast the bend, veered the horse for the sharp grade. The buckskin slowed, gathered his muscles, and lunged. His hoofs stabbed into the baked soil, churned furiously, and then abruptly he was on the top. Keegan wheeled him around, halted on the level ground. While the others followed the trail dug by the buckskin, he threw his glance toward the lower end of the wash.

There was no sign of the Seevert party, but that could mean nothing. The arroyo whipped back and forth many times during its course to the lower flats, effectively cutting off the view of anyone hoping to see for any distance.

Bradford paused beside him. "Think we shook them?"

Dave shrugged. "Doubt it. Pride'll realize there was only one way out of that trap . . . south. He'll have his look, and, when he gets to the arroyo, there'll be plenty of tracks to follow."

"Hadn't we better keep goin' then?"

"Got to give the horses a breather. Five minutes'll mean a lot to them . . . not much where Seevert's bunch is concerned."

"Where does this trail lead?" Hannah asked, looking off into the brush.

"To the lower end of the mountain," Dave replied. "We'll come to a fork about a quarter mile this side. Want you and your pa to take the left hand. It'll put you on Ed Corrigan's place, get you out of this."

"You and the others heading up onto the mountain?" Bradford said.

Keegan nodded. "Figure we can give them the slip there. If we don't, there'll be plenty of good places where we can make a stand."

Five minutes later, he cut the buckskin around and pointed him up the narrow path, scarcely visible in the thick growth. The others fell in behind him, maintaining a close column. When they reached the point where the brush cut off a final glimpse of the arroyo, Keegan looked back. Pride Seevert and his Seven Diamond men were just coming into view. Dave stiffened involuntarily. Weems, watching him at the moment, turned, followed his gaze.

"Sure didn't take 'em long," the old cowman said grimly. "Reckon we can outrun 'em?"

Keegan said—"We've got to."—and urged the buckskin to a lope.

An hour later, with the horses laboring under the strain, they reached the split in the trail. The Seeverts had trimmed their lead some, but they were still a safe distance to the rear. Dave faced Bradford and his daughter.

"We're leaving you here," he said, ducking his

head toward the path that led directly to the mountain. "You ride south. Corrigan's ranch is six, maybe seven miles."

Cass Bradford glanced over his shoulder to the oncoming riders, now taking definite shape and form in the distance. He shook his head.

"I'm through bowing and scraping to Pride Seevert. Know I should have felt that way years ago but I was fool enough to string along with the rest of the people around here . . . or most of them. I'm making a change right here."

Dave cast a worried look toward the approaching horsemen. "Don't be a fool. You've got too much to lose. Take Hannah and get out of here before it's too late."

"Too late," Bradford echoed bitterly. "Maybe I am late in admitting to myself how things are around here . . . but it ain't too late to change. Had me a real first-class look at Pride Seevert and how he does things there this morning and it fair turned my stomach to realize I've had a part in letting him get away with it. If it's all the same with you, I'll stick."

"Up to you," Keegan said. "We can use another gun, but you ought to know the chances are plenty slim."

"I figure they'll be pretty good," the rancher said, looking toward the rocky slope of the mountain. "Half a dozen men could hold off a fair-size army up there."

"Well, we better be hightailin' for them rocks, or we'll never get the chance," Pete Weems said in a worried voice.

The old cowman was right, Dave saw, glancing back down the trail. The Seeverts were closing the gap fast. He nodded to Bradford.

"We're glad to have you. Maybe . . . if things go right . . . we can settle things once and for all with the Seeverts."

"Just what I'm hoping we can do," Bradford said, and turned to Hannah. "You get on down the trail for the Corrigans, girl. Don't worry none about me. We'll make it all right. Soon as this's over . . ."

"I'm not running, either," Hannah broke in flatly, and drove spurs into her horse. The startled black she mounted spurted ahead, started up the slope at a fast gallop.

"Head her off!" Keegan shouted, jabbing his own horse and waving the others forward. "Be no place for a woman up there when . . ."

A splatter of gunshots coming from their back trail cut off his words. He twisted about. The Seeverts were close—still out of bullet range, but close. Anger and frustration rushing through him, he turned to the others.

"Let her go. Too late now to do anything."

XVII

With Hannah a good fifty yards in the lead, they pounded up the rock-studded path. Raging inwardly, Dave kept his eyes on the girl's crouched figure. Her presence changed everything. He'd have to avoid an out and out showdown with Pride Seevert and his men now; he couldn't risk her getting hurt. The little fool—didn't she realize what she was doing?

More shooting erupted from the Seevert party. Dave didn't trouble to look back; they were still well beyond range. Pete Weems, directly in front of him, turned.

"How high up we goin'?"

"Place about a mile farther on!" Keegan shouted. "Trail bends left, goes by a rocky cañon! We'll fort up there!"

The old cowman bobbed his head in understanding. He pointed to the girl. "What about her?"

"She'll double back when she sees us pull off the road." Temper again rolled through Keegan. "She dealt herself in on this! She'll have to look out for herself!"

Weems grinned, nodded again, and spurred forward to relay word of their destination to Henley and Cass Bradford. Dave twisted, looked to the rear. The Seven Diamond riders were now strung out in a long line on the lower portion of the trail. Pride Seevert was pushing them hard. Once they reached the rocky cañon, Dave realized, he and the others wouldn't have much time in which to get set.

The horses began to wilt under the steady climb. Keegan raised himself on the saddle and looked ahead. The bend in the trail was in sight. He drew his pistol, pointed it aloft, and fired a single shot. Hannah glanced over her shoulder. He motioned to her to stop and she pulled in the black at once.

As they caught up with her, Dave waved her in. "Stay close," he yelled, moving to the fore. "We're turning off."

Hannah nodded. Her eyes were bright with excitement and her lips were compressed to a tight line. Keegan wondered if she really understood what she had gotten herself into, or had any idea of what lay ahead for them. Likely not, he decided, anger once more stirring him. Hannah Bradford would soon find out. The Seeverts weren't there for a Sunday picnic. His only hope, and worry, was that he could prevent her from getting hurt. He had a brief wonder at the possibility of Pride's allowing her to leave before matters reached the critical stage. Immediately he dismissed the thought. Pride Seevert would never agree—and, if he did, he could not be trusted to stand by his word. Like as not he would seize

Hannah the moment she rode out, and use her as a hostage to gain a quick victory.

Dave reached the bend in the roadway, rounded it, and urged the buckskin on toward the narrow mouth of the cañon 100 yards farther on. Gaining the opening, he swung into it immediately. There was no identifiable trail, only a maze of brush, boulders, and stunted trees. The buckskin faltered on the rough terrain and Dave dropped from the saddle, motioned to the others to do likewise.

"That pile of rocks," he said, pointing to a jumbled mass of jagged granite and twisted junipers nearly dead center of the high-walled gash. "Be the best place."

Leading their horses, they struggled over the rough, uneven ground and moved in behind the natural fortification. Picketing their mounts in the deep brush beyond, they returned to the rocks.

Pete Weems glanced to the sheer palisades rising on either side. "Sure ain't nobody goin' to be slippin' up on us from there," he said. "How about back of us?"

"Box cañon . . . runs for a mile or so," Keegan replied. "Only way they can get at us is from the front."

Pete grunted his satisfaction, moved to a place where he had a commanding view of the trail. "Might as well get ourselves sot. Reckon Pride and the boys'll be along right soon now."

Dave only half heard. His gaze was on Hannah

Bradford, standing a few paces to one side with her father. The rancher caught his eye, smiled lamely.

"Sorry about this, Keegan . . . Hannah just wasn't thinkin' . . ."

"Tried to figure a way to get you out of this," Dave said, placing his attention on the girl. His tone was angry, impatient. "Couldn't come up with an answer, so you'll have to stay."

"Don't make allowances for me," she said stiffly. "I can use a gun . . . as good as most men."

"You'll keep out of it!" Keegan snapped. "We're up against enough trouble without you getting yourself shot."

Hannah tossed her head angrily. "I'll do what I like!"

"The hell you will!" Keegan exploded, thoroughly aroused. "You'll do exactly what I tell you . . . or I'll stake you out with a rope. That stubborn streak of yours has already put us in a bad way. I won't have you making things worse."

Startled, the girl stared at him. "I . . . I'll . . ."

"You'll listen and do what you're told. I want you back there with the horses. And you're to stay there. Understand?"

For a long moment Hannah faced him, defiant, strong-willed, and then she dropped her head. "I understand," she murmured, and, wheeling, started for the brush where the horses had been picketed.

Dave brushed at the sweat clothing his face, glanced at Cass Bradford. The rancher was regarding him with a quiet smile.

"How you fixed for bullets?" Keegan asked.

Bradford ran one hand over his cartridge belt. "Couple dozen, more or less."

"Going to have to make every shot count if Pride means to make a fight of it."

"He will," the rancher said flatly. "Knows he's got us backed into a corner. Not like him to pass up a good chance. Anywhere special you want me?"

Dave shook his head. "Pick your own . . ."

"Here they come!" Pete Weems sang out. "Now, you all harken to me . . . I got first claim on Pride. You hear? He's my meat."

"Forget it," Keegan said harshly. "Hold your fire until I give the word. Goes for everybody."

XVIII

Weems turned, his weathered face furrowed into a frown. "What's that mean?"

"Just what I said."

Pete continued to stare. "Thought you was out to settle with the Seeverts."

"Aim to . . . only things have changed a bit."

"The girl . . . that it?"

"Could be," Dave replied, and let it drop.

"Then what're you figurin' to do?" Henley

asked, shifting restlessly. “Make up your mind. They’re gettin’ close.”

“Try talking Pride out of it. There’ll come another time.”

Weems swore in disgust. “Ain’t never goin’ to be a time good as this’n’.”

Keegan’s attention was on the bend in the trail. Seevert and the men with him were just rounding the dark shoulder of rock, walking their horses slowly. Apparently they expected trouble.

Again Pete Weems swore, stirred irritably. The barrel of his rifle clanged against the rock he was crouching behind. Instantly Pride Seevert lifted his hand, halted.

Keegan flashed an angry look at Weems. He had planned to let the Seven Diamond riders advance until they were directly opposite—to where they would be within easy reach of their guns—but that advantage was lost now.

“Keegan!”

Pride Seevert’s tone was impatient. Dave made no answer, hoping the men would continue. But the eldest Seevert was not to be fooled.

“Keegan . . . I know you’re holed up in those rocks. I’m giving you one minute to come out . . . with your hands up!”

Dave edged forward to where he was partially visible. “We’re holed up all right. What’s more we’ve got every man with you covered. First one to make a wrong move is dead.”

Seevert half rose in his stirrups, glanced over the riders clustered around him. He laughed. "Big talk when you figure the odds. There are a dozen of us!"

"But we're holding all the aces. Want to talk it over?"

"Why talk?"

"Because there's a rifle pointed at your belly, ready to go off when I give the word."

Pride Seevert relaxed gently. Chancy crowded in close, said something in a quick, anxious way. One of the riders behind him looked over his shoulder as if wishing he were nearer the protective shoulder of rock. Gabe Seevert, at Pride's immediate left, continued to slouch and wait.

"What's the deal, Keegan?"

"Couple of people here that're not mixed up in what's between us. Let them go."

"Sure. Tell them to ride out."

Dave laughed. "Your word's no good to me, Pride."

Again Chancy spoke hurriedly to his brother. Pride shook his head. "What are you wanting me to do, then?"

"Take your bunch on up the trail. Keep going for an hour. . . ."

"And give you a chance to run?" Chancy broke in. "Hell, no!"

"I'm not running. I'll be around. Just want my friends out of it."

"Well, I sure ain't goin' no place," Weems grumbled. "You can tell 'em that for me."

"That mean you'll be waiting when we come back?" Pride asked.

"I'll be here."

Seevert shrugged. "You won't take my word, but you want me to take yours."

"About the size of it," Dave answered.

He was pushing his luck, he knew, but he was trying hard to prevent a standoff—a standoff that would eventually erupt in gunfire. Without Hannah on his hands he would not hesitate to take on Seevert and his men. Well entrenched in the rocks he with Pete Weems and Joe Henley could more than even the odds; but with the girl—and her father who likely would prove more a liability than an asset—he had to avoid a shoot-out.

Pride Seevert's voice brought him from his thoughts. "What if I say no?"

"You'd be a fool. You don't have much choice."

"Could make a run for the rocks."

"Maybe half of you'd make it. Probably less."

Seevert made an angry, frustrated gesture. "All right! Deal is we ride on, double back in one hour. You'll be here."

"He won't be by hisself!" Pete Weems yelled suddenly, springing to his feet. "Damn you to hell, Pride Seevert! Had my way, I'd cut loose on the whole passel of you right now!"

Seevert stared at the trembling figure of the old man. After a time he shook his head.

"Who else you got up there, Keegan?"

"Don't see as it matters." A thought came to Dave. "You want to keep this strictly between us . . . just you and me?"

"Meaning?"

"Send your men on. I'll do the same with the people with me. Then you and I can settle this alone."

"Why not?"

Cass Bradford came about, his features strained. "You ain't thinking of doing that, are you?" he asked incredulously. "You'd be a plain fool."

"I'm looking for a way out of this . . . any way at all," Dave said grimly. "We haven't got a prayer if they decide to wait us out."

"But . . ."

"Thing I'm interested in is getting Hannah and you in the clear. Goes for Pete and Henley, too, if they're of a mind."

"I ain't lookin' to pull out," Weems declared. "Don't figure Joe'll be, either . . . but you're plumb loco if you make a bargain like that with Pride."

"Pete's right," Bradford said. "Pride'll never face up to you alone. If he don't ambush you, he'll have his whole bunch standin' by, ready to cut you down."

"Have to figure on that," Keegan said.

Weems groaned. Bradford wagged his head helplessly.

"Where you want to meet?" Pride called.

Keegan considered. Important thing was to keep the Bradfords out of it. Seevert evidently was unaware of their being with him—and it should be kept that way in event the showdown backfired.

"Hell Cañon," Dave said, choosing a point well distant and in the opposite direction. "You've got a liking for the place."

"Suits me. When?"

"This afternoon. Say three o'clock."

Pride nodded. "I'll be there. What guarantee I got that you'll show?"

"My word . . . and I don't go back on it."

Seevert stirred indifferently. "Won't make no difference. If you don't, I can still hunt you down. It all right if we move out?"

"Go ahead . . . up the trail. Any of your bunch turns back, I'll figure the deal's off and start shooting."

Seevert turned, said something to the men behind him. Chancy protested but Pride waved him to silence, put his horse into motion. In single file the riders fell in line.

"Sure a mistake," Pete Weems muttered, squinting at the procession. "We had them skunks by the short hair. Should've blowed them off the map."

Henley released the hammers on his shotgun, reached for his plug of tobacco. "Had old Pride stopped cold, sure enough, else he wouldn't have been so agreeable. You really goin' up there and havin' it out with him?"

Dave nodded as he continued to watch the departing riders. "Nothing's changed, far as the Seeverts are concerned."

Bradford looked down. "Reckon it was my fault . . . me and my daughter's . . . that you lost a good chance. I'm obliged to you for thinkin' of her . . . but don't go counting me out. Done made up my mind about Pride and his bunch and I ain't drawing a full breath until I see them crawlin'."

Keegan turned to the rancher as hope pushed through him. "Cass, there a chance you could talk some of the others into seeing things your way? They wouldn't listen to me."

Bradford rose, holstered his weapon. "Might be a couple . . . Ed Corrigan for one, Ollie Miller for another. Maybe more. Why? What're you thinkin'?"

"I'm not fool enough to believe Pride'll be at Hell Cañon alone . . . but I still aim to meet him like I promised. Occurred to me that if you and some of the other ranchers came along . . . not with me but behind me . . . we might get this problem settled for everybody."

"See what you mean," Henley said, catching on quickly. "We can bank on Pride ringin' in his outfit once you show up, but if he sees a bunch of the ranchers standin' by, backin' your play . . ."

Dave prodded Bradford gently. "What do you think?"

"Sure as hell worth a try," the rancher said. He glanced to the sun. "Ain't got much time, however. Expect I'd better be ridin' if I aim to do much talkin'."

Keegan's shoulders relaxed slightly. Perhaps the end of Pride Seevert's rule over Tenkiller Flats was in sight, after all.

"Good," he said, "and this time lock that daughter of yours in a room somewhere so she won't get in the way," he added with a grin.

"I'll do that," Bradford said. "Where'll we meet?"

Dave looked off to the north. "Hell Cañon."

XIX

Bradford studied Dave closely as if uncertain of his hearing. Then he shrugged. "Could be crowdin' things a mite," he said, "but I reckon you know what you're doin'."

Joe Henley shifted his double-barrel from right hand to left. "He's maybe got somethin' there. Might be smart to sort of hold back, see who all's comin' to the party."

"Was me who set the time," Keegan said. "Means that's when I'll be there."

Complete silence followed Dave's words, broken finally by Bradford.

"You're calling the shots," the rancher said, and started for the horses.

Keegan motioned to Henley. "Take a look up the trail . . . see if the Seeverts are sticking to the agreement."

The older man nodded, moved out of the rocks toward the path. Dave turned, and with Pete Weems at his heels followed Bradford to where the mounts were picketed.

Hannah was already in the saddle when they reached the brush. She passed the reins of her father's horse to him, smiled down at Keegan.

"I'm sorry," she said contritely. "I didn't realize I was going to ruin things for you."

"It'll work out," Dave said gruffly. "Maybe better."

"I hope so."

He glanced up, met her eyes. She was smiling softly. "Good luck," she murmured. "I'll be . . ."

"Come on, girl!" Cass Bradford broke in. "Got to get movin' if I'm to make all them calls."

He pulled away at once, and Hannah, with a final smile at Dave, swung in behind him. Keegan looked toward the trail. Joe Henley had his arm up, signaling that all was in order.

Keegan knew it would not be otherwise. Pride Seevert figured the meeting at Hell Cañon would be a cinch deal—all his way. He wouldn't risk queering it with a false move now. And Pride *would* have it all his way unless he could come up with a good idea, Dave thought, stepping up to the buckskin. So far everything had worked fine. He had been able to get Hannah and Cass Bradford out of the way before a shot was fired—and without the Seeverts being aware of their presence. Next would be the confrontation at Hell Cañon—and a plan of some sort that would afford him at least an even chance of coming out alive. He would, of course, like nothing better than a showdown with Pride Seevert alone, but Pride didn't operate that way. The eldest Seevert would start things off, then leave it to his brothers or his hired guns to finish.

He went to the buckskin's saddle, delayed while Pete Weems mounted and gathered in the reins of Henley's horse. When the old cowman was settled, he wheeled about and headed for the trail slowly.

Weems said: "Where's Joe and me fit in this?"

"Still feel like cutting yourself in?"

"You're dang' right . . . leastwise I do," Pete answered. "Ain't nothin' changed."

They reached the trail, halted. Henley crossed to his horse, climbed stiffly to the saddle. To his right Dave could see the figures of the Bradfords diminishing into the distance. To the left the way was clear; the Seeverts were out of sight. He heard Weems speak.

"Joe, you still comin' along?"

"Wouldn't miss this here hoe-down for a peck of money," the old man replied. "Where we goin' now?"

Dave realized the question was directed to him. He glanced to the north. "Just thinking about a ledge up near the cañon. On the west side of the mountain, sort of overlooks everything below. Be a good place to watch the Seeverts from."

"That'd be a right smart thing to do," Weems said, bobbing his head vigorously. "Get us an idea of what old Pride's plannin' to pull. But how we goin' to get there without them spottin' us?"

"Trail forks about half a mile on up, swings to the other side of the mountain. If we follow it, we can come in from behind, and be above them. Long ride but we've got plenty of time."

"How long?" Henley asked.

"Couple hours, maybe little more. Why?"

"Was just thinkin' we could use a bite to eat. Never did get around to that breakfast I cooked up this mornin'. You figure it might be a good idea for me to drop back to your place and get us some vittles?"

"I'm for that," Pete Weems said. "My guts is growlin' somethin' fierce. Reckon it's 'cause I'm hungry. How about you, Dave?"

It dawned on Keegan then that he, too, was in need of a meal. He had eaten little that previous night and, like the others, had been interrupted before he could touch his food that morning.

"Go ahead," he said. "We'll leave a marker on the trail showing you where to turn off for the ledge."

"I'll find it," Henley said, and wheeled about. "*Adiós*."

"*Adiós* . . . and don't you be takin' all day!" Weems said. "This here shindig comes off at three o'clock sharp!"

"I'll be there!" Henley shouted as he put his horse to a lope. Keegan and Weems moved up the trail. They rode in silence the short distance to where a faint path led off the main course and cut its steep way up the slope.

"Goin' to be mean," the old cowman said, eyeing the area critically. "Way it looks everything's been washed out."

"If it has," Dave answered, "we'll make a new one." They clambered over a rock slide, broke out onto smoothly washed ground. Dave looked upslope and pointed to a low butte. "Trail goes around that bluff. I remember it now."

"I'd say you ain't the only one rememberin'," Pete Weems commented in a low voice.

Keegan looked back. The old cowman was staring at the ground, his features sober.

"Them's fresh tracks."

Dave dropped from the saddle, squatted over the hoof prints pressed into the smooth soil. They were no more than an hour old, if that. Rising, he probed the country before him carefully; there was no horseman in sight. But there was a man up there, somewhere—one dispatched by Pride Seevert. That meant Pride knew about the ledge, that he was stationing one of his gunmen there as an additional precaution.

"This could be Pride's ace in the hole," he said half aloud. "He'll make a show of sending all the rest of his bunch away, but all the time he'll have this jasper on the ledge looking down on me over his rifle sights."

"Sounds like Pride, sure enough," Weems said dryly.

Keegan stepped back onto the buckskin, eyes still on the lifting slope. "Don't think whoever it is up there will be looking for us on his back trail, but we won't gamble on it. Keep it quiet and stay behind me."

Weems for once had no comment, simply followed orders. They climbed the grade slowly, approaching the butte at an angle that closed them off from view of anyone beyond it. Reaching that point, Dave signaled a halt and, again dismounting, made his way to the flat-crested bulge of rock. Keeping low, he worked around to the opposite side. The trail, definite and unmarred by storms, stretched out before him toward the rim of the mountain. He could see no one moving along its winding course.

Dropping back to Weems, he reported his

findings, adding: "We'll stay to the side . . . in the brush. Be harder going, but nobody'll see us."

The old cowman grinned tightly. "Sort of gives a man a creepy feelin' knowin' somebody's up ahead just waitin' for a chance to put a bullet in his brisket."

"He won't get the chance if we're careful," Dave said.

"Sound carries a far piece up in the hills like this."

"Doubt if he'll be listening or watching. Pride gave him orders to get on that ledge and lay low. That's all he'll be thinking about."

"And Pride'll be figurin' on him bein' there . . . a bushwhacker all cocked and primed to cut down on you when he gives the high sign."

"Just about the way it's set up," Keegan said, and added: "Wonder if he's the same one who took those shots at me at my place that first day?"

Pete Weems looked down. "That was me," he said in a low voice.

Keegan whirled on his saddle. "You! Why in the . . . ?"

"Was afeared you'd change your mind once you seen your place and keep on goin'. Wanted to make you mad enough to stay and fight the Seeverts. Figured throwin' a couple a shots at you from the brush'd do that."

Dave, over his surprise, smiled wryly. "Guess it worked."

"Maybe so . . . only I can see now there weren't no need. I'm plumb sorry, Dave."

"Forget it," Keegan said. "Let's get to that ledge and take care of a real bushwhacker. Think maybe this time Pride Seevert's outsmarted himself."

XX

Around noon they paused to rest in the shade of a wind-tipped juniper. They were just below the rim and less than a quarter mile, Dave estimated, from the shelf of rock, but the horses were blowing from the stiff climb and lathered with sweat.

Weems, sprawled full-length, looked off down the long slope, and mopped at his face. "Sure wishin' Joe'd turn up with that grub . . . powerful hungry. . . ."

Dave Keegan had thought little more of food after the ascent of the mountain had begun. His mind was on the Seeverts and what lay ahead. He had gone into the situation glowing with anger at the injustice being dispensed by the owners of Seven Diamond. This became more intense when they endeavored to force him into line with the other ranchers, but when he had learned that his father had also suffered the brutal pressure of the Seevert brothers, the fires within him had leaped to a high pitch. Now the time of reckoning was at hand, a reckoning he had, perhaps, deliberately provoked. Dave had no liking for what faced him—death for Pride Seevert and possibly for himself—but he was a man who knew that such a problem must be met head-on and settled definitely, once and for all. Only the end of the Seeverts would write finish to the trouble on Tenkiller Flats, but he wished there were another answer besides a gun; there was no glory in killing, only a revolting sickness, yet he knew he had no choice. It was the only thing Pride and his brothers understood and thus the only means by which their grip on the country could be broken. Still, if he talked to Pride, gave him a chance to pull out . . .

He stared up at the cloudless sky, gleaming blue through the heat. Two vultures high overhead dipped and soared on broad, tireless wings. *Waiting,* he thought, *just waiting.*

"Reckon we ought to be movin'?"

Pete Weems's question jarred him. He nodded, got to his feet, and walked to the buckskin. Halting next to the horse, he glanced to the rim above them.

"Up on top," he said, "the trail forks. The one going straight leads to the ledge. Other one follows the ridge for a spell, then drops off."

Weems said: "You figurin' we ought to part, come in on the ledge from two sides?"

"Be the smart way to do it. You take the ridge. Best we go quiet . . . and no shooting. Don't want Pride and the rest to know something's wrong."

The old cowman signified his understanding. "What about the horses?"

"We'll leave them on the ridge."

Pete groaned softly. "Never was much for walkin'."

"Be only a couple of hundred yards."

Weems grumbled something, climbed onto his saddle. Dave mounted and, again keeping to the brush, much sparser at the higher elevation, pressed on.

The buckskin broke out onto the top of the slope and walked slowly down into a small, grassy basin. Dave halted, waited for the old man to appear. A moment later Weems came over the edge and drew up near Keegan. They sat in silence, letting their tired horses graze for a time, and then Dave pointed to a rocky pathway leading on to the north.

"Stay on that. It'll cut to your right just beyond those cedars and take you down to the ledge. Leave your horse there and double back. Expect we'll find our bushwhacker somewhere near the middle."

Pete said: "I savvy. One thing . . . if you get there first, be mighty careful. Them snakes Pride hires can be plenty tricky."

"Same goes for you," Keegan replied, and headed across the basin.

He would reach the shelf first—he had planned it that way. Not that he didn't trust the old cowman; he simply believed it was his job and he wanted no man assuming a risk rightfully his.

Keegan gained the far side, found himself in a dense stand of scrub oak. Wishing to avoid noise, he veered right, circled the irregular patch, and entered a grove of towering ponderosa pine. Halting there, he picketed the buckskin in a shady hollow where grass was plentiful. The ledge was dead ahead, below and beyond a ragged hogback.

Moving quietly, he crossed to the rocky spine, picking his way with utmost care. One click of a stone, he knew, would alert the man now somewhere close by. A moment later he saw a blur of motion, froze. It was a horse, tied well back in the brush that covered the ledge. Knowing the rider would not be far away, Dave dropped to his belly, wormed to the face of the hogback, and looked over.

Gabe Seevert, rifle across his lap, sat near the edge of the shelf, smoking a cigarette. He was turned sideways to Keegan.

Dave studied the land briefly, and then withdrew. Dropping to a point some thirty or forty feet below the man, he again made his way to the ridge. Glancing over, he gave a grunt of satisfaction. Gabe's broad back was now to him.

The problem was getting down to the ledge unheard. Keegan mulled that puzzle about in his mind, spurred by the need to get the matter handled before Pete Weems came onto the scene, and arrived at a hurried decision. Sitting down, he removed his boots, hooked them under his belt, and began a slow, crawling descent of the embankment.

Reaching the bottom without incident, he paused, stifling his labored breathing. The sound of voices coming up from the clearing adjacent to the cañon was clear. Dave gave thanks for that; Gabe, not suspecting anyone was behind him, was keeping his attention on the men below.

Drawing his pistol, Dave drew himself to a crouch and cat-footed it to where the man sat.

"Don't move," he warned, jamming the muzzle of the weapon into Gabe's thick neck.

Seevert stiffened with shock and surprise. The cigarette fell from his lips.

"Who . . . ?"

"Not a sound," Keegan murmured, throwing the rifle aside. "Start scooting back from the edge, quiet."

Immediately Gabe began to hitch his way from the lip of the shelf. He still had not caught a glimpse of his captor and he continually tried to see from the corner of his eye while beads of sweat thickened on his ruddy face. Well back from possible view below, Dave stopped.

"Far enough," he said. "Now sit until my partner gets here."

Gabe Seevert sighed heavily in relief. He twisted his head around. His eyes widened.

"Keegan . . . where in the hell . . . ?"

"Maybe you're forgetting I grew up in this country," Dave said. "Knew about this ledge, too."

Gabe's shoulders went down. He shook his head. "Always figured things'd blow sky-high someday. Kept tellin' Pride that . . . only he wouldn't listen."

Keegan glanced to the north. Pete Weems had reached the fringe of brush at the end of the ledge, was peering at him questioningly. Dave waved him in.

"Maybe you should've talked harder," he said.

Gabe frowned. "You aim to shoot him down from here?"

Anger rushed through Keegan. "That's what you were sent up here for . . . to put a bullet in me, wasn't it? Where's the difference?"

Gabe dropped his head. "Was Pride's idea."

"But you went along with it. You could . . ."

"You got him! By God, it's Gabe!" Pete Weems exclaimed, coming in, crouched low.

"Yeah, it's Gabe," Dave said. "All set to pick me off like we figured." He pointed to the brush at the lower end of the ledge. "Saw his horse down there. See if he's carrying a rope. This is one Seevert that's not going to do much moving around for the rest of the day."

Weems hurried off. Dave reached down, plucked Gabe's pistol from its holster, thrust it under his own belt. Gabe watched him steadily, suspiciously.

"What're you goin' to do?"

"Not hang you . . . I'll leave that to somebody else. I'm just tying you up."

Keegan was suddenly conscious of the quiet below in the clearing. Shortly Pride Seevert's voice sounded.

"Gabe . . . you ready up there?"

Dave shoved the gun barrel deeper into Seevert's flabby neck. "Answer him, damn you," he said savagely. "And you better say the right words or this war'll start right here with me blowing your head off."

XXI

Gabe Seevert swallowed hard. "All set," he croaked.

There was a brief silence and then Pride's voice, suppressed and irritable, came again. "What's the matter with you?"

Keegan pressed harder. Gabe flinched. "I'm all right!" he shouted desperately. "Everything's fine!"

"Well, keep your eyes peeled," Pride said, satisfied. "Keegan'll be showing up pretty soon."

Immediately the murmur of voices resumed below. Dave relented, lowered his arm. "Keep playing it smart," he said, settling back, "and maybe you'll live to see the next sunrise."

Pete Weems trotted up carrying a coiled lariat over his shoulder. Keegan motioned Gabe to a stump at the extreme rear of the ledge and directed him to sit beside it. After they had bound and gagged the man securely, Dave and Weems returned to the edge of the shelf and, lying flat, looked down on the clearing. Pride Seevert, with Chancy close by, was sitting on a large rock. Gathered around them, some squatting on their heels, others taking their ease full-length, were nine of their hired hands.

Pride was just concluding a story of some sort and all were laughing. Pete Weems shifted angrily.

"Mighty sure of hisself."

Seevert could hardly be otherwise, Dave thought. He'd had everything his way for so long that he had no comprehension of opposition, much less of defeat.

"What's the time?" he asked in a hushed voice.

The old cowman dug about in his pocket until he produced a thick nickeled watch. " 'Most half past one."

Over an hour to wait. Keegan rolled to his back, glanced toward the spine of rock. He, too, was feeling hunger and wishing Joe Henley would put in an appearance. And the ranchers. There was no sign of them—not even of Cass Bradford. He stifled his impatience. There'd scarcely been time enough yet. Give them another hour. Anyway, there was no assurance they would come; like

Pride Seevert, except in reverse, they had been dominated by a ruthless power for so long they'd forgotten how to resist.

The minutes dragged. Weems dozed, as an old man will, in the hot sun. Gabe Seevert twisted and turned, seeking comfort that could not be found. Up on the rocks two striped chipmunks scampered about, eventually drawing the attention of a piñon jay that came to stare at them with beady eyes from behind his black mask. Where the hell was Henley? Had he, somehow, missed the turn off on the trail? He should . . .

"You boys better get moving." Pride Seevert's words reached Keegan clearly. "Don't want to scare our rabbit off before he comes to the snare."

Chancy laughed. "You reckon you're goin' to be safe, big brother?"

"I'm always safe," Pride answered, and also laughed. "Sort of a rule of mine."

Dave watched the Seven Diamond riders rouse, stroll leisurely to their horses, and mount, Chancy leading them. When all were in the saddle, Pride stepped to his younger brother's side. There was no levity in his manner now.

"You sure you got things right?"

Chancy frowned. " 'Course I have," he replied in an injured tone. "What the hell . . . you'd think I didn't have a lick of sense."

Pride made no comment, simply wheeled and returned to the rock. He sat down, watched

Chancy and the others ride slowly out of the clearing and up the trail. *Up the trail.* Keegan's eyes narrowed as he gave that thought. If Chancy and his men intended to return to Seven Diamond headquarters, they would have taken an opposite direction. To the north lay the higher levels of Tenkiller Mountain, and little else. There were a few game trails, he recalled, that dropped off and wound through the arroyos and lesser cañons to the flats, but no man was likely to choose such a rugged route intentionally. It could mean only one thing: they weren't actually leaving.

Back in his mind Keegan had known all along that Pride Seevert would devise such a plan; he simply hadn't given it any consideration. Undoubtedly Chancy and his followers would draw off a short distance, hide in the brush or possibly one of the many side draws that slashed the area. There they would be at Pride's call every moment.

Dave grinned tightly. The eldest Seevert left nothing to chance; not only had he stationed Gabe above on the ledge where he had absolute control of the clearing, but he also was positioning Chancy and nine of his hired guns where they would be handy. It wasn't going to be easy. Danger from Gabe had been removed but Chancy and his crowd posed a serious problem. He would be forced to depend more on Pete Weems than he had intended—and on Joe Henley, if only he'd return. The wiry old man and his shotgun would really be a big help.

Weems stirred, muttered something unintelligible. Dave reached over, shook him gently.

"Time?"

"Quarter past two," the old cowman replied, fumbling with the heavy piece. "Anythin' happen?"

"Chancy and the boys rode out . . . north."

"North? Where they goin' that way?"

"Expect Pride's got them hiding out nearby."

Pete swore. "That'd be him, all right."

Keegan drew back from the edge and sat up. Pulling his pistol he checked the cylinder for loads, then returned it to its leather pocket.

"I'll be going," he said. "Take me a little while to circle around, come in by the trail."

Weems frowned, looked to the lower end of the clearing. "Seen anything of Bradford and them folks he was bringin'?"

"Not yet."

"By dingies, they'd better be comin'. This here ruckus is all for them."

"Better not figure on it," Dave said. "Comes right down to it, it's my fight."

"No more'n theirs."

"Maybe, but they were willing to go along with the Seeverts. I wasn't . . . and that drops it in my lap."

Weems cast an angry, sidelong glance at Gabe slumped against the stump. "Well, don't you be forgettin' I'm in it."

"I'm not. I'm figuring on you staying put right up here. If things get out of hand, I'll holler, and you cut yourself in. Otherwise, leave it up to me."

"You ain't thinkin' you got a chance against the whole bunch, are you?"

"Pride won't call in Chancy unless he has to . . . and, long as he's sure Gabe's sitting up here with a rifle on my back, he won't. I'm going to try and settle things with him before it comes to that."

"Comes to what?"

"Shooting."

Pete's jaw sagged. "You mean you're goin' to try and talk sense . . . ?"

Dave nodded, got to his feet. Keeping low, he started for the end of the shelf.

"You're a plumb fool," Weems said in genuine alarm. "You'll be handin' Pride the chance he'll be lookin' for. I know him."

"So do I," Keegan said quietly. "Keep a sharp watch, and be careful. Want Pride to think Gabe's still up here, ready."

The old cowman mumbled a dissatisfied reply that was lost to Dave as he moved into the brush and began a slow, cautious descent to the clearing.

He reached it half an hour later, coming in at a point fifty feet or so below where Pride Seevert was waiting. Halting behind a thick stand of mountain mahogany, he turned his head to the trail and listened. He could hear nothing that would indicate the approach of Bradford and any of the ranchers he had succeeded in enlisting to the cause. Dave swung his attention again to the eldest Seevert.

Pride had forsaken the rock and was now upright and lighting a slim black cigar. He drew in deeply, exhaled a cloud of smoke, and watched it drift lazily away. Coming around then, he looked up to the ledge.

"Gabe!"

His voice was soft as though he were making certain it would carry only a short distance. He rode out several seconds, and, when there was no reply, he repeated the summons more insistently. Worry lifted within Dave. If Gabe made no answer . . .

"Yeah?"

Keegan felt relief trickle through him. He grinned faintly. Pete Weems's imitation was surprisingly close.

"What the hell's the matter with you . . . you sleeping up there?"

"Nope. Just waitin'."

Pride was satisfied. "All right. Time's about up. Keegan ought to be showing . . . if he's going to."

Dave touched the butt of the pistol at his hip, took a long breath. "I'm here," he said, and stepped into the open.

XXII

In the sudden hush Pride Seevert stood absolutely motionless for the space of several breaths. Then, with great deliberateness, he reached for the cigar clenched between his teeth and removed it. Smoke trickled from the corners of his mouth.

"Thought you'd be smarter than this, Keegan."

Dave closed in slowly, a step at a time. "Said I'd be here."

"Yeah, guess you did. Makes things easy for me."

"Maybe, but before you start anything you'd better listen . . . hear me out."

Pride watched Keegan ease into within a dozen paces, halt. "I'm through talking. Nothing more to be said."

"Could be worth your life."

"Doubt that, but go ahead."

"This is going to end in a killing . . . one or could be both of us. I'm offering you the chance to call it off, ride out of this country, take your brothers."

"You what?" Seevert exclaimed in amazement.

"You heard me. You're through here on the Flats, one way or another."

"Me . . . walk off . . . leave everything? Hell, I own this country, Keegan! It's mine, lock, stock and water bucket!"

"Not any more."

Pride Seevert stared at Keegan, finally began to laugh. "Beats all," he said, shaking his head. "You telling me to move on . . . you! What makes you think you're big enough?"

"One thing . . . you're going to decide here and now. There's just the two of us, and either you agree to pull out, or you reach for that gun you're wearing. It's that simple."

"Not quite. I've . . ."

"No. Gabe's not up there on the ledge with a rifle. He can't give you any help. And if you sing out for Chancy, I'll kill you."

At Dave's flat, quiet words Pride Seevert froze. Color began to drain from his face. He threw a hasty glance toward the shelf of rock.

"I . . . I don't believe a god-damn' thing you're saying," he managed.

Dave shrugged. "Pete," he called, "show yourself!"

He came to stunned attention as the voice of Joe Henley reached him.

"Things is all right up here, Mister Seevert. You go right ahead. I'll turn Gabe loose in a minute. Dassen't take my eyes offen Pete here just yet."

Relief crossed Pride's features, and the old confidence returned. "Joe's working for me again," he said. "Hired him back when he came out and told me he was signing up with you. Figured he'd be useful."

The shock of being double-crossed faded into

anger within Dave Keegan. He looked to the ledge. Weems was upright, arms aloft. Henley, shotgun muzzle pressed into the old cowman's back, was standing warily behind him. Keegan smiled grimly. With Henley thus occupied, Pride was little better off.

"Still makes it you and me," he said. "What's it to be? You pulling out or . . . ?"

"The hell with you!" Seevert yelled, and jumped for the protection of the rock. "Chancy!"

Dave drew fast, snapped a bullet at Pride. He threw himself to one side as Seevert fired an answering shot, winced as the slug plucked at his sleeve. He tried for a second time at Pride but Seevert was crouched low and offered no target.

Then, beyond the rock, Dave saw Chancy and his riders burst from the trees and charge into the clearing. Tight-lipped, Keegan rushed for the brush to his left. He heard Pride yell, saw him rise, and level his pistol. Dave triggered instinctively. Pride jolted, staggered back, and fell against the rock. More yells lifted as Chancy and the Seven Diamond riders pounded in. Guns began to crackle through the rising dust and smoke. Dave felt a solid smash against his leg, went down. Dirt spurted over him.

He threw two shots at the oncoming horsemen, rolled frantically to get farther into the brush. He caught a glimpse of Chancy Seevert, out in front, bearing down upon him. Pulling himself up slightly, he emptied his gun at Chancy, saw him buckle and fall from the saddle as his frightened horse veered off sharply.

Fighting the searing pain in his leg, Keegan fumbled at his belt for cartridges with which to reload. He paused, suddenly aware of the quiet. Drawing himself upright slowly, painfully, he glanced to the clearing where the spinning dust was beginning to settle. Seevert's riders were sitting motionlessly, hands above their heads.

Dave shifted his eyes to the opposite direction. Cass Bradford, Corrigan, and two men he didn't know were advancing slowly. Each held a leveled rifle. Well beyond them he saw a fifth figure—Hannah.

Keegan finished reloading and hobbled into the open. Bradford grinned at him hurriedly, then swung his attention back to the Seven Diamond riders.

"Drop them guns . . . all of you!"

There was a series of *thud*s as the men complied. From above on the ledge Pete Weems's voice sounded: "What about Dave? He all right?"

Moving deeper into the clearing, Keegan looked up. "I'm fine. You?"

The old cowman waved. "Nothin' wrong with me a shot o' rye won't cure. What'll I do with these two skunks?"

"Bring 'em down here!" Keegan called.

"Pride's dead," Ed Corrigan said, coming up. "So's Chancy. Where's Gabe?"

"Up with Pete, tied to a stump. You got here just in time. Obliged."

"Seems the thanks better go to you," Bradford said. "Big favor you done us all . . . even them that wasn't in on it." He paused, ducked his head toward the captive Seven Diamond men. "What'll we do with them?"

Dave leaned against the rock, favoring his throbbing leg. "Turn them loose, long as they promise to get out of the country, and stay out. Just hired hands."

"Could hold them for a trial."

"You've got Gabe to answer for anything you want to bring up."

"Figure that'll be plenty, once we have a look at what's in the bottom of Hell Cañon," Corrigan said.

Bradford nodded and grinned at Keegan, who was looking past his shoulder at Hannah, now entering the clearing.

"Tried to make her stay home but she wouldn't listen. Said most likely some of us would need doctorin'."

"Guess she was right," Dave agreed. "And I reckon I'm her first patient."

Outlaw's Promise

I

Wayne Trevison, grim and silent, stood in the murky, dim shadows of the way station waiting for the hostler to make his team change. The planes of his hard-bitten face were gaunt, toned to the color of winter's dry leaves, and his eyes, dark and splintery under their shelf of heavy brows, were but partly open as he watched the shape of the deputy standing near the off back wheel of the coach.

The late spring wind was cold. It had been cold all day long and the heat from the rumbling sheet-iron stove was a pleasant thing. Behind him the drummer, his only fellow passenger, was having a final whiskey at the makeshift bar and telling another of his pointless, rambling stories.

"And then this here sodbuster went and tried to take the wagon . . ."

The hostler was buckling up the final straps. The driver crossed the yard and pushed open the door. "All right, folks. All aboard."

The deputy eased around behind the stage, moving deeper into the yard. Trevison's glance sharpened; the man's presence worried him. He studied the lawman's bland face, but it was showing no emotion, revealing nothing of what lay behind it. Trevison hitched up the small carpetbag under his arm. He heard the drummer, speaking hurriedly: "Never knew what hit him, it was that sudden."

Trevison stepped into the wind-swept open, small flags of danger waving within him. He crossed the drive in slow, leisurely strides, a tall, wide-shouldered man of cool, arrogant carriage. He wore the usual clothing of the country—black boots, Levi's, wool shirt, canvas jumper, and broad Stetson hat.

"Come on, come on," the driver muttered from his seat.

The deputy slid forward. Trevison slowed. The deputy said—"Hold it, *amigo*."—in a flat voice and drew his gun.

Trevison halted and wheeled slowly around, allowing the carpetbag to slide lower under his arm. His eyes had become flat, empty; his lips a long slash of gray.

"Well?"

The deputy surveyed him closely. "You look a bit familiar. I know you?"

Trevison shrugged. "Doubt it," he said brusquely.

"You got a name?"

Trevison considered the man in the hard, disfavoring way of his. "Crewes. Jim Crewes."

"From where?"

Trevison stirred. All that way from Miles City. Across Wyoming and Colorado, part of Kansas and the Indian Territory strip. All that distance to this hole of a town in Texas without being stopped. And now, by a deputy sheriff. He considered his chances of coming through if he reached into the carpetbag for his gun. They were slim.

He said—"Dalhart."—mainly because that was the last town of any size he had been in. And no one knew him there.

"Dalhart, eh?"

The deputy remained still, thinking of that. The drummer was leaning through the window, watching and listening with avid interest, his eyes popped and round.

The driver threw a disgusted look at the lawman. "Hell, Mapes, why didn't you start this sooner? I got a schedule to keep."

The deputy made no answer. He said to Trevison: "Just you keep your hands from your sides."

Holding his pistol in one hand, the deputy explored Trevison's belt for a weapon. Finding none there, he patted the tall man's armpits for a hideaway gun. Satisfied as to that point, he stepped back. "Where you headin' for?"

Trevison breathed easier. He was glad now his gun had not been on him, that it was in the carpetbag. He had been extremely careful all the way from Dodge City, doing nothing that might draw attention to himself. In towns where guns were worn, he strapped his on; in the few where they were not, he kept his in the carpetbag. Handy but not in sight.

He said: “Fort Worth.”

“Come on, come on,” the driver grumbled in lifting temper.

The deputy cast an unswinging glance toward him, and then came back to Trevison. “All right, Crewes, get on board. Can’t help thinkin’ you look familiar, however. You been in Bowie before?”

Trevison said—“No.”—and climbed into the coach.

The deputy slammed the door and stepped back. The drummer grinned brightly, showing his collection of gold teeth. “Must have been two other fellers, eh, Marshal?”

The lawman favored him with a brief, sour look and spat. “Yeah, could be.”

The driver shouted at the team and the coach lurched ahead, harness metal jingling from the sudden motion. Trevison settled back in the seat, laying the carpetbag across his knees. Tension was draining slowly from him. He reached into his jumper pocket for tobacco and papers.

“How about a cigar, Mister Crewes?” the drummer said.

Trevison shook his head. He pulled a slip of paper off the fold and, shielding it with a cupped hand, tapped a quantity of dry grains into it, riding easily with the sway of the coach, running full tilt now, beyond the scatter of town. He half smiled.

That had been a close one. Evidently the deputy had seen the Reward dodger somewhere, the one offering $1,000 for him, dead or alive. Luckily he had not been sure.

The drummer struck a match with his thumbnail, leaned forward, and held it for Trevison. "Give one of these yokels a gun and a badge and they're just a-brimmin' with authority," he observed knowingly.

Trevison nodded and settled back, closing the man out. Outside, the driver's shouts flung back on the sharp breath of the wind. It was colder now and he settled the jumper a little closer about his body. But that was the only concession he made to the discomfort. He was accustomed to it, as are all men who drift restlessly on, never tying down. How many months now? Eighteen, almost nineteen since that day in Miles City when he had ridden out of town with fresh earth still damp on the sheriff's grave.

It was an endless trail. Large towns, small towns, railroad camps, road gangs, ranches, never at any of them for long. The letter had caught up with him at Dodge City, seven weeks after Tom Washburn had written it. Tom had once been foreman for Cass Goodman's Rocking R spread in Montana. He had taken Trevison and his kid brother, both orphans, under his wing and turned them into good cowboys, a substitution of some sort for his two sons back in Texas. Someday, Tom was always saying, he was going to have enough money salted away to go back to Texas and have his own ranch with his two sons to help run it.

Strangely enough it had come to pass. It took years, but Washburn did leave, and to Wayne Trevison it was like losing his father all over again. He had stayed on at the Rocking R, hearing once or twice from Washburn in the years that followed. And then had come the trouble and he was ever afterward on the move. Tom Washburn had not known of this when he wrote his letter from a sickbed in Fort Worth. Cass Goodman had placed it in another envelope, sealed it, and addressed it to—**James Crewes, c/o The Dodge House, Dodge City, Kansas**—knowing that Trevison turned up there periodically. Trevison had read the letter, nearly two months old by the time it came to his hands, and started immediately for Texas. Any favor Tom Washburn needed was an obligation that nothing would keep him from fulfilling.

Trevison idly watched the landscape rush by, thinking of that letter. Things had not gone well at the ranch, Tom said in his heavy-handed scrawl. His sons weren't much help, although they were now both grown men. Rustlers were picking the place clean and they seemed powerless to stop it. The bank was crowding him over his notes, which were long overdue. He was presently laid up in Dr. Rogers's home in Fort Worth. Could Wayne manage to come down and help an old friend straighten things out? He could take on the foreman's job long enough to see them through the roundup and the spring trail drive. Cass Goodman would let him off that long, he was sure. One good season was all it would take to put Triangle W on its feet. Would he come? And bring the kid brother, too; they could always use an extra rider on the place.

It was no problem to pick up and leave. At the time the letter came he was working on the railroad that had stalled at Dodge City, while Eastern money circles floundered in a money panic that threatened to throttle operations. He had simply sold his horse and boarded the stagecoach. In his pockets he had five gold eagles and a few silver dollars. He owned the clothes he wore, his gun, a battered carpetbag, and a saddle and other such gear, now in a gunny sack that was stowed in the boot of the coach.

He realized that traveling would be dangerous. He would get there, do what was necessary to get his old friend's ranch on a paying basis, and then move on. It was never healthy to stay overly long in any one place—bitter experience had taught him that. The one thing that bothered him most was the fact that Washburn referred to him as Wayne Trevison. The old rancher did not know about the trouble in Miles City, and therefore did not understand the danger that lay in the use of his real name. He hoped Tom had not done much talking about his coming down. That could make things much tougher. "Fort Worth!" the drummer called out, glancing through the window at the gathering houses. "Sure made that in fast time."

Trevison stirred his long shape and pushed his hat to the back of his head. It was growing late and a few lights were beginning to appear in windows. They pulled up at the station. The driver came down at once, wiping his gritty mouth and saying: "Night stop, folks. Hotel inside." He turned away and struck across the street in a direct line for the saloon.

Trevison waited while the drummer crawled out, and then followed. Guns were in evidence on the sidewalk, and he paused long enough to procure his from the carpetbag and strap it on. Inside, he registered for his room, glancing again to the outside where daylight still lingered. The man's natural caution swung him toward the dining room, warning him it was wiser to wait until full dark before making the one call he had in mind.

Ignoring the drummer's frank invitation, he sat down at an empty table and ordered a meal. When it was finished, he laid down his dollar and returned to the desk. The clerk, a bald man with weak, watery eyes and spectacles perched far down on a thin nose, met him with a questioning look.

"Doctor Rogers . . . where's his place from here?"

The clerk peered at him. "You sick?"

Trevison said—"No."—in a curt voice. He waited a moment. "Well? Where is it?"

"Right down the street," the man then replied hastily. "Brown house on your right."

Trevison nodded and swung through the doorway. Rogers's place was but a short distance, a rusty-looking shingled affair that apparently served in the triple capacity of home, office, and hospital. Trevison mounted the creaking porch and rapped on the door.

A voice from the inside said: "Come on in."

He cntered, finding himself in a large waiting room, once the parlor of the house, he guessed. A small man in a dusty blue suit came to meet him.

"Yes? What's your trouble?"

"You Doctor Rogers?"

The man blinked. "Yes, I'm Rogers. Who are you?"

"Crewes. Looking for a friend of mine. He was here a few weeks ago. Thought he might still be around. Name of Washburn."

"Washburn? Oh, yes, that rancher from over around Canaan way. He's gone. Been gone for some time."

"I see. Just how long?"

"About a month I'd say. I wanted him to stay here longer but he wouldn't listen to it. Bull-headed as they come. Said he had to get back to his ranch."

That sounded like Tom Washburn. He had a strong way about him once his mind was set.

The physician said: "He should have stayed. He wasn't in any shape to travel, much less work. He'd been gored. A bad wound it was. But he wouldn't listen to me. Some of those old-timers are like that, though, can't tell them a thing. That wound needed tending right close, it being deep like it was. Anything else I can do for you?"

Trevison shook his head. "No. Just thought he might still be here."

"He ought to be," the doctor replied tartly. "You see him, tell him it would be a good idea for him to drop back and let me look at that thing."

Trevison pivoted on his heel. "I'll do that," he said, and turned to the street. "Obliged to you."

II

There was a third passenger for the stage that next morning. A slim girl dressed in a dove-gray suit over which she draped a blue velvet cape. Trevison held the door of the hotel open for her, and she passed him with a slight nod of her head. The wind had not lessened during the night hours, and now it whipped along the street in persistent gusts. The drummer was already in the coach settled in the fore seat. Cigar smoke lay trapped in a pungent cloud within the vehicle as the girl hesitated on the step, wrinkling her nose in distaste. From behind her Trevison slanted a glance at the cigar, and then to the man, his meaning plain as spoken words. The drummer grinned weakly, and tucked the weed into the breast pocket of his check suit.

The girl sat down in the back seat and Trevison moved in beside the drummer. The driver shouted his—"Hey-up!"—and the stage rolled off down the street. There was a blurring of buildings, of houses, of faces turned toward them, the staccato barking of dogs, the shrill cries of children. Then they reached the outskirts and were rushing westward. The houses gave way to open prairie with its few trees and the mixed sounds of the steady rapping of the running horses, and the grating slice of iron-tired wheels cutting through loose sand.

Trevison settled back, tipping his wide hat to the bridge of his nose. He studied the girl from the shelter of its brim. She was pretty in a regular sort of way and the straight lines of her suit did little to hide the interesting contours of her figure. She had, he noticed, cool gray eyes beneath dark brows and her lashes were so long they tipped and curled at the ends. Her hair was a deep chestnut, and it lay around her face in shining folds like a burnished halo. The kind of woman he would choose if ever he had a choice. But that was not for him. A man on the move constantly had no right to press such a life upon a woman, any woman. She should have things that did not come out of cheap hotel rooms, dirty restaurants, and windy railroad camps.

She was wearing one of those small name pins, currently in style, on her lapel. It was of fine gold wire and the script read: **Halla**. An odd name, he reflected. The drummer twisted beside him. "Live around here close?" he asked, leaning forward.

Trevison shifted his attention to the girl's face. She was gazing out the window, her eyes lost in the brown and gray world beyond.

The drummer, not discouraged, tried again. "Great country! Real estate's sure movin' . . . movin' right on by, that is!"

The man laughed uproariously. The girl did not turn, evidently preferring the swirling dust and sand to his humor.

"Once knew a feller, travelin' man like myself, that made this country every spring. He got acquainted with a girl in a ratty little honky-tonk . . ."

Trevison saw the girl stiffen slightly, and a slow flush begin to rise in her face. His own thrusting anger began to lift. The damned fool—he should have sense enough to see she was no dance-hall chippy!

He said—"Forget it."—in a harsh voice that brooked no opposition.

The drummer choked on his words and

swallowed hard. He turned then to Trevison. In an injured tone, he said: "Was just tryin' to pass time. Make it a little more pleasant."

"We'll do without it," Trevison answered. The drummer got off at Abilene to await the Lordsburg-Tucson coach, then they swung north for Canaan on the last leg of the journey for Trevison. The wind now struck at them from right angles, buffeting the stage with fierce, sporadic blasts that filled the swaying vehicle with sand and spinning clouds of dust.

Trevison reached for the curtain and, finding it gone, shifted and placed his back to the open window, thus shutting it off to some extent. To the girl he said: "You care to sit over here next to me, maybe I can afford you a bit of shelter from that sand."

It was placed as a suggestion rather than an invitation, and his tone plainly indicated he cared little whether she accepted or not. But she did, moving across to the empty seat beside him, settling back against the bulk of his body. She made no sound, thanking him only with her eyes.

At this close range he could see a faint spray of freckles across her small nose. Her hands, lying still in her lap, were firm and strong; they were no strangers to work. There was a faint perfume about her, a light sweetness that reminded him of the flowers Mrs. Goodman grew around the house in Montana.

The driver's cries were a ceaseless howl in the wind, and the dust grew and fell in varying intensity. As the sun swung lower in its copper arch, the cold increased and bit deeper. The girl shuddered and pushed closer to him.

At once he said: "I've a blanket with my gear in the boot. If you want it, I'll stop this coach and get it for you."

She shook her head. "It's not far now. But thank you just the same."

It was fully dark when they rolled into Canaan, a small cluster of a dozen buildings huddled together along a short, crooked street. Trevison stepped from the coach and held the door for the girl, assisting her down with his free arm. She gave him her brief, serious smile and moved for the hotel, a single-story structure in which a feeble, yellow light burned above the desk. Canaan apparently was an overnight stop.

The driver was digging in the back of the stage, and Trevison swung to him to claim his sacked gear. Throwing it over his shoulder, he headed for the Longhorn Saloon that, besides the hotel, seemed to be the only place awake. A half dozen saddled horses stood at the tie rail, and, when he pushed through the swinging doors, he came to a halt. Dropping his gear in a corner, he let his gaze run the room.

A dozen men were bellied up to the bar. Three poker games were in progress at as many tables, and in the far corner a piano was thumping out a tune under the slack attention of a man wearing a derby hat. Trevison, his throat dry and dusty from the long ride, moved to the bar. The bartender met him with uplifted brows.

"Water. And whiskey."

The bartender poured a glass from a pitcher and slid it to him. He followed this with the liquor. Trevison emptied both glasses. Afterward, he stood quietly fingering the whiskey tumbler, revolving it between thumb and forefinger. The smells and the smoke and the boil of talk moved about him in a never-ending circle. He was having a lonely man's keen enjoyment of them.

The bartender poured another drink. "On the house. Sad day to be traveling."

Trevison nodded his thanks, making no other comment. He downed the fiery liquor and reached into his pocket for a coin.

"Come far?" the bartender asked absently.

"Not far today," Trevison replied, flipping the coin on to the counter. The man took it and returned his change. "Where's Washburn's place from here?"

The man's eyes pulled down. "You headed there?"

Trevison said: "Could be. Where is it?"

"About fifteen, sixteen miles west of town."

"Place around here where a man could rent a horse?"

The bartender was looking over Trevison's shoulder, to one of the poker games near the door. The piano began afresh, and a girl began to sing a ballad about a lost cowboy wandering the cold prairie in the dark. Sound was a low din in the shadowy depths of the room. The game near the batwings broke up, the four riders leaving at once.

"Where can I rent a horse?" Trevison repeated.

The bartender said: "Livery stable at the end of the street. Other side of the hotel."

Trevison nodded, and wheeled about. He picked up his gear and moved out onto the porch. For a moment he paused there, feeling the strong beat of the wind while he located the dim bulk of the stables 100 yards or more to his left. He debated briefly the wisdom of waiting out the night in town and reporting to Washburn in the morning. But he decided against that; it was not late and they could get things talked out that evening. Coming to that decision, he swung off the porch and started up the street.

He heard the scuff of boot heels even above the moaning of the wind. Instinct prompted him to take a swift side-step. A blow, directed for the back of his neck, fell short and came down hard upon the sacked gear dragging at his shoulder. A curse ripped through the blackness as flesh and bone thudded into the solid wood and leather. Trevison, knocked off balance by the sudden application of force, dropped the sack and spun away.

A fist caught him high on the arm and he, veteran of many similar experiences, continued to dodge and wheel away. Three, perhaps four, dimly outlined shapes swarmed in upon him. They were coming from the alleyway that separated the Longhorn from its adjoining structure. Trevison fell into a crouch, trying to get at his gun. A shadow closed in, pinning his arm. With the other he struck out, feeling his fist drive into yielding flesh, hearing a grunt of pain. Blows began to hammer at him, coming from all sides.

He braced himself, standing, straddle-legged, striking out with both hands. Time after time he felt his blows reach home, but they seemed to have little effect, and there was no slackening in the punishment he was absorbing. From out of the blackness a blow caught him squarely on the point of the jaw. A great roaring rushed through his head and lights popped before his eyes. He staggered back, hearing faintly a strained voice gasp: "He's a tough bastard!"

Hands caught at him, pinning his arms back. Fingers clutched at his hair, jerked his head up. Vaguely he could make out the tall, wide shape of a man standing before him his face half concealed by a bandanna.

"Hold him up!" The man's voice was a rasping, harsh command.

Trevison struggled against the hands that pulled him to a stiff, upright stance. Then pain rocketed through him as the big man drove a balled fist into his belly. Breath gushed from his lips and the night was a swirling, pain-filled void through which the wind howled. He fought to breathe, stemming the sickness that the blow had lifted.

"You sure you got the right man?" he gasped.

"We got the right man," the towering shape before him replied, and again sank his fist into Trevison's middle.

Trevison folded. He hung that way, swimming in a world half present, half gone. Through glazing eyes he had a close-up view of the tall man's shirt front and vest corners and the heavy buckle on his belt. In the smoky, filmy depths of his mind, he registered the buckle.

A voice said: "You got off that stage. Come mornin', you get back on it. And keep right on movin'. Understand?"

A sharp blow to the chin snapped Trevison's head up. Fingers entwined his hair, held it back, and then the tall shadow made a brutal game of slapping him first to one side, then to the other. Starch was running out of his legs, his arms were great, leaden weights. Through a haze of flashing light he saw a clenched fist coming straight at him. He tried to move away, to escape it, but the hands holding him upright kept him pinned to the spot. It caught him directly on the chin and abruptly it was totally dark.

III

Trevison came to with the moaning of the wind, the faint tinkle of a piano, and the shouts of laughter—all blending in his ears. He lay still, there in the street, dust and sand sifting over him. He was listening for any other noises, any tip off that the big man with the engraved buckle and the men who sided him were still present.

After a full five minutes he concluded he was entirely alone. He sat up slowly. His head throbbed and his sides and shoulders ached dully, and his face was tender to his exploring fingertips. They had made a good job of it. They had really worked him over. He might never know who the others were, but he would know that belt buckle anywhere—and the big man who wore it. He groaned as he got to his feet, the muscles across his chest and stomach complaining mightily at the effort. He felt around in the dark until he located his gun and hat. He dusted himself off, after a fashion, and picked up his sacked gear. He then headed for the hotel, knowing he was now in no condition to show up at Tom Washburn's ranch.

The clerk was sleeping on a cot behind the desk. Trevison rapped sharply on the counter and the man roused. He shuffled up, turned up the wick on a smoky lamp, and peered at Trevison.

"Yeah?"

"Room," Trevison said shortly. "How much?"

The clerk, getting a better look at Trevison, came more fully awake. He stared hard.

"How much?" Trevison snarled impatiently.

The clerk jumped. "Two dollars . . . in advance."

Trevison tossed the silver coins onto the desk and laid a cool glance on the man. "What's wrong with you, friend? Never see a man that's been in a fight before?"

He reached out and pulled the register to him and signed—**James Crewes, Dalhart, Texas**—in a bold hand and shoved the book at the clerk. "Which one?"

"Number Two," the man murmured, and ducked his head at the hallway to his left.

The room was stuffy. Trevison, ignoring the dust, threw the single window wide and let the wind have its rushing way for a few minutes. He closed it after a time, locking it, as he did the door. Pulling the ragged shade, he struck a match to the lamp and then, standing high and broad-shouldered in the center of the small cubicle, he thought back over the fight, considering its implication and possible meaning. Someone did not want him around, that was sure. The big problem was—who? Washburn's sons? Rustlers? The banker? He shrugged. At this stage of the game it would be difficult to tell, but whoever it was would show themselves again when they saw he had not left. He glanced around. The room was bare and plain. Rough planking formed the walls, their intervening cracks stripped by paste and old newspapers. A small circular rug lay on the unpainted floor in front of a sagging, iron bedstead. On the washstand, scarred by many a boot, stood the usual china bowl and pitcher, and behind these hung a broken, irregularly shaped piece of mirror, once a part of a whole. Large, square-headed nails driven into the west wall supplied pegs for his clothing. He began to undress, stripping to the skin.

After scrubbing himself vigorously with the cold water, he felt much better. The tenderness had become more localized, mostly along his ribs and over his belly. Peering into the dim mirror, he saw, with some satisfaction, his face was not too badly marked up. He stretched out on the lumpy mattress, tired and suddenly hungry. But it was too late now to eat. Canaan's only café had been dark. He would have to wait until morning, and, thinking of that, he fell asleep.

Daylight pushing against the drawn shade awakened him. The wind had finally blown itself out and he rose, somewhat stiffly, but much better for the night's sleep. The same clerk was behind the desk when he came down into the lobby. The man nodded unsmilingly and Trevison deposited his sack of gear, saying: "I'll be back for it."

It was early but the sun was warm. He stood for a minute in the street enjoying its touch, a tall, muscular, wedge-shaped man with a dark and bitter face. He swung his gaze toward the Longhorn, to the spot where he had been jumped that previous night. He was remembering the actions of the bartender, and he wondered now just how much that man knew about the ambush. It might pay to have a talk with him. But after he had eaten, he decided, and crossed over to the Canaan Café.

He chose a table near the back and sat down. A frowzy woman came from the rear, wiping her hands dry on a soiled apron. He said: "Breakfast . . . coffee, steak, and potatoes. I'll have the coffee now."

The woman nodded and returned to the kitchen. She brought him a cup of steaming black liquid, and placed it before him, saying nothing. Trevison drank the coffee steadily, finishing it long before she brought his meal.

Canaan was even less in the day's revealing light. Two or three stores: the Longhorn, the stable at the far end of the street, the café in which he now sat, a barbershop, and several such minor places. And then the bank. Trevison viewed the building critically. It was a single-story structure of frame that had been fronted with red brick. **WEST TEXAS STATE BANK**, the sign over it read. Tom Washburn had mentioned it in his letter as having a big stake in the success or failure of the Triangle W. He decided he would have a few minutes' talk with the banker before he left town. He might even be able to learn a little about the events of the preceding night.

The woman brought his meal and he ate it with the relish of a strong man accustomed to outdoor living. He consumed three cups of good, strong coffee before he was finished. When he got up to leave, he saw the waitress standing just behind the partition that shut off the kitchen. She was watching him with disturbed, fearful eyes, afraid perhaps he might ask her some question she would find hard to answer. He gave her a hard grin, laid a dollar on the table, and left.

He paused outside the door, once again enjoying the sun's warmth. Few people were abroad. A lone horse stood at the Longhorn's rail, weary and drooping. Farther down, a man swept vigorously at the accumulation of sand and dust piled into the corners of his porch by the wind. A nondescript dog sauntered from the stable, and made his way to the general store, and there lay down on the step.

Trevison swung into the street and walked to the bank. The door was open and he entered. A short, heavy man with a fringe of gray hair circling his head rose to meet him. Trevison crossed the small lobby to the counter that separated the customers from the desks and vault.

The banker smilingly offered his hand. "Gringras,"

he said, looking Trevison over carefully. "Frank Gringras. I imagine you're Trevison."

Trevison said: "Possibly."

"Fit Tom's description. Little older, maybe."

Trevison nodded, again wondering how much talking Tom Washburn had done. He said: "For the time the name is Crewes. Just forget the Trevison."

Gringras gave him a close look. He shrugged and held open the hinged gate for Trevison to enter the enclosed area. Motioning to a chair, he dropped into his own. "Just ride in?"

"Last night."

"You have some trouble?"

"Only a scrap," Trevison replied. He watched the banker for some sign of surprise, or perhaps guilt. But he detected nothing. Then: "How's Tom?"

Gringras frowned, his mouth dropping open a little. He said: "Of course you wouldn't know about it. I'm sorry to tell you this, but Tom's dead. Been dead for near onto a month now."

"Dead?"

Gringras shook his head. "He should have stayed with that doctor there in Fort Worth. Got himself gored by a bull but wouldn't take care of it. Came back before the doc wanted him to and the next thing you know, gangrene had set in."

The shock of this information traveled through Trevison. Washburn was dead. He had arrived too late. That changed matters considerably, throwing an entirely different light on matters; Tom was beyond the need for his or anyone else's help now.

He said: "That's the way the chips fall sometimes. Sorry I didn't get here sooner. I would have liked to have seen him and do what I could for him."

Gringras knitted a frown again. "You don't figure to stay? You're not going ahead with the job?"

"Why?" Trevison asked coolly. "I came to help Tom. He's gone and don't need me now. I owe nobody else any favors."

"Maybe so," the banker said slowly. "But remember all the things he started, the matters he wanted your help on are still here. His hopes, I guess you might call them. I would like to see them finished up right."

"A natural thing," Trevison observed dryly.

Gringras shook his head. "Of course, there's my stake in it, too. But I can live through it. Tom was a good friend of mine. I hate to see everything he slaved for go down a rat hole."

"What's wrong with those two boys of his? They're old enough to take over."

Gringras snorted. "Doubt if either of them will ever be old enough for that. Virgil's twenty-two, and all he thinks about is that woman he married and acting like a big-time rancher. And that woman! Married her up in Dodge City, and she's got him so confounded balled up he can't think of anything but her. She's a real good-looking girl and Virgil is so jealous of her he's about to shoot up any man that looks at her twice."

"What about the other one?"

"Troy? Wilder'n a swamp rabbit! Never done an honest day's work in his life. Thinks only of gambling and helling around. Not worth the powder it would take to lift his hat. Neither of them is, for that matter. Both of them were a great disappointment to Tom."

Trevison was watching the banker closely, seeing the heat rise in him and color his neck and face. He felt very strongly about it, there was no doubt of that. It was hard to believe Tom Washburn's sons could be that way. Tom was so solid and dependable. For him to have a pair of mavericks like Frank Gringras had described did not seem right.

But then, he remembered, Tom was apart from them for the greater part of their growing-up years. They had lived, along with Tom's wife, with an uncle or some such relative down near Austin. It was an ironic thing, Tom's saving and working all that time to build something for himself and his sons, and then having it all turn out as it had.

He said, asking the question for no particular reason: "What kind of shape's Tom's ranch in?"

"Good and bad. Unless somebody steps in and

takes it over with an iron hand, those boys will run it into the ground fast. Them and the rustlers."

"Rustlers are not hard to stop," Trevison commented.

"First you got to want to."

Trevison considered that strange statement, trying to ferret out its meaning. Abruptly he shrugged it off. It was now no concern of his—why waste time thinking about it? He had come nearly 500 miles to help a friend, and now that friend was dead and needed no help. He could move on, a smart thing he should do anyway, before some overly zealous lawman, like the deputy in Bowie, got bright ideas.

"Still don't figure it any affair of mine now," he said, rising to his feet. "My sticking around would do Tom no good."

Gringras said: "Just a minute. I got a letter here for you. Probably should have given it to you sooner." He turned to the vault and from its interior of pigeonholes and drawers procured a long envelope. He handed it to Trevison and settled back into his chair.

Trevison ripped the flap. There were two separate sheets and a letter of several pages. He glanced at the signature at the bottom.

Dear Wayne,

I figured you'd show up sooner or later. Looks now like I've got me some misery I won't be around to tell about. Like I said in my other letter, I'm needing your help bad at my ranch. Somehow I can't seem to stop what is going on, or even put my finger on it. And the boys aren't much help. They're good boys but they don't have the knack of it.

Now if you could take over the foreman's job and run things for a spell, I know you could straighten it all out. Do something about that danged rustling and get my 2,500 steers to Dodge for shipping this summer and you'd have it licked. There's plenty of beef there on my range. All you need to do is get it together and you'll be all right.

I won't be trying to tell you who to trust and who to look out for, because I know you'll be doing your own choosing. But you'd better keep an eye on everybody. I've been fooled myself pretty bad. I hope it won't make any difference, my not being there to work with you. I'd like to have the ranch straightened out anyway and my obligation to Frank Gringras taken care of. He's been a good friend and he went way out on a limb for me. I don't want to let him down.

And maybe there's something you can do about my boys. They're not bad, maybe a bit wild and hare-brained but not bad. Maybe you can just sort of straighten them out, too, as you go along and make something out of them.

We had good times in Montana, Wayne, and I used to think about them a lot. Sure wish I was there to hash them around with you but I guess it's not in the cards for me.

Keep that fast gun of yours handy and do what you can for your old friend. So long.

Tom Washburn

The signature was genuine. The handwriting in the body of the letter was not. Trevison finished it and for a long minute studied it. Then: "Who wrote this?"

"I did," the banker said promptly. "Tom just never gave up the idea that you would get here. Then, when he got bad sick, and knew he wasn't going to make it, he called me out to the ranch, closed the door to his room, and gave it to me. I wrote it down just as he said it. Then he signed it. Just to make sure it would stick, he made out a will, also, left everything to his two boys, but made me executor with the right to run the place and appoint a foreman until the bank's loan is paid off."

Trevison nodded. It sounded like Tom, the words he would use, the way he would say them. He unfolded the first sheet of paper. It was a copy of the will, short and simple and just as described. The second sheet was a formal authorization of him to take over the Triangle W as foreman, at a salary of $100 per month and keep, and operate it as he saw fit. It was signed by Washburn and countersigned by Gringras.

Trevison remained silent, his thoughts on the long letter Washburn had left. He could leave, push on to a new place, and keep running. That was the usual pattern. Or he could stay and take over Tom's ranch long enough to get it on its feet, thus fulfilling a dead man's request. After that was done, he could move on, hoping it would be before someone got suspicious and did a little checking on him. It was a gamble, but with a small amount of luck he could last out a few months. He folded the papers and thrust them into his inner pocket.

"How much Tom owe you?"

"Near thirty thousand dollars."

Trevison's hard-planed face broke a little with its surprise. "That's a lot of money."

Gringras said: "Like Tom told you, I went out on a limb for him. A big limb. That place of his goes under so does this bank and a few other places."

Trevison nodded, his face again a solid mask. "Keep my coming here to yourself. And the name is Jim Crewes. Don't forget it."

Gringras smiled with sudden relief as he realized what Trevison's words meant. He came up from his chair quickly, reaching for Trevison's hand. "You don't know how good it is to hear you say something like that. Tom will rest easy in his grave now, knowing you've taken a hand in the game." The banker paused. Then: "About this name business. Tom didn't know you'd changed it. He's talked Wayne Trevison around here for the last year. Doubt if there's anybody, especially there at the ranch, who won't guess who you are."

"Probably right, but just keep saying Crewes anyway."

He swung about to leave, Gringras trailing him to the doorway. Stopping there, the banker shook his hand again and murmured: "Good luck."

Trevison nodded his thanks. Good luck—he would need a lot of it, especially if the whole country knew him as Wayne Trevison.

IV

Trevison angled across the empty street to the hotel and picked up his gear. He continued on to the stable, the matter of questioning the bartender out of his thoughts. The stage had already pulled out and he had a moment's memory of the girl, Halla, wondering what her final destination had been. It had been a pleasant thing, that long ride with her sitting tightly against him as the wind whistled through the coach. Women were no strangers to Wayne Trevison. He had the strong, normal instincts of any man, and the masculine appeal of him usually brought him more attention than he desired. In almost every town in which he had spent any time, there had been a woman with whom he had become acquainted. In Dodge it was a dance-hall girl named Roxie. In Santa Fé, there was Carmelita; in Denver, it was Grace. And there was a rancher's daughter in Laramie. But he was always careful to keep a tight rein on his emotions, never allowing any affair to become too involved.

The hostler, an unkempt man in filthy, stained overalls, came from the gloomy depths of the stable and faced him.

"You wantin' somethin'?"

Trevison said: "A horse."

"Buy or rent?"

"Rent."

The hostler rummaged through his tangled hair with crooked fingers. "Well, now, I don't know about that. I know you?"

"Name's Crewes. I'll be working the Washburn Ranch. Just got in and need a horse to get out there on."

"Why didn't they send one down for you?" the man asked in a suspicious voice. "They got plenty of 'em."

"Forgot it, I figure," Trevison said calmly. "Go talk to Frank Gringras at the bank. He'll tell you it's all right."

"He know you?"

The old impatience began to needle through Trevison. "You think I'd tell you to go see him if he didn't?"

Trevison's harsh tone brought an injured look to the man's watery eyes. "Well, we don't rent no horses to people we ain't regularly knowin' . . ."

"Talk to Gringras," Trevison said wearily.

The man shrugged and turned away. He walked the length of the street to the bank, and in a few minutes he was back. He said nothing but disappeared into the stable, returning later with a wiry little buckskin.

Trevison dumped his gear from the gunny sack. He tossed the blanket over the buckskin and swung up his saddle. "Leave on that halter," he said to the hostler. "We'll use it to bring him back."

The hostler nodded and picked up Trevison's bridle, pulling it on over the makeshift hackamore. "When you get him back here?"

"Tomorrow. Maybe later today."

"You want to pay now?"

Trevison said: "Let it wait. Might even keep him for a month." And he rode out of the stable, leaving a perplexed man staring after him.

He struck due west, following the directions he had obtained. Within a mile he was out of the swale in which the town of Canaan lay, and was riding across a high and level prairie. It reminded him a great deal of the country west of Dalhart; the high plains they called it. He noted, critically, the grass along there was not too good. It had not been a wet spring, he guessed. More wind than rain likely.

He rode steadily onward, the sun at his back. He came finally to a gentle dropping away of the land. This would be Nine Mile Valley. It looked much greener than the plateau, and it extended both north and south as far as he could see. Trees, a deeper green band snaking along the valley's floor, marked a stream's course and the flash of silver in the strong light proved there was ample water within its banks. Almost the entire breadth across he caught the faint, bluish smudge that indicated a ranch. That would be Washburn's Triangle W. Tom had chosen a mighty fine place for his spread.

He approached the ranch from its southwest corner, not following the well-cut wagon tracks that bent away toward the town. A windmill grated in the breeze, making dull clanking sounds in the morning air. Several horses stood in the corral, and, as he walked the buckskin quietly into the yard, he saw a half dozen men gathered before the bunkhouse.

Trevison was a dozen yards away when he came to an abrupt, attentive halt. Something about the high, broad shape of one of the riders arrested him. The way he was wearing his hat or carried his shoulders, he didn't know which. But it struck a hard, familiar chord within him, stirring up a vague anger and drawing his eyes down to slits. He urged the buckskin forward, coming in silently. The men had not heard him and paid no heed until he was almost upon them. They wheeled in surprise and stared. Trevison checked the pony, his face suddenly hard-cornered and bleak.

The big man had turned, a frown on his coarse-featured face. He said: "What do you want?"

But Trevison did not hear. His eyes were on the heavy silver buckle the man wore. Wicked, black anger swept through him like a flash flood. He said—"You."—and launched himself from the saddle in a long dive.

He hit the cowpuncher at the waistline and they went down in a threshing heap. Trevison came up, hearing the startled yelps of the others. He stopped them cold with a bitter, warning glance that left them still.

"Keep out of this!"

The big rider was back on his feet, shock and pure amazement still slackening the lines of his face. He dropped into a crouch, long arms outreaching as he circled Trevison. He had lost his hat in the first violent collision and now his hair hung down in dusty disarray. A thin grin split his lips; a sullen anger began to push through his eyes.

"Get him, Jeff," a cowpuncher muttered.

As if at a signal, the man rushed in. Trevison met him full on—with a flashing left fist that stalled him. He followed this with a whistling right that cracked when it landed. But Jeff was not hurt badly. The blow had been too high on his head. Trevison moved in quickly, following up the small advantage he had gained. Hammering with both fists, he drove the man back, the memory of the attack at the Longhorn fanning his temper.

Jeff did not give ground for long. He hauled up, braced himself, and began to counter. For a long minute they stood there like that, toe to toe, slugging it out. The dull, meaty *thud* of fists was a steady drumming sound in the hushed yard. It was Trevison who, seeing his blows were gaining him little except his own weariness, stepped back and aside. The movement caught Jeff off guard, and he went slightly off balance as his swing missed. Trevison, moving fast, brought a down-sledging blow to his ear and dropped him flat.

A murmur went up from the watching riders. Trevison backed away, shooting another glance at them. If they had any intentions of helping their member, they did not show it.

Jeff came up slowly to his hands and knees, wagging his head. He came unsteadily to his feet. Blood trickled from one nostril and from a corner of his mouth. Dust plastered a side of his face, matted his hair, and covered the front of his clothing. He pivoted slowly about, the light in his eyes wild, murderous. He lunged suddenly. Trevison had been watching for the move, but he was a fraction late. His punishing right and left landed in rapid succession, but Jeff grabbed and managed to reach his arm and hang on.

Trevison lashed out with his free hand. It struck Jeff hard in the face, just across the eyes. But the swing was short and Trevison had no steam behind it. He wrestled with the man as they reeled about the hard pack in a tight circle, Jeff hanging on as he tried to regain his footing, Trevison beating him savagely about the face and neck. Suddenly he felt Jeff's leg behind him, tripping him up. He tried to throw himself to one side, to escape falling, but the rider's weight was now against him, pushing him back. He went down, Jeff falling heavily upon him.

"Now you got him!" a voice yelled.

The big rider, bearing down with everything he had, squirmed around until he was straddling Trevison's body, pinning him fast to the ground. A triumphant look was on his face, the grin was back, much wider. With one hand he knocked aside Trevison's lashing fists. With the other, he sent a blow smashing into the bridge of Trevison's nose.

Pain surged through Trevison in a great wave. He struggled to displace the man's weight, but it was an overwhelming burden, held steadily in place by Jeff's bridging legs. He struck out at the rider's face, felt that blow miss, and clawed for the man's eyes, his mouth—anything that would offer purchase. His hand skated off Jeff's face, greasy with blood. Another blow, this time to the side of his head, rocked his senses and set the lights to dancing. He fought to keep consciousness, knowing only the worst could await him once he ceased to fight.

Jeff was grinning down at him. "Maybe a knot on your head would help you lay still," he said.

Through the haze Trevison saw him lift his gun, butt foremost, and prepare to bring it down. He sucked in wind deeply and heaved upward, lifting his hips off the ground. Jeff, impelled by the unexpected movement, dipped forward. In that small movement Trevison doubled his leg and struck out at the man's head. It was low. The boot missed Jeff's head but the spur rowel caught him in the neck, raking a long gash that spurted bright red.

The man yelled in pain. Trevison felt his muscles relax. With another demand upon his reserve strength, he shoved, and Jeff spilled over and off him. Trevison rolled free and came up at once, drawing for wind in great gasps. His legs were trembling from the efforts of those last moments. Hand near his gun he watched Jeff still sitting there, dabbing at the steady flow of blood in his neck with a dusty handkerchief.

Trevison said: "Get up! You're not hurt bad. We'll finish this now."

Jeff glared at him with dull hatred. "Later. We'll finish it later."

"There'll be no later. If you work for this outfit, you're through."

The big cowpuncher got to his feet, holding the cloth to his wound. "What's that? Who you think you are, mister?"

"You ought to know," Trevison said evenly. "You said you did last night."

Jeff spat. "A smart man would have taken that advice."

Trevison said: "Advice is a thing I don't often take, even from friends. But here's a little for you. Get off this ranch and stay off. You're not working for it any more."

A voice, reaching over Trevison's shoulder from the yard said: "Who's not working here? Who's running this place, anyway?"

Without turning Trevison said curtly: "I am."

V

"The devil you say!"

Trevison remained where he stood, his gaze close and watchful on Jeff and on the others who now ranged about him in a half circle. In a low voice he said: "Come around front where I can see you, friend, if you've got some talking to do. I don't cotton much to men standing at my back."

He heard the light scuff of boot heels as the man who spoke moved by him and took up a stand near Jeff. He was young, handsome in a weak sort of way. He wore expensive boots, costly broadcloth breeches, and cream-colored silk shirt. The broad Stetson hat he wore would have set him back no less than $50. There was a smiling quality about his features, a sort of reckless gaiety that looked out of his blue eyes, and quirked the corners of his mouth. The resemblance was there, hidden somewhere. But it was there. This would be Troy Washburn, Tom's younger.

Washburn surveyed Trevison, looking him up and down in a swift, encompassing glance. A smile pulled at his lips. "Guess you must be Trevison."

"I am."

"You're a little late. The old man's dead. I'm running the ranch now . . . me and my brother."

Trevison said: "No, not quite. Beginning now I'm foreman, range boss, trail boss, and manager of Triangle W. Not that I give a hoot about taking the job. But a dying man asked me to do it, and, because he was a friend of mine, I'll take it on."

Troy considered this, taking no apparent offense at Trevison's words. After a time he said mildly: "You're a little high-handed with your methods."

"The way it will be until the job's done. Once it's over and finished and Tom Washburn's obligations are settled, I'll leave. You can damn' well do what you please with it then. Until then, it's my way."

"Still happens I own this ranch . . . ," Washburn

began, the smile fading a bit. Light anger began to push at his eyes and color his neck and face.

"You'll own it when I'm through," Trevison said dryly. "Meantime, I'm doing the running of it. You got two choices . . . pitch in and work, or get out of the way."

"Just what you figuring to do?"

"Good many things. Straighten out this outfit, mainly. And get two or three thousand steers to market this summer and collect for them."

"That's all?" Troy Washburn said in a faintly sarcastic tone. He was fighting to maintain some semblance of authority before the crew.

"Don't worry about it," Trevison murmured, and dismissed the conversation by turning to the man called Jeff.

"I want you off this place in fifteen minutes. And the next time you walk up behind me, daylight or dark, you're a dead man."

The big cowpuncher swung a hasty, questioning look at Troy Washburn. Trevison stopped him cold.

"Don't think that will help you. He's no more than any of the hired hands around here now."

"Looks to me . . . ," Troy began hotly, but Trevison sliced across his words.

"What things look like to you don't matter to me. You let a good man down when you didn't stand by your father, and I'm not forgetting that. He was a man you're not fit to clean boots for.

Let's get it straight, Troy, once and for all time . . . you and that brother of yours can rot in quicksand for all it means to me. I'd not turn a hand to help you." The yard was hushed, tension lying tightly over the small group. One of the horses in the corral blew noisily and stamped. Somewhere down in the trees near the river a crow *caw*ed harshly.

Trevison turned his bitter attention to the man called Jeff. "You're fifteen minutes are near up. Get moving." He swiveled his glance to the others. "This goes for all of you. Either you work for me or get off. Now's the time to make up your mind."

Jeff gave Trevison a seething glare and stomped off toward the corral. There was a moment of indecision among the riders, then three of them shambled off after him. A cowpuncher with graying hair and mustache remained where he stood, his hawk-like face calm and pleased.

"What about it?" Trevison demanded.

The rider stirred. "Why, I reckon I'm staying."

Trevison gave him a brief nod and came back to Troy Washburn. "Any more committees like that one you sent to meet me last night, and I'll come looking for you, not them."

Washburn showed surprise. He started to say something, thought better of it, and shrugged. Trevison reached into his pocket and withdrew the letter of authority Tom Washburn had left for him. He handed it to Troy, saying: "Here, read this."

Washburn read it and handed it back, making no comment.

Jeff and the others had collected their gear and were pulling out of the yard. They swung by, the big cowpuncher giving Trevison a close, burning glance as he passed. A quarter mile down the road they stopped, coming abreast of a light buggy.

"My brother," Troy announced. "We'll see what he has to say about all this."

"I'll not go over it again," Trevison stated. "If he needs to know anything, I'll be in the bunkhouse."

He wheeled away to the rented buckskin. Taking up the reins, he led him to the barn, issuing orders there to the wrangler for its care. Coming out, he found the old cowpuncher awaiting him.

"Name's Farr. Jay Farr, Mister Trevison. Come on, I'll show you where you can wash up."

Trevison followed him to a small shed-like building at the rear of the bunkhouse, where there was a pump and a bench, lined with a row of tin wash pans. Trevison cleaned up as best he could, removing the dust and blood smears from his face and arms. When he was finished, he turned to Farr.

"You a friend of Tom's?"

"Been workin' for him ever since he come back from Montana. He was tellin' me about you. Said he'd sent you a letter and asked you to come down. 'Bout give you up, myself."

Trevison walked deeper into the yard, away from any possible listeners in the barn. He said: "What's wrong around here, Jay? Looks like a right good spread to me."

The old cowpuncher hitched at his Levi's. "One of the best in the country. But it's a dang' sight easier to say there's nothin' right. The boys don't give a hang about the place, only for what cash they can dig out of it. Just bleed it dry all the time. Jeff Steeg, that ranny you tangled with, was supposed to be foreman but he never did no bossin', leastwise of ranch work. Plays around with Troy and does his fightin' for him . . . and Virgil's dirty work."

"Virgil any help around the place?"

"Same as Troy. Worthless."

"How about the stock?"

"Good shape. Ought to wind up the roundup pretty soon. Looks like they wintered good."

"Understood from Tom's letter you were having a little rustler trouble."

Farr scratched at his chin. "Yep. Mostly piddlin' stuff. Ten, twenty head at a time. Never more than fifty."

Trevison clucked. "Still runs into money after a while. Any idea who it is?"

"Got my own idea about some of it," Farr said promptly. "And they's some small, jackleg outfits around us. I figure they just help themselves when they need beef."

"What's wrong with Steeg? Didn't he try to stop them?"

"Never did. Says it's just somethin' a big outfit like this had to expect."

"And the Washburns . . . didn't they worry about it?"

Farr snorted. "They just left everything to Jeff."

Trevison gave this some thought. There was the possibility Steeg was connected in some way with the rustlers. But it was also possible the foreman ignored it simply because of the Washburn boys' lack of interest in the ranch itself. What of the time when Tom Washburn was alive? Trevison knew that man well enough to know he would countenance no such neglect of duty.

"Couldn't Tom make Steeg toe the mark when he was here?"

"Jeff wasn't no foreman when Tom run the place," Farr said, shaking his head. "He was just one of the crew. Virgil was the onc who made him foreman, after his pa got hurt."

The buggy had pulled into the yard and halted at the rail near the front of the main house. Trevison watched as Troy Washburn met his brother and sister-in-law. All three went immediately inside.

"Figure I ought to tell you about Steeg," Farr said then. "He's a bad one. You'd better keep your eye on him from now on." He paused, a frown pulling at his weathered features. "I heard you say somethin' 'bout last night. What happened?"

"Steeg and two or three others jumped me when I came out of the Longhorn. Warned me to keep moving."

Farr chuckled. "That figures. Sure never forget the look on Jeff's face when you come sailin' off that saddle after him. You'd thought the devil hisself was on his trail."

Trevison grinned. "Had my hands full there for a few minutes." Thinking again of the Washburns, he said: "What kind of man is this Virgil?"

Farr shook his head. "Virg don't do nothin' at all. Leaves everything up to Troy and Jeff. Got hisself a right pretty woman up in Dodge about a year ago, and keeps hisself busy foolin' around her. Guess he's afraid she'll look twice at another man."

"Jealous, I hear."

"Worst I ever saw. Causes him to get a mite rough with her now and then." The old rider hesitated. "Reminds me. Where you figurin' to bunk? Up there at the main house like Jeff did?"

Trevison shook his head at once. "No, not there. Better out here where I can see what goes on. What's in that shed over there?"

Farr swung his glance to the small frame building standing a short distance from the bunkhouse. "Nothin' right now. Missus Washburn used it for doin' her washin' when she was alive. Ain't been used in years."

"I'll move in there if you'll rustle me up a bed and some furniture."

“Good enough,” Farr said, and pivoted toward the barn. “I’ll get one of the boys to help me clean it up and tote in some fixin’s.”

“One thing more,” Trevison added. “How are we set for a crew? We’re short Steeg and three others now.”

“We just about got no crew,” Farr stated. “They had Jeff cut down to save expenses. So’s they could have more money for themselves, I reckon.”

“How many men working night guard?”

“Two’s all. And they don’t do much work. They figure the two of them ain’t doin’ much good, so they just put in their time out there sleepin’.”

“What do you figure we need?”

“To get the herd in shape and drive it to Dodge . . . about ten more riders.”

“Any ’punchers around we can hire?”

Farr nodded. “Always a few boys in town lookin’ for work. And if there ain’t enough there, we can sure enough find plenty in Abilene.”

“Pass the word along then. Forty dollars and chuck.”

“I’ll do that,” Farr said, and went on toward the barn.

Trevison remained where he stood, thinking over the information he had obtained. It all jibed with the things he had been told by Frank Gringras, and it was not hard now to understand why Tom Washburn had needed help, why he had feared for the future of Triangle W. With two self-centered and useless sons, a foreman of no consequence, little if any crew, the ranch was fair game for any rider with a long loop. But that was over now, finished. The days of easy come, easy go for Troy and Virgil, and all others who had taken advantage of things, were gone. Even if he had to resort to the rule of the gun.

VI

Trevison was sitting on the edge of his bed in the new quarters, feeling some of the bruises along his ribs beginning to throb, when the knock came. He was alone, Jay Farr having already started for town in quest of new riders, and taking back the rented buckskin with him. The day was late, nearly over.

He called: "Yes?"

A heavily accented voice said: "Supper is ready. You come eat with Mister Virgil at the house?"

Trevison considered the invitation. This would be the other Washburn's way of getting acquainted. It was not a pleasant thing to anticipate. But he might as well go.

He said: "All right. In a minute."

Some time later he stood at the door of the main house and rapped. A voice bid him enter and he complied, passing through the parlor into a small dining room. Troy Washburn sat at one end of a square table. His brother was at the opposite end.

He did not offer his hand, merely ducking his hand at an empty chair. In this simple lack of courtesy Trevison read the shape of things to come.

Trevison sat down, his mood changing from the easy familiarity he had felt with Jay Farr to one of stiff, uncompromising reserve. He had scarcely settled himself when a woman came from an adjoining room. Trevison rose to his feet, shock and surprise tracing swiftly through him. It was Roxie—Roxie Davis of Dodge City.

"My wife, Trevison," Virgil Washburn said, watching him narrowly.

Trevison nodded, seeing that familiar, provocative smile upon her full lips, the cool recognition in her eyes. She had changed little since he had last seen her in Dodge. Virgil said: "You've met before?"

Trevison made no reply, leaving it up to the girl. He was remembering the words of Jay Farr and Frank Gringras, and he would say nothing that might cause her trouble.

"A long time ago, dear. In Dodge City," she answered easily. "Before I met you."

Virgil relaxed. Roxie sat down and for the next few minutes they were silent, bending their attention to the meal. It was good food, the best Trevison had tasted in many months. Tender steak, gravy, hot biscuits, fried potatoes that were soft and mealy. And coffee just the way he liked it—strong and black. He had his quick suspicion that Roxie had had something to do with its preparation; it was so like those meals she had once prepared for him in Dodge. When he was finished, he sat back, drew a sack of makings from his shirt pocket, and spun up a cigarette.

Virgil's eyes were upon him. "My brother tells me you are taking over the place," he said coolly, adding: "whether we like it or not."

"He's right," Trevison said briefly.

"I suppose you realize I could appeal to the law in this matter? I could get you thrown off."

"I doubt that," Trevison drawled.

"Watch out, Virg," Troy said in mock alarm. "He's pretty tough. Don't rile him."

Trevison pushed back from the table, all the patience gone from him. "I didn't come here to get whipsawed by you two," he said coldly. "If you got any business to talk over, I'm listening. But to get things straight, Washburn, I'll tell you just what I told your brother. I'm taking over this ranch long enough to clean up your father's obligations. When that's done, you can do what you please with it."

"If there's anything left to take back," Troy said with thick sarcasm.

Virgil watched him with sullen, suspicious eyes. He had a thin nose and a mouth that was hardly more than a gray line. His hair was a sandy brown, his eyes light blue, like Troy's only with a piercing, bird-like sharpness to them. Neither of the boys favored Tom to any extent. "Mind telling me your plans?" Virgil asked then.

Trevison shook his head. "Prefer not. Something I don't want bandied around at present."

Washburn flushed hotly. Troy laughed loudly. "See? I told you he was a tough one."

"My cattle you're figuring to sell. I think I've got a right to know what goes on."

Trevison was blunt. "You don't have any rights. You threw them away a long time back, when you laid down on the job of helping your father. If you had been any help to him at all, I'd not be here today. But you weren't. And it's plain he couldn't trust either of you, so I'll just keep it that way."

The last of the day's sunlight reached in through the window and flooded the hushed room.

"You seem," Virgil said then with icy calmness, "determined to do this thing without us, regardless of whether we agree. You realize how big a job that can be if we take it in mind to buck you?"

Trevison's square jaw settled into a grim line. "I expect as much from you. And you might make it tough but remember . . . it's a two-sided game."

"Real rough, eh?"

"You name it," Trevison said softly, "and I'll accommodate you . . . or Steeg or anybody else you can get to do your fighting for you."

Again Virgil flushed.

Troy laughed. "Jeff sure didn't do so good, Virg."

"Shut up, Troy," Washburn snapped.

Troy laughed once more. "Just leaving. Anybody wants me, I'll be at the Longhorn Saloon, town of Canaan. So long."

He got up, crossed the room, and went into the parlor. Moments later he slammed out the front door, angled across the hard pack to the corral. Trevison saw him swing up to his saddle and ride away.

Trevison, weary of the talk, rose to his feet. "I'm obliged for the dinner," he said, and moved for the door.

Virgil lifted his hand to stay him. "Before you go, Trevison, I'd like to see this letter of authority Troy was telling me about."

Trevison fished the letter from his inside pocket. He handed it to Washburn who unfolded it with deliberate care and read it slowly. "Means absolutely nothing now," he said, and ripped the sheet of paper into shreds.

A thrusting temper flooded through Trevison. He took one step forward, grabbed Washburn by the shirt front, and jerked him to his feet. The chair skated back and crashed into the wall, dislodging something that fell to the floor with a loud clatter.

"I should break your face in," he ground out harshly between clenched teeth. "Only the fact you're Tom Washburn's kid keeps me from doing it."

Across the table Roxie had arisen. Her eyes were open widely and a bright light sparkled in their depths. The fear that had swept through Virgil Washburn died away. He said: "Take your hands off me, Trevison."

Trevison relaxed his grip, allowing the man to slide back into his chair. Without saying more, he wheeled about and left the room. He heard Washburn say to Roxie: "Troy's right. A hardcase if ever I saw one."

Outside, in the gathering dusk, Trevison let his anger drain. He walked slowly toward the corral, thinking of Virgil Washburn and the things he had said. And he thought of Roxie and of Dodge City. She was a far cry from that now. But she had changed little. It was still there, lying in her eyes, inviting, almost challenging, it seemed. She might be married to Virgil Washburn but that would mean little to her. Hearing the sound of dishes in the long mess shack, he changed his direction toward that point. Entering, he found a half dozen men gathered at the table eating. He poured himself a cup of coffee from the big pot and sat down at one of the vacant places. The Mexican cook came in from the kitchen and cast an enquiring glance at him. "You want to eat, Mister Trevison?"

He shook his head, and the cook slid back through the doorway. He placed his cup back on the table and faced the riders.

"My name's Trevison. I'm ramrodding this outfit until we can get a herd to Dodge and shipped. It's going to be a tough job. You can expect plenty of hard work and plenty of trouble along with it. If you want to work, you've got a job. If you don't, be off the place in an hour."

There was a moment's long silence and then one of the cowpunchers got to his feet. He cleared his throat and swallowed. "Reckon we done made up our minds, Trevison. We heard about Jeff and his bunch leavin', which suits us to a T. We hired out to this outfit to punch cattle, but there's been dang' little of it done around here, leastwise the kind of cowboyin' we figure needs to be."

Trevison nodded. "I sent Farr into town to hire on some more men. Nobody's going to have to work longer than his share of time."

"We ain't mindin' that so much," another of the riders spoke up. "It's what goes on around here."

The man paused, seemingly uncertain in his own mind whether he wanted to pursue the subject or not. Trevison waited, making no comments. If the man knew something, he would tell it if he desired.

The rider apparently decided he had said enough. He sat down. The first cowpuncher, still on his feet, grinned and said: "Reckon you'd like to know who we are since you told us who you was. I'm Jules Bryant. That bushy-headed gent there is Jesse Shelton. Then there's Carl Miner and John Frazer and Dub Erickson. There's two more 'punchers and the horse wranglers, not here now."

"Only two men with the herd?"

Bryant nodded. "Yeah. Chuck Collins and Nemo Wilson."

"I want four more out there tonight. Anybody want to volunteer?"

He had them immediately. Despite the long day in the saddle, they all were willing to do more. Trevison voiced his thanks, adding: "Soon as Farr rounds up some new men, I'll set up regular shifts for you."

The riders filed out, and Trevison followed. He was suddenly conscious that he was tired, that his muscles ached, that there were several places on his body that throbbed. It had been a long and hard day. But he felt better about things. They all knew where he stood, including the Washburns, and just what he expected of them. What crew he had was willing; whether they were able was something he would reserve judgment on.

He dropped onto the bed, too tired to remove his clothing. The last thing he heard was the rapid drumming of the night crew pulling out for the range.

VII

The early, pre-dawn hour was cold. A light wind, rushing in from the Texas plains to the north, slipped down the furrow of Nine Mile Valley, touching all things with its chilling finger. It reminded them that spring was late, winter was yet master and had not fully relinquished entirely its clutch upon the vast, rolling land of grass and cattle. Trevison shivered as he stood at the bench and performed the morning wash ritual. Yellow light blocked the windows of the dining room and the kitchen where the men were having their breakfasts. A rider, Jesse Shelton, brushed by grousing at the coldness. Another man, hearing this, made his observation: "And you'll be bellyachin' about the heat, come another thutty days!"

Trevison entered the long room, steamy from the plates of hot food and coffee. There was little conversation at this hour, only the clatter of metal against crockery, and the inhaling sound of coffee being sucked in cautiously. Farr had recruited four new men who were having their first meal at Triangle W expense. He had sent word on to Abilenc, he told Trevison, and they could expect a half dozen more cowpunchers before the day was over.

Trevison took a place at the table, helping

himself from the big platter. When he had finished, he stood up. The clatter decreased as the men paused and lifted their attention to him.

"We'll start today shaping the herd," he said. "I'm going to look things over. Meantime, you'll take your orders on the range from Jay Farr."

There was a low murmur of approval to this announcement. Farr said: "You want to start driftin' them to the north water hole?"

"It big enough to handle them?"

Farr said: "Yes. Pretty fair-sized pond. And then we got the creek there."

"That's where to put them," said Trevison.

Farr drew an old pipe from his pocket and stuffed it with tobacco. "You not figurin' on bein' around?"

Trevison shook his head. "Not today. I'm paying the neighbors a little call."

Farr looked up quickly. "Old man Helland and his boys?"

"If he's a neighbor. Understand there are three or four."

"Four. Helland's to the west. Noble Greer to the south along with the McMahon Ranch. And then there's Pewter Quinn on the east side."

"Nobody north?"

"Nobody anyways close."

"Good," Trevison said. "Now, starting today I want every man in this outfit wearing a gun. The understanding is going to be with everybody that

Triangle W range is shut down, tight-closed. Any man found on it, not working for this ranch, stands a good chance of getting a bullet in his hide."

There was a dead silence following those cold, matter-of-fact words. Rustling was a difficult thing to cope with. A steer now and then was hard to account for, and that was the way many thieves worked. The range was a wide and rolling area filled with a multitude of gullies, draws, swales, cañons, and low hills, and at night the herd was especially vulnerable. The only sure defense was reprisal, the fear of being caught, of being shot down while on another man's land, or of being the principal attraction at a lynching party. For the past year there apparently had existed little, if any, fear of consequence. But by sundown that day the old order would have changed, the new taken over.

"By dang!" Jay Farr exclaimed finally. "Sure looks like we're off and runnin'!"

Jules Bryant wagged his head. "Too bad old Tom couldn't be here and listen to that. Reckon that's just what he was wantin' all the time."

Trevison said quietly: "Tom's who we're doing this for. Remember that." Turning, he left the room.

A few minutes later in the barn, Farr caught up with him. The old cowpuncher laid a gnarled hand on his arm. "I know I ain't got no call tellin' you about things like this. Kind of like tellin' your grandma how to pick ducks. But you be a mite careful around them Hellands. There's three of them. The old man, and Willie, the oldest boy. Then there's Orville. He's just a younker. But they're all plumb no good, and tricky as they come. None of them ain't past drillin' a bullet into your back when you ain't lookin'."

Trevison said: "Thanks, Jay. I'll watch them. You and the boys get that stock moving."

He had chosen a deep-chested bay from the corral as his own horse. Now, as he moved out under the breaking day, he had again that feeling of well-being that always filled him when in the saddle. A rider since he could recall, he was never fully at home on the ground. Like all such men, walking was a painful chore. The times when he did jobs on the railroad gangs were sheer misery, since they called for his being on his feet. Forking a horse was a natural part of him. Loping easily along with the keen slice of the breeze upon him, he had a moment's brief wish that it could always be that way. It would be a good thing to believe he could spend the rest of his life aboard a fine animal like the bay, covering the range of a ranch like the Triangle W that was his own. But it was an empty wish, a lost hope. They would never let him rest. To kill a sheriff was a crime second to none, and every lawman automatically assumed the rôle of avenger for his fallen clansman. Few people ever stopped to consider that there could be black sheep in that order also, that a lawman could be anything but honorable and true. It did things to a man. It filled him with an understanding of life's futility, of its temporal quality. It made high-flung ambitions and beautiful dreams of little value, and placed a price of exaggerated importance upon escape and freedom.

The grass was better on this part of the range than he had expected it to be. In the down-flooding sunlight that spread swiftly once released from the imprisoning hills far to the east, it sparkled brightly. As the chill began to lift, the sweet smell of it lifted and became a perfume in the air.

Trevison rode for a good hour, striking due west. He saw scattered patches of cattle grazing, and, riding close to such clusters, he found them to be Triangle W stock, all unattended. He paused to think of that, but passed it off after a moment. That would be taken care of now. Farr and the crew would start that day rounding up the stray parts of the scattered herd, collecting them eventually on the north section of the ranch.

He rode on and a few minutes later topped a low ridge and looked down upon a decaying group of old buildings. This would be the Helland place. For a time he studied it, noting the gray structures, the sagging corrals, the absence of activity. A half dozen steers were milling about in a small yard near the barn. Three horses dozed at the tie rail. A lopsided wagon, its tongue canted to an odd angle, stood in the center of the hard pack. The whole place had the forlorn appearance of abandonment.

Trevison dropped back below the ridge and followed out its full run, thus coming into Hellands' from its extreme western end. He wanted to have first a look at those steers in the pen. He eased up to them from the off side of the barn, which was little more than a hollow shell. They lifted their heavy heads at his approach. All young, surprisingly fat animals for this time of year. Trevison circled them, suspicion riding him hard. They were unbranded, having no marks of any sort, and that, in itself, was wrong. He drifted quietly deeper into the yard, narrow eyes prying sharply for hides or other evidence that would prove the conclusion he felt certain was true. But he could find no more. Only the empty structures, long unused. Onc thing certain, whatever it was that kept the Helland bunch alive, it was not ranching.

He rode the bay to the front of the largest shack that seemed to be the housing point. Then, scanning the range at his back, he called out: "Helland!"

Almost at once the door kicked back and a man stepped out onto the porch. He threw a hard, questioning glance at Trevison and moved on into the yard, a short and heavy man with thick shoulders, bull neck, and flaming red hair that extended down the sides of his face into a matching beard.

"You Helland?"

The old man nodded. "What do y'want?"

"Give you a little advice. I don't know where those steers in your corral came from, but I've got a pretty fair idea."

The door opened again. Two more men came out, younger duplicates of the elder Helland. This would be Willie, wearing a gun on his hip. Orville carried a single-barreled shotgun. Trevison waited while they lined up, one on either side of their father.

"When I want advice, I'll ask for it," Helland stated in a flat voice.

"Here's some you're getting anyway. Stay off Triangle W range. I'll tell you this one time . . . not again. Hereafter, any of you or your bunch caught on Triangle land will end up dead. That clear?"

The boy with the shotgun stirred angrily. Helland calmed him with a backward sweep of his hand.

"You accusing me of rustling?" he demanded in a loud voice.

"Take it any way you like. I'm here to tell you and your pups what you'd better not do."

Helland said something out of the corner of his mouth to Willie that Trevison could not hear. Then, in a mocking voice, the old man said:

"Mighty big talk coming from a Washburn hired hand. You reckon you can back it up?"

Trevison was watching Willie, the Helland with the pistol on his hip. If there was trouble coming, that was where it would spring from. And come it did. Trevison saw the sudden, betraying break in the man's expression in that fragment of time before he clawed for his gun. Trevison, in a single, fluid motion, drew and fired. He laid the bullet at old man Helland's feet, kicking dirt over his boots. The red-headed man yelled and jumped back.

Willie, his gun still holstered, let his hand fall slowly away. Trevison said: "The next one will be in your belly. But I don't think it will be necessary. Now toss those guns out there into the middle of the yard."

He waited, watching narrowly, while Willie pulled the heavy pistol and threw it to the indicated spot. Orville did not at once follow suit. Helland muttered something to him and he dropped the shotgun.

"Where's your herd?" Trevison asked unexpectedly.

"What herd?" the old man answered without thinking. Then, with a wave of his hand: "Oh, I reckon it's over there on the other side of the hill. Drifts around right smart."

Trevison's laugh was a harsh, grating sound. "You're a damn' poor liar, Helland. You don't have a herd. You're rustling beef, every pound that you get. You're butchering and selling. That's how you're living. Well, think up something else, old man. That's finished now. You'll rustle no more Triangle W stock and live to enjoy it." He slid his gun back into its holster and pulled the bay around. "Any of you interested in dying right now, just make a move for one of those guns before I'm out of sight."

Keeping half turned in the saddle, he rode slowly from the yard. His last glimpse of the Hellands, before he dropped into a draw, was the coppery shine of sunlight on their flaming hair. No doubt that was where some of the Washburn beef was going. But in his own mind Trevison knew the quantity was small. Just a few head now and then to keep them in cash. But it all counted up. At fifteen or twenty dollars a head, it graduated into real money. And if Helland was getting away with it, so also must the others.

He followed out a long valley coming upon a small herd at its termination. They wore an NG brand, for Noble Greer no doubt. A mile later he spotted the ranch, lying in a semicircle of trees, with the bright slash of a stream cutting across the back of it. Here again he swung wide, approaching the buildings on their blind side. The place was clean, well kept, in sharp contrast to the Helland Ranch.

Reaching the barn, he heard the steady *thud* of a

blacksmith working at iron. Directly ahead was the calf yard, and in it he saw a bunch of steers. He rode quietly up to the pole fence and threw his sharp glance at the animals. Anger brushed swiftly through him. Every steer in the pen bore the Triangle W brand! Methodically he counted them: twenty-five. Twenty-five head of Washburn stock penned there in brazen, impudent disregard of all who might come and see, awaiting a running iron.

He sawed the bay around and rode straight up to the house, his mouth a hard line, eyes glittering, fires beneath their dark brows. A cold, driving anger was rushing through him. He pulled up a dozen feet away from the door.

"Greer! Come out!"

The steady strike of the hammer in the barn ceased. Trevison moved in the saddle, sliding half about to where he could keep his gaze on that building, also. The door of the house opened. Trevison's thudding temper focused on that point. He would actually be justified in shooting Greer down where he stood. Any man who would rustle stock and pen it right in his own yard must be dead certain of himself, and have absolutely no fear whatever of retaliation.

A slim figure came through the doorway of the house and stepped off the porch. Trevison stared. A frown broke across his face. It was the girl from the stagecoach—Halla. She met his gaze with that serious, half smile he remembered so well, and that he had not been entirely able to erase from his memory.

"Hello! What brings you way out here?"

Trevison, shock stiffening his tongue and making words hard to come by, said finally: "This your place?"

"My father's," she answered. "I'm Halla Greer."

VIII

The recollection of the Triangle W steers in the corral brought Trevison back to the moment. In a terse voice he said: "Your father here?"

Halla looked at him closely, aware of the brittle change in his manner and tone. "Why, yes. He's in the barn." She swung her glance to that building. A man was coming through the doorway, tossing aside a leather apron as he did so. Apparently it had been Greer himself working at the forge. He crossed the yard leisurely, a thin, slight man with a noticeable limp. When he drew up beside the girl, Trevison saw he had the same gray eyes.

"What is it, Halla?"

She shook her head, frowning slightly. There was some danger here, she sensed, some threat in the big man sitting silently on the bay horse. "I don't know. He wants to see you."

Greer turned then to Trevison. "Something on your mind?"

"Like to know what you're doing with Triangle W stock in your corral?"

"Doing with it?" Greer echoed. "Why, I'm getting ready to slap my own brand on them! Why? Who are you and what business is it of yours?"

"Name's Trevison. I'm running the Washburn spread and I'm looking for missing stock."

Halla Greer and her father exchanged looks. He said: "You're running Triangle W?"

Trevison said: "I am. Now, what about those steers?"

Greer wagged his head. "Those are mine. Bought and paid for in hard cash."

Trevison gave the man a slanting look. "Bought from whom?"

At this inference Greer bristled. "Since that's a deal that took place some days back, I don't figure it any of your business."

"I'm making it my business," Trevison stated in a winter-cold voice. "Either you show me a bill of sale, or I'm taking them back with me."

He was aware of Halla's close gaze. She was watching him with something like distaste in her eyes. Yet there was a trace of fear there, too.

"Could be a fair chore," Greer said coolly. "I've got a few men around."

"Not enough to keep you from getting hurt," Trevison said brusquely. "Do I see that bill of sale or not?"

Halla spoke then, the first time since her father had arrived. "I guess I made a mistake. You're not the same man I was with on the stagecoach," she observed with womanly candor. "Show him the receipt, Papa. Then maybe he will move on and leave us alone."

Greer had turned to her. "You say this is the man you saw on the stage?"

She nodded.

Greer shook his head. "You must have had a touch of sun," he commented and, wheeling about, started for the house. "I'll get that receipt."

Halla remained in the yard. She was wearing Levi's and a faded checkered shirt. Lifting her eyes suddenly, she caught Trevison frankly appraising her. She returned his study coolly. After a moment he turned away, a heaviness within him. Odd how some things got into a man, and never let him completely rest, never fully left him. He had tried to forget this Halla Greer ever since they had got off the stage in Canaan. And just when he was making some progress along that line, wrapping himself in a job that was to be done, here she was again, standing before him, proud and unyielding as lava rock.

Noble Greer was back in short minutes, holding a slip of paper in his hand. He paused in front of Trevison, uncertain of his trust in the dark-faced man who watched him so narrowly.

Trevison ended that. He said—"It's safe."—and, reaching, plucked it from his fingers.

It was a bill of sale. Made out to Noble Greer for twenty-five steers. Sum $250. It was signed by Troy Washburn.

Trevison handed it back to the rancher, anger once again having its strong way with him. That was Troy's way of keeping himself supplied with cash for his gambling and drinking, actually rustling his own cattle and selling them to other ranchers. And the price—$10 a head. Barely half their worth.

A hard twist to his voice, he commented: "A real good buy, Greer. A bargain."

Greer grimaced. "Sure, otherwise I wouldn't have bought them. Troy said he needed to raise some quick money and offered them to me. I bought them. Any rancher would have done the same."

In a tone that left no room for misunderstanding, Trevison said: "It's a bargain you can forget. We're selling no stock to anybody. I'll send word in to Frank Gringras to give you your money back. Tomorrow I'll have a couple of riders here for the steers."

"Now wait a minute," Greer protested. "I bought those from Troy. . . ."

"Makes no difference. It's no deal. And if he ever shows up here again trying to peddle you any Triangle W cattle, leave it alone. I'll be right behind him to take them home. And next time there won't be any refund."

"You mean Troy's got no authority . . . ?"

"Troy or Virgil or anybody else around here . . . but me. And while we're talking about it, Triangle W is closed. Orders are to shoot anybody found on it. You got any business to transact, use the road and stay on it all the way."

Halla still watched him with that disturbed, almost repelled air. In a brave voice she said: "I do believe Mister Trevison is accusing us of rustling."

Trevison saw no humor in that. He said: "No, not that. I can't put you in the same wagon with the Hellands. But I want no mistakes made. I don't want to bury anybody that doesn't have it coming."

"No, of course not," she said. "You're the kind of man that never does such things."

Trevison's glance settled upon her as he attempted to fathom her meaning. "Only when necessary," he said soberly.

"Killing . . . when necessary?"

"If necessary," Trevison replied quietly. He swung his attention back to Noble Greer. "No hard feelings, I hope. But something like this has to be set straight, once and for all time."

"Sure, no hard feelings," the rancher agreed. "I just never questioned Troy's motives. If a man can't figure on his own future son-in-law, then I don't know who he can figure on."

Trevison touched the brim of his hat to Halla, nodded to the rancher, and wheeled out of the yard. Minutes later, Greer's words caught up with his thoughts. Future son-in-law—Halla was planning to marry Troy! It came as a mild shock, and he considered it for some time. Finally he shook his head. Halla Greer was entitled to something better than Troy Washburn. She was a mighty fine woman to be wasted on such as he. She deserved more. . . .

McMahon's place was a duplication of Greer's, only years older. The rancher and his wife were not there, Trevison learned after he had made his quiet examination of the premises. A cowboy, aroused from the bunkhouse, said they were in town.

"Back soon?"

"Prob'ly not before dark."

"You bought any Triangle W stock lately?" Trevison asked then.

The cowboy shook his head. "Not that I can recollect. Month, maybe two months back."

"Troy Washburn handle the deal?"

A frown crowded the man's face. "Say, who the hell are you, anyway? Comin' 'round here askin' questions?"

"Answer the question," Trevison snapped. "Was it Troy?"

The rider gave Trevison a startled look. "I reckon it was. He always did handle it."

Trevison settled back in his saddle, his face dark and stern. “You tell McMahon from now on he’s not to buy Triangle W stock from anybody. You got that? And tell him, and everybody else around here, that Triangle W range is closed. It’s a dangerous place to be if you’re not working there for them.”

Before the rider could make any reply, Trevison pulled the bay around and loped from the yard.

One more stop. Pewter Quinn. It was sometime after midday when he rode out of a draw and saw the place. Small, no larger than Greer’s, but in much worse condition. Yet there appeared to be considerable activity about the yard and around the buildings. It was not going to be possible to look over the place first, as he had done the others. At least a half dozen riders were in plain sight.

Trevison rode straight in, heading for a corral fence upon which several hides had been draped to dry. While a surprised cowpuncher watched, he probed about the skins until he found what he wanted—the triangle with its center W burned into the hide.

He wheeled to the man. “Where’s Quinn?”

The man ducked his head toward another corral. “Over there, workin’.”

Trevison walked the bay to that point. A stocky, bare-waisted man wrestled with an untamed buckskin in a square of yard. The horse was fighting the leathers, and, as Trevison approached, he reared and struck out with his forelegs. The stocky man ducked away neatly, seeing Trevison in that moment.

He said—"What do you want?"—in an impatient, demanding sort of way. "I don't need no riders."

Trevison was brief. "Where'd you get those hides hanging on your fence?"

Quinn, sweat and dirt streaming down his face and neck and onto his hairy chest, wrapped the reins of the bronco around a snubbing post. He moved closer to Trevison, placing his hands on his hips. "What's it to you, mister?"

"Plenty," Trevison shot back. "I'm looking for rustled Triangle W stock. Looks like I've found it."

Quinn's eyes flared. He took a quick step forward, his arms going down.

"Hold it!" Trevison barked. "And keep your hand away from that gun. I don't want to kill you."

Quinn halted abruptly. He covered Trevison with an appraising look. A slow smile came to his mouth. "Just how far you think you'll get pulling that hardcase stuff on me? One yell and I'll have a half dozen men on your back."

"Fine. They can dig the bullets out of your belly," Trevison said coldly. "Now, show some sense and answer my questions. How did that Triangle W stock get here?"

Pewter Quinn searched Trevison's grim face for

a cue to something that was in his mind. Apparently finding it, he shrugged. "Bought them. How else?"

"Bought them from whom?"

"Troy Washburn. Last week."

Trevison thought for a moment. "You bought many from him?"

"Whenever he comes along with a good price. That's what I'm in the business for . . . to make money."

Trevison said: "That's over with now. Don't buy any more from him, no matter how good the price is."

Quinn squared himself. "Reckon that's up to me. I see a bargain, by granny, I'll take it."

"Not if it's Triangle W stock. You buy any more from him, or anybody else, I'll be here after it. That's a warning, Quinn."

"You talk a little wide. Think you can back up that kind of talk?"

Trevison smiled. "Try me and see."

The threat of the man was a solid force, making its presence felt in the small yard. Pewter Quinn watched silently for a full minute. Then his gaze wavered and fell. "Well, of course, if he don't make me no offer . . ."

"Offer or not," Trevison slashed through his words, "forget it. Don't buy. And here's one more thing for you to remember. Triangle W range is closed. Keep off it and keep your riders off."

"Who says we're on it?"

"Nobody. I'm just telling you it's closed."

Quinn shrugged. "So it's closed. All right. What did you say your name was?"

"I didn't say, but it's Trevison."

"You take over the Washburn Ranch?"

Trevison said: "Right. Any business you've got to handle, see me about it."

"What about Troy and the other boy . . . Virgil, or whatever his name is?"

"They'll be around, but no more than that. What did you pay Troy for the beef?"

"Ten dollars a head."

"You didn't buy then, you got them as a gift," Trevison commented, and wheeled about. "Don't take any more bargains from him, Quinn. It's likely to cost you a lot more than you're ready to pay."

He did not wait for the rancher's reply but rode from the yard. Ten dollars a head for good beef. The very thought of it angered Trevison. But Troy Washburn had rustled his last beef at Triangle W. He could mark that down for a dead certain fact.

IX

When Trevison rode into the yard at Washburns', he was thinking again of Halla Greer and this disturbed him. There was no place in his future for a woman such as she. Affairs of short duration, like that with Roxie Davis, or the *señorita* in Santa Fé, were all right. They were soon over, forgotten in a few weeks. But Halla Greer was affecting him differently. She was threatening to upset the carefully calculated void of future he had programmed for himself.

It was near suppertime and the long ride had built a hunger within him. He rode straight to the corral and released the bay. Farr and two of the new riders were washing up, and the old cowpuncher, finished, waited aside for Trevison to complete his own chore.

When he finished, Farr said: "Well, you meet the neighbors?"

Trevison said: "All but the McMahons. He wasn't home. I left word with one of his crew."

"Any trouble?"

"Not 'specially. Helland's got a pair of anxious boys."

Farr threw him a quick, shrewd glance. "You have to do anything about that?"

Trevison shrugged. "Just dusted off the old man's boots. Nobody hurt."

Jay Farr chuckled. "Bet that hurt his pride some. He's so all fired proud of Willie, and thinkin' he's such shuckin's with a gun."

Trevison said: "I dropped a warning to them all. They know this range is closed and we'll back it up with guns if need be. The crew understand that?"

Farr ducked his head. "Includin' the new boys in from Abilene. Three of them."

Trevison pivoted toward his quarters. Abruptly he halted and swiveled his attention back to Farr. "You know Troy was selling beef to these other ranchers?"

The old cowpuncher plucked at his chin. "Nope. Not for sure, anyway. Had me an idea or two about it. Jeff and him sort of kept things like that to themselves."

"Looks like he had a regular market going. Seems every time he needed some cash, he'd run a small jag of cattle down and sell off to one of them."

"Bill of sale, too?"

Trevison nodded. "Everything just right. Can't very well blame the ranchers for not picking up a bargain when they found one. But I don't figure they'll be buying any more."

He turned back for his bunkhouse. Some slight noise from within that small building laid its quick caution upon him as he reached for the knob. He hesitated, old wariness, born of suspicion for every unknown sound and shadow, making him careful. It came from the endless trails, from never knowing what was around a corner, or who stood on the far side of a closed door. It was a part of the cloth, a piece of the whole pattern that had begun that day in Miles City.

He drifted to the side, easing away from the

door. One hand resting on the gun at his hip, he reached for the knob and threw the door wide.

"Come out!"

There was the immediate sound of a chair scraping against the floor, the dry rustle of corded clothing. And then Troy Washburn stood framed in the doorway.

Trevison relaxed slowly. In a low voice he said: "Don't ever do that again."

"Do what?" Washburn asked, his face puzzled.

"Sit in a dark room and wait for me. Next time light the lamp."

Troy Washburn stared. A slow smile broke across his mouth. "You afraid of the dark?"

Trevison shook his head. "Only like to know who's in it."

Troy regarded him thoughtfully. "You don't like a man standing behind you . . . at your back. You don't like somebody to wait for you in the dark. You've got some strange ideas, Trevison."

"Nothing strange about them," Trevison said shortly. "Something on your mind?"

Washburn said: "Yes, you. I stopped by the Greers' on my way back from town. Understand you were there today, doing a lot of big talking."

"I was there," Trevison agreed.

"You're a bit out of line, throwing your weight around with people like them. They're close friends of mine."

"Friends or not, they're buying no more beef

from this ranch. You're not selling them, or anybody else, any more Triangle W stock."

"Anybody else?"

"McMahon . . . Quinn . . . Helland. Anybody."

The mention of Helland's name was a shot in the dark. But it apparently struck true. Trevison waited for Washburn to make a denial but he did not.

Instead, he said: "I don't appreciate your sneaking around behind my back talking about . . ."

"Makes no difference what you think," Trevison cut in. "I'm doing the things that have to be done around here. If you don't go for it, best thing you can do then is get off the place, and stay off until I'm through. As for talking behind your back . . . don't fool yourself. You're not worth that kind of trouble. I've said it all to your face to start with."

"You didn't say anything about me not having any authority to sell my own beef."

"Only because I didn't know about it. I had no idea you were rustling your own herd."

Washburn was visibly startled. His face colored and he stared hard at Trevison for a long moment, then his eyes shifted, going off into the night. After a time he said: "That's the way of it, eh?"

"That's the way it is," Trevison assured him coolly.

Washburn murmured—"All right, Trevison."—and started for the main house. Several more of the crew rode in, clattering across the hard pack on their way to the corral. A voice, deep in the gloom behind the bunkhouse, called: "Hey, Dub? You goin' into town tonight?"

A dozen steps away Troy Washburn halted. He wheeled slowly around and, for a fraction of time, Trevison thought the man had gun play in mind. But he said, almost in a friendly tone: "You're calling the shots, Trevison, and we'll let it go for now. But don't think I'm going to take this lying down. You're making few friends and plenty of enemies in this country. I'm wondering if you'll be big enough to handle it when the chips go down."

"Don't worry about me," Trevison answered softly, and turned into his quarters.

After the evening meal was over, he called Jay Farr aside.

"Send two men to Greers' in the morning. There's twenty-five steers there that belong to us. We're taking them back."

Farr nodded. "Be any trouble doing it?"

"No. Greer's getting his money back. How can I get word to Frank Gringras to pay him?"

"Couple of the boys goin' to town tonight. Could send a note to him."

Trevison wrote out the information and Farr delivered it to the Canaan-bound riders. Afterward, the two of them sat in front of the bunkhouse talking of Tom Washburn, of ranches, of the job that lay ahead of them. Farr was one of the few men Wayne Trevison found it easy to converse with, and he thoroughly enjoyed the old rider's company.

It was late before he realized it. All the lamps were out. Feeling the need for sleep and rest, he got up. Farr murmured his good night and went off to the bunkhouse. Trevison moved for his own small quarters, thinking back of Troy Washburn's last words, of their underlying threat. He was sitting on the edge of his cot, drawing at a final cigarette, when he heard the tapping at his window.

He swung his attention to that point immediately. In the pale starlight he saw Roxie's face, an indistinct oval beyond the glass. She beckoned to him. A faint forewarning of trouble running through him, he dropped the cigarette to the floor and ground it out. She rapped lightly again. He got up and quietly left the cabin, circling to where she waited.

She was standing in the shadows when he reached her side, smiling softly. She was wearing some sort of nightdress, over which she had drawn a thin robe. Her hair was loosely gathered about her head and tied with a ribbon. In the weak light it looked silver.

"I thought that old man would never go to bed," she said in a husky whisper. "I've been standing here for hours, it seems."

Trevison was gruff, impatient with her. "What do you want, Roxie?"

"To see you," she replied frankly. "I was never so glad to see anybody in my life, as yesterday when you came."

"Why? You and I were through back in Dodge. Besides, you've got a husband now."

She made a small sound of distaste. "He's an animal, not a man."

"But still your husband," Trevison said. "You shouldn't be here now, dressed like that."

She gave him a wide, tantalizing smile. "Still bother you, don't I, Wayne? Makes you think of Dodge and all the good times we had there."

He said: "A thousand years ago."

"But so easily and quickly regained," she said, moving in close to him. She laid her arms against his chest and leaned her weight upon his tall shape. "It could be the same as then, Wayne. Just like before."

The strong attraction of her was a powerful force hammering at his emotions. But he said: "A thing like this means only trouble. I've got enough of that."

"But worth it. You know that, Wayne. I can stand anything from Virgil . . . his jealousy, his possessiveness, even his beatings . . ."

"Beatings?" Trevison echoed.

She drew away from him. Turning her head and drawing back her hair, she showed him a bluish swelling near the cheek bone. "That's for knowing you in Dodge."

Trevison shook his head. That would be Virgil's way, all right. He was the kind. A man, ineffectual with other men, feeling their contempt, would take it out on a woman. They all ran true to form. A rider came into the yard, sitting, heavy-eyed and slack, in the saddle. Trevison waited until he had reached the barn and clumped his way to the bunkhouse.

"It's risky here for you," he said. "We're stretching our luck. Somebody is bound to see you."

"Meet me tomorrow then? I'll wait until Virgil takes his afternoon nap. I can go for a ride."

Trevison said firmly: "No, Roxie."

She pulled away from him, petulant and disappointed. "Why? Why not? He'll never know. And I can't stand him any longer, Wayne. You've got to help me. . . ."

Again Trevison shook his head. There was too much at stake to risk trouble of this sort with Virgil Washburn. Under other circumstances he might look at it differently. Roxie was a beautiful woman, soft to touch and hold. But not now, not here while he had so many other problems on his shoulders. And besides, she was married.

She said: "I'll do anything to make you see it my way. You know that. I'm not weak and I get what I want, one way or another."

"Meaning what?" Trevison asked, his tone going a little stiff.

"Just this. Unless you meet me tomorrow like I ask, I'll tell Virgil about Miles City. The way he feels about you, I think he'd like very much to know about that, about your being a wanted man. It would solve all his problems."

In the vast stillness that followed her words, Trevison was a tall, rigid figure. He was suddenly hard against a blank wall, facing a problem that offered no solution. He knew Roxie, knew she would do as she promised, that she would think nothing of upsetting all his plans to obtain her own objective.

"Well?" she pressed softly.

"All right," he said in a descending tone. "Where do I meet you?"

"At the picnic grove below the ranch. Three o'clock?"

"Three o'clock," he repeated.

She reached up, going to her tiptoes, and kissed him fully on the mouth. A moment later she was gone.

X

Trevison had a restless night. He was up early and in the saddle long ahead of the crew, striking northward. He wanted a good look at that section of the ranch, and the point at the water hole where the herd would be assembled.

He lifted out of the shallow valley after a short

time coming up on to the long-reaching prairie. Here the grass was not so good and this he gave some thought to. He had hoped the grazing in this area would be in better condition, since the entire herd would soon be moving across it. But it was not, and there was nothing that could be done about it; one thing more he could chalk up to Steeg and the Washburn boys. In their negligent short-sightedness, they had permitted the stock, in small broken herds, to graze anywhere and everywhere their fancy took them.

One thing was heartening. The water stand was better than he had anticipated. It was a good two acres across, and, walking the bay horse from one shore to the other, he found the bottom firm, although not boggy as such places generally are. The creek was running full, fed farther to the north by some underground spring. There would be no water problem at the start of the trek at least. That was some consolation.

He drifted out of the swale wherein the pond lay like a broad, dark mirror under the sun, and rode to the crest of a small hill a mile east. From that point he could see the roll away of the flat table land in all directions. He had no way of knowing where Washburn's boundaries lay. He assumed he was still within them but in this huge, unmarked world there was nothing to show where one man's property ended, and another's began.

Coming off the bay, he dropped to his heels and

established his directions on a smooth spread of sand with a greasewood twig. He was facing east. To the north, a good 500 miles away, lay Dodge City and the railhead to which the herd must be delivered. The best route would be up the near center of Texas, along the Western Trail as some called it. It followed the best course and water was assured since the herds crossed the Brazos, the Red, both forks of the Canadian and the Cimarron Rivers—the latter where it laced the Kansas and Indian Territory border.

In the past, Farr had told him, it was customary to start the drive at the Brazos crossing. Trevison studied the lines he had scratched in the sand. This meant they would start out, striking due east until they hit the Brazos, and then swing north up the trail. The thought occurred to him that, as such, it was a long route; why not slice diagonally across the prairies and join the trail where it intersected the Red? Several days might be saved in such a move. Every day less on the road meant better beef at the railhead.

He glanced upward to the sun, estimating the time of day. He still had a few hours before he was to meet Roxie. He rode on, changing his direction to a northeasterly route. That was the way the herd would go if he decided to attempt a more direct trail.

He kept his watch on the grass, throwing a glance far ahead in search of a stand of green that would indicate a water hole. It never appeared, although the grass did improve after he had dropped off a shelf of mesa into a wide and sweeping valley. It would be nearly 100 miles from water at Washburn's extreme north range to the Red River crossing, he figured. Four to five days march for the herd, at least. And three days were about all you could expect cattle to go without a drink.

After a while he swung the bay around, heading back. He had spotted no water stands but he was not ready to give up the idea. He would ask Jay Farr about the chances for water farther north. One place, if only a small creek, was all they needed to make the short cut worthwhile.

He swung wide of the ranch on his return, keeping well to the west of it. He ran into several segments of the herd, all moving northward, pointing to the valley where the pond lay. The cattle, as a whole, did not look too good, he noted. But it was soon after winter and little more could be expected. A few days of good grass and water would help considerably. Also, if they had average grazing conditions on the trail, they would arrive at Dodge City in pretty fair condition. He waved to several riders and passed on.

It was a full three o'clock when he reached the grove. It lay below the ranch a few miles. He had noticed it casually before, but given it no particular attention. It was a thick, circular stand of spreading cottonwood trees clustered about a small spring. In days gone, Tom Washburn and his family had built a rustic table and several benches there, and quite often held their Sunday picnics in its shaded depths. Once it had been a friendly place where other ranchers also came, and many a trail-weary rider had stopped there to rest his bones and water his horse.

Trevison, never entirely off guard, approached from the far side, walking the bay at slow pace through the dense growth. A blur of white dead ahead brought him up short. He threw a sharp glance to that point and saw it was Roxie. When he came softly from the thickets of willows into the open, she wheeled in alarm to face him.

"You frightened me!" she exclaimed, throwing a hand to her throat. "Was it necessary to come creeping through the bushes like that . . . like an Indian?"

"Never know who might be around," Trevison answered, shrugging.

"No one ever comes here any more," she said, watching him tether the bay. She was wearing a full-flowing riding skirt with a white shirtwaist. A small hat perched jauntily upon her head, like a brightly colored straw crown. The shirtwaist fitted snugly, accentuating the full swell of her breasts. As Trevison sat down beside her on one of the crude benches, she unfastened the long buttons, allowing a greater expanse of white skin to show.

She met Trevison's grave eyes with a faint smile. "Warm today. If that spring was larger, I'd be swimming right now."

Trevison allowed his gaze to patrol the grove. "You've been here before?"

"A few times."

"Family place. Makes a man think of things like that."

"I was never here with Virgil," she said, "if that's what you mean. Having to live with him is enough." She laid her hand upon his arm. "We don't need to make all this small talk, Wayne. Why are we? Old friends like us know each other and talk is such a waste."

He shook his head. "This is no good, Roxie. No good for either of us. And dangerous for you."

"Dangerous?" she scoffed. "What's Virgil Washburn? A mean, dried-up excuse for a man with a nasty temper." She paused, shuddered. "His hands are like snakes. Just as slimy and cold."

"He's your husband," Trevison reminded her patiently. "You picked him. You married him. You didn't have to."

"No, I didn't have to, but I did. All his talk about a big, fine ranch. And money and clothes and trips to the big towns . . . everything I've always wanted. He made it sound real good."

"That's not the way it turned out?"

She shook her head. "No trips to far away places. A ranch he doesn't even own. No money and lots of quarrels. Some men can change quickly, and he is one of those."

"There's a hitch to most good things," Trevison said absently. "You have to take the bad to have the good."

"But this is all bad, not much good," she answered, adding: "but I can take the bad if I can find the good some other place . . . with you, Wayne."

She rose swiftly and came around to stand directly in front of him. She put her arms about his neck and drew him in close, burying his face in her bosom. Trevison laid his hands upon the curve of her hips and pushed her gently away. She resisted, holding him tightly.

"Wayne . . . you don't know, you can't know how I've waited for this."

Trevison, fighting himself, got to his feet, the movement only bringing her hard against him. He reached for her hands, noting the bruise on her cheek and several more on the snowy white of her shoulders and neck. He said: "Roxie, you can't do this . . . I've had nothing to do with another man's wife. I'll not begin now."

"You will," she murmured, swaying against him. "Put your arms around me, Wayne. Hold me tight."

He found her hands and broke their tight clasp and tried to step back. She clung to him. And for a moment they stood there, in the shadows of the grove, two figures struggling slightly. It was then

Trevison saw the two horses standing a short distance away.

He said—"Visitors, Roxie."—and pulled forcibly back.

Roxie let her arms fall. There was no fear in her eyes, only a dismay at being thus disturbed. She turned slowly to look.

"My good brother-in-law and his bride-to-be," she said, her tone tipped with sarcasm. "Fine time for them to show up!"

Trevison's gaze was upon Halla Greer, reading the shock in her eyes. She pulled her pony about and faced the other way. Troy Washburn rode in closer, a sardonic smile twisting his thin lips.

"Regret the interruption." He smirked. "You have a great many talents, Trevison."

He gave them a down-curling smile and swung about to rejoin Halla. They were riding north, toward the ranch, and they continued on.

Trevison watched them leave. Virgil Washburn would have news of this moment before much time elapsed. He said to Roxie: "Why don't you ride on to town? I'll handle this with Virgil."

Roxie buttoned her blouse with languid indifference. "No. Not that way. Let me handle Virgil. I've been through it before." Then: "Tomorrow, Wayne?"

Trevison said wearily: "No, Roxie. Not tomorrow, not again any time. So long as you're married to Virgil."

She moved toward her horse, swinging her hips. He helped her to the saddle. Settling herself, she smiled down to him. "Tomorrow . . . on the other side. Don't forget it, Wayne."

Standing beside the bench Tom Washburn had built, he watched her ride off.

XI

Two hours later Trevison rode across the hard pack of Triangle W's yard. The crew was still on the range and the only horse in view was Roxie's at the tie rail. Halfway to the barn, Virgil Washburn's voice, shrill and demanding, ripped through the quiet.

"Trevison! Come over here!"

Trevison half turned in the saddle, giving the man an acknowledging glance, and continued on. He stabled the bay and returned to the yard. For a minute he stood just outside the wide, double doorway, building himself a smoke and thinking about Virgil Washburn. Evidently Roxie had not been as successful as she had anticipated.

He crossed the yard in deliberate steps, presenting himself at the side door of the main house. Before he could knock, Virgil pulled back the door and stepped aside for him to enter. The man was in a high state of agitation, his eyes burning brightly with a wild anger. In one hand he held a pistol, and with this he waved Trevison deeper into the room. Roxie stood in a far corner, her face calm. Trevison closed the door at his heels. In a level voice he said: "Put that gun away, Virgil."

Washburn covered him with a murderous glance, his face working with unchecked emotion. "I will like hell! I'm going . . ."

"Put it away," Trevison repeated the order. "You try using it on me and I'll kill you before you can pull the trigger. You know that."

Washburn gave the weapon a long, hopeless look and tossed it on to the table. The defeat of that moment culling some of the fury that trampled him. A sigh escaped Roxie's throat and a faint, sneering smile came to her lips.

Washburn wheeled away from the table, circling the room, an inner frustration driving through him ruthlessly. He was a raging bundle of nerves. He snatched up the short riding crop and stopped in front of Trevison.

"My brother said he saw you with my wife this afternoon!"

Trevison lifted his gaze to Roxie. She nodded, almost imperceptibly. "He did," he said.

"What were you doing? What was going on?"

"Your brother told you that, too."

"He said he saw you standing there . . . holding her in your arms! He didn't know how long you'd been there. . . ."

Trevison, still watching Roxie for his cues,

ducked his head. He was trying to say as little as possible, not knowing what Troy had said, or what explanation Roxie had made of the incident. Virgil Washburn struggled with himself, punishing himself brutally with his own thoughts.

"How long had you been there?"

"Not long," Trevison murmured.

Washburn whirled upon him, his face pushed close. "My wife said you forced yourself upon her!" The muscles of Virgil's face were writhing in agonized, tight lines.

Trevison saw Roxie's glance slide away, and go searching for something beyond the window. Anger stirred within. He shook it off. It was not worth it. If this was the way she had explained it, then this was the way it would be.

"She said she was there alone, resting. You came along and forced your attentions on her, presuming upon your acquaintance of Dodge City. You deny it?"

Trevison shrugged his wide shoulders. "You seem to have all the answers."

Washburn spun away, his face going pale as a jealous fury racked his body. "You . . . you dog!" he screamed. "Maybe you can come here and take my ranch away from me . . . but not my wife! Not my wife! You hear that?"

The dam broke suddenly. Washburn lunged across the room and struck out at Trevison with the riding crop.

"You leave her alone! Leave her alone!" he cried, lashing with the whip. "You stay away from her!"

Trevison stood motionlessly, taking some of the blows on his shoulders, some on his arms. They hurt but little, and in those moments he was feeling only pity for this man, this small excuse for Tom Washburn. He allowed Virgil's anger to spend itself, and then, having enough of it, he seized the riding crop and hurled it across the room. Washburn made a frantic grab for the pistol, lying on the table. Trevison reached it first, and calmly tucked it into the waistband of his trousers. Roxie, silent through it all, watched with indifferent interest.

Trevison turned on his heel for the door. He paused there, throwing a look at the gasping, breathless Virgil leaning weakly against the table.

"Keep your wife inside," he said. "Otherwise be with her when she's not."

He stepped out into the dusk and slanted for his bunk. Remembering Washburn's gun, he flipped back the loading gate and punched out the shells. Afterward, he dropped the weapon into the dust near the step and moved on.

He washed up with that part of the crew who were in, having some conversation with Farr about the herd. A few places around his shoulders smarted from Washburn's blows with the riding crop. But that bothered him little. It was the necessity that had forced him to stand and take the beating that hurt the most. But even this passed after a time; it was better, he reasoned, that Washburn take his anger out on him than on Roxie.

After the meal was over, he called Farr to one side and outlined his thoughts for driving the herd directly to a Red River crossing rather than taking the east route to the Brazos.

Farr puffed at his pipe. "Well, now, I don't know about that," he said. "Pretty risky."

"Any water that way, to the north?"

Farr said: "Injun Creek. About fifty miles up."

"Pretty good stream?"

"Don't know. Never set eyes on it."

"Tomorrow send a man up there to look it over. Like to know how big the stream is and how much water it's got in it."

Farr nodded. "Save a heap of time, goin' that way."

"Why haven't they used it before?"

"Water for one thing. Sometimes Injun Creek's dry. And raiders. That's the worst thing."

"Indians or whites?"

"Both, I hear tell. Mostly Injuns."

Trevison considered this information. After a time he said: "How long since anybody tried it across there?"

"Five, maybe six years."

"Tom ever try it?"

Farr shook his head. "Nope. Always figured it

too risky. Things bein' like they was, he played it pretty close to the belt. Losin' a herd would have wiped him plumb out, I reckon."

Trevison said: "If there's water in that creek, we'll chance it."

Jay Farr struck a match to his pipe and sucked at the stem. He stared at the flame for a moment, waved it out, and flipped it into the yard. "Don't get me wrong now," he said slowly, "but I'm thinkin' that would be a mistake. It's a big chance to take."

Trevison said: "With a full crew and all wearing guns, the odds shouldn't be too bad. Main thing is the water. Get a man off for there tomorrow."

Farr murmured: "I'll send Jesse Shelton. He's been around long enough to know about what it would take."

A door at the main house slammed. Virgil Washburn stepped out into the yard, a thin shape in the dim light. Trevison watched him start toward them, pause, bend down, and pick up his revolver, lying where Trevison had dropped it. He thrust it into his holster and came on.

He crossed the hard pack, bearing straight for Trevison and Farr. Trevison stiffened, anger stirring through him. The matter of Roxie was concluded so far as he was concerned. He would take no more abuse from Virgil Washburn. Washburn pulled up before them but his attention was on the old cowpuncher.

"You seen anything of Troy?"

Farr shook his head. "Sure ain't, Virg. Been out on the range all day. Why? Something wrong?"

Washburn said: "I don't know. Looks like most of his clothes are gone. You sure he didn't say anything to you or anybody else around here?"

"Like I told you, I been gone all day," Farr replied.

"Then, get on your horse and ride into town and find him," Washburn said in a clipped tone. "I want to see him."

Trevison pushed a step closer to Washburn. "You want him, you go after him yourself. This man's been working all day, same as all the rest of the crew around here."

Washburn swung his burning gaze on Trevison, hate and fury working his jaws. Words formed on his lips. But he could voice no sound. A moment later he spun about and stalked back to the main house.

XII

Alone in his small quarters Trevison thought of Virgil Washburn's words. Troy was gone. Maybe that was good; possibly it was bad. Around Triangle W he was of no value. Trevison would have viewed any offers of help from him with considerable caution, believing there could be only some hidden reason back of it. But why had he gone, if, indeed, he had? Was he pulling out, giving up, feeling there no longer was anything at Triangle W for him since Trevison had taken over? Was it because his featherbed had turned stone hard and the days of easy-come money were over? Or was he drawing off, like some wounded animal, to lick his wounds and plan his revenge? In Wayne Trevison's direct and logical mind there had to be a good and valid reason.

He fell asleep thinking of this, and he came awake, moments later it seemed, to a furious hammering on his door. He sat bolt upright, reaching automatically for the holstered gun hanging at the bedside. It was a habit he likely would never break.

"Trevison!" It was Jay Farr's voice. "There's trouble!"

Trevison hit the floor and wrenched the door open. The old cowpuncher stood before him, his face gaunt and strained.

"Rustlers! They hit the small herd the boys were bringin' in from the breaks."

Trevison was pulling on his clothing. "How many head gone?"

"Don't know. Can't tell yet. They shot Jules up a bit."

"Bad?"

"Bullet in the shoulder, another in the leg. They're bringin' him in now."

Trevison came through the doorway at a run,

buckling on his gun belt. The bunkhouse lamp was on, light from its windows laying yellow squares in the yard. Four men waited near the corral with saddled horses. Trevison joined them, and they whirled away, heading due west.

Farr led the way. It was the stock they had been popping out of the brush, he told Trevison, yelling his words. Jules Bryant and two other cowpunchers were doing the job. They had finally got them out around dark, and driven them a few miles to the north, there bedding them down. Jules had sent one of the riders in for a sack of lunch to tide them over until daylight. The rustlers had struck then.

Trevison cursed under his breath. He leaned lower in the saddle. The horse lengthened his stride and the others, drumming along behind, were pressed to keep up. There was little time to lose. The night was a dark one and the raiders could easily make away with the stolen stock in quick order.

They reached the night camp, a small spot of fire in the long-reaching blackness. A man rode out to challenge them, rifle ready across his saddle. Farr yelled—"It's us, Carl!"—and the cowboy trotted in close.

"You see Jules?" he asked.

Farr said: "No. Reckon we must have missed them on the way. Any more trouble?"

"No. They haven't come back, anyway."

They rode to the fire. Trevison turned to the rider.

"You alone here?"

The cowpuncher shook his head. "Jay sent a couple of the boys out to help. They're up with the herd."

"How was Jules makin' it?" Farr asked then.

"Not good," Carl replied. "He was bleeding right smart. We stopped it best we could."

Trevison was staring off into the darkness. "Where were you when the rustlers hit?"

"About a mile south."

Trevison was thinking of Troy Washburn, of his disappearance from the ranch and the things he had speculated upon. "You any idea who it was?"

"Nope. I was up at the lead point. Old mossyhorn up there kept trying to stir up the rest and get them to running. Was having myself a chore trying to settle them down when I heard the shooting. I started back, but the herd was up and milling around so bad I had a hard time getting through. I finally did and found Jules setting there in his saddle, all humped over."

"You didn't see which way the rustlers took off?"

Carl shook his head. "No, they was gone when I got there. And Jules was in such bad shape I didn't spend any time looking for them."

Trevison swept the men who had come with him in a single glance. "Two of you stay here with Carl and the herd. Rest of you come with Jay and me." When they were under way, he yelled: "We'll fan out and do a bit of looking! I know it's dark and we can't do much about tracks. But walk your horse and listen. Maybe we can pick up the sounds of the cattle moving."

They separated, branching out like fingers of a hand, and began a series of sorties across the prairie. A long two hours later they had found nothing. Trevison passed the word along and they returned to camp.

"Give it up until daylight," he said.

One of the riders had dragged in a clump of greasewood and built up the fire. Coffee, made in a lard bucket, boiled over the flames. While it was well watered for the sake of quantity, it was good. For two hours more they hunched about the fire, smoking and taking turns sipping from the bucket.

When the first light began to break, Trevison was in the saddle, Farr and the two other riders with him. The rest he left with instructions to push the cattle on northward where they could join with the main body of stock. He headed straight for the broken, brushy country that lay to the south and west. He had not covered it before, but he had heard the others speak of it and realized it would offer quick and adequate cover for rustlers.

They rode in a widely flung line, traveling slowly. Each man had his eyes on the ground now, searching for the telltale tracks. It was difficult. So much stock had passed across the range in recent days that a myriad of prints lay everywhere on the open ground. And where the grass grew thick, there was none at all.

They got their break just before daylight. Trevison saw Farr, riding some distance to his right, haul up and leave the saddle. He watched as the old rider spent a few moments on his hands and knees, exploring the ground, then stand up and wave. Trevison relayed the signal and loped his horse to where Farr waited.

"Looks like here's what we been lookin' for," he said as Trevison pulled up. "Been a little jag of beef go through here, headin' back into the breaks."

"That's it," Trevison said. He touched his horse with spurs and started along the clearly defined trail. They were on the lip of a small cañon in which buck brier and greasewood and other brush grew in thick, tangled profusion. Trevison pushed along hard, Farr close behind. The other riders had caught up as he could hear them starting the rough descent.

The bottom of the draw was sandy. The tracks were clear and sharp. He paused there, throwing his glance ahead, hoping he might spot motion or some indication of the missing steers' whereabouts. But there was nothing.

He moved on, knowing the cattle could be ten

yards or a mile ahead, it was that difficult to tell. Once he checked the gun at his hip, reassuring himself that the clutching brambles had not dragged it from its scabbard. A good pair of leather chaps would be a welcome bit of clothing here in this wood of sharp thorns and tough brush.

It seemed to Wayne Trevison, riding grimly along in the early light, there was little time for anything. In the past, he was never permitted to stay long in any one place because of the imminence of capture; now, it was necessary he move as fast as possible to fulfill his obligation to Tom Washburn—and then move on. And Halla Greer. He wished he might have the chance to explain his position to her, to make her understand his problem. But no such opportunity had been afforded him and likely never would. Time, since that day in Miles City, had become an all-important and critical factor in his life.

It seemed to Trevison the brush was getting denser, more intertwined, more difficult to break through. His horse fought every step, tossing his head nervously, plunging and shying as the briers dug at his hide, and limbs snapped back and lashed him. It came to Trevison that the rustlers were undoubtedly having the same delaying trouble, for the steers would be just as reluctant to travel with any degree of haste. Small draws were gashing the low hills on either side. Trevison began to search them with his eyes. But the tracks of the moving cattle were still plain in the sand before him. They continued, bearing straight ahead.

They broke out into an open place where the ground was fairly smooth. A sharp, upthrusting of rock lifted some ten feet above the surrounding area, and Trevison called a halt. He climbed to the tip of the uprising, and found that from such a vantage point he had a commanding view of the country. From there he spotted the missing cattle. They were in a dead-end draw, a quarter mile or so to his right. Not more than a dozen head, half of which were lying down, their legs doubled under them in cow fashion. This could mean only one thing: they had been here in their natural corral for some time.

Trevison shouted the information to Farr and the other two riders, and they moved out, following his directions to the arroyo. Trevison kept his eyes roving the land ahead, searching for horses and men. He saw nothing, although he remained there on his perch until Farr and the men had hazed the steers out, and brought them back up the trail of the main cañon.

Farr paused as the cattle lumbered unwillingly by. "Any signs of the rustlers themselves?"

Trevison said—"No."—and climbed down to his horse. Something was not right. It clawed at his mind, leaving him disturbed and unsettled.

Why should the rustlers deliberately drive the stolen stock into a dead end and abandon them? To come back later? That was not reasonable. They had a good enough start to preclude being overtaken and caught. And they would have realized they were leaving a plain trail that could easily be followed to the hidden stock.

He mulled it over the entire distance of the cañon. When they had climbed the steep slope and were once again on the range proper, he said to Farr: "Jay, none of this makes sense. I've got a hunch we've been played for suckers."

Farr drew in close. "How you figure that? We got back the steers."

"Sure. That's just what they wanted us to do. They had it figured that way. While we were following out an easy trail through the brush, they were driving a bigger herd they cut out last night . . . in another direction. Probably taking the same route we brought the main herd over so no tracks would show. That jag there in the breaks was just a decoy."

Farr stroked his mustache. Then: "Danged if it don't look like you're right! Sure makes sense anyway. They didn't have to stash them critters there in that box."

Trevison shook his head. "What we've done is give them another half day's start on us. Half a night and half a day. They're a whole day ahead, somewhere."

"Could be anywhere by now," Farr said morosely. "Lot of good hidin' country farther south."

Trevison nodded. "If they've reached there, we can about figure them gone. A few places I think I'll look first, though, before we give them up. See you later."

XIII

He rode straight to the ranch. The horse was beat, dead tired from the hard trip through the brush-locked cañon, and capable of little more work that day. Also, Trevison wanted to talk with Jules Bryant. He released the bay and roped out a likely looking buckskin from the corral. It took a few minutes to swap gear during which the cook came out and asked: "You want dinner?" Trevison nodded, remembering there had been no breakfast, other than weak coffee. When it was finished, he stopped by the bunkhouse where Jules Bryant lay. The doctor had come and gone, leaving the cowpuncher bandaged and resting easier. He grinned as Trevison entered.

"Dang' country's gettin' tough again! You catch up with them rustlers?"

Trevison shook his head. "Located about a dozen steers hid in the breaks. My hunch is that we were supposed to find them while they drove a big bunch away."

Bryant stirred, his brow pulling into a frown. "I been hopin' you'd come by. I think I know who was in that bunch."

"You get a look at the rustlers?"

"Mighty quick one," Bryant said. "There was six or seven of them. Maybe more. They all come yellin' and shootin' at me. But I saw the jasper that plugged me . . . Jeff Steeg, sure as I'm lyin' here now! I didn't make no mistake about that big hoss, even in the dark. And maybe one of the others was Troy, but I ain't so sure."

Trevison got slowly to his feet. He was thinking: *Where you find Steeg you find Troy*. "You're sure about Jeff?"

"Dead sure."

The pattern was becoming increasingly clear. Troy and Steeg would not have driven a dozen head of stock into the box cañon and left them there. It was part of a plan. While a couple of men drove the few deeply into the rough country, Troy and Steeg and others struck off in another direction, with a much larger bunch. But where had he taken them? The Hellands, the McMahons, the Greers, and Pewter Quinn had received their warnings, yet it did not necessarily follow that they would heed them. And Troy was an engaging talker.

He nodded to Bryant. "You take it easy here for a few days. Anybody asks for me, I'll be back when they see me."

He wheeled out of the bunkhouse and stepped to the saddle. Cutting the buckskin out of the yard, he started at a long lope toward the Helland place. He doubted he would find anything there but every possibility had to be checked.

It was straight up noon when he reached that ranch. He did not go in close, having little time to spare on words. He circled the structures seeing no stock at all, also finding no sign of any having passed that way. To be doubly sure, he rode a few miles farther south, to a low-running hogback, from which he could send his search for a much greater distance. But the prairies were empty.

He doubled back for the Greers', intending to do no more than give it a quick inspection, as he had done the Helland spread. But topping the low rise that lay behind the place, he came suddenly head on into Halla, drifting a few steers to the water hole where the main part of the herd grazed. The unexpectedness of his appearance spooked the animals, and they immediately split and began to run.

Trevison grinned at the vexation spreading over the girl's face. He kicked the buckskin into quick action and, pulling free his rope, swung to head off the lead steers. In a few minutes he had them back in line, following out the path that led to the water hole. He coiled his rope and rode to meet her.

Removing his hat, he said: "Sorry. Didn't mean to break up your drive."

She nodded coolly. "Did you check them for brands?"

He said soberly: "No, ma'am. Should I?"

"I supposed you were still hunting rustlers."

"Matter of fact, I am."

"You'll not find them here!"

Trevison said: "I doubted it myself, but a man has to check everywhere. And they might have passed this way."

Halla thought that over for a moment. Then: "Who would have been with them? Troy?"

Trevison shook his head. "Hard to say. Did you see or maybe hear a herd passing?"

"No," she answered at once. "But they could have been in the cañon north of us. We wouldn't have seen them or heard them, either, if they went that way." She was watching him closely, interest breaking in her eyes. She said: "I can't understand you, Mister Trevison. One minute I think I like you, the next minute I'm sure I don't. One thing I am positive of is that I believe you are a very great threat to this country."

"Threat?" he echoed. "In what way? I'm just here to do a job."

"But a job that is setting neighbor against neighbor, friends against friends. Maybe even brother against brother."

Trevison's voice was stiff. "If that's the result,

I'm sorry. What I am doing is a thing that should have been done a long time ago. I have no intentions of stirring up trouble."

"Does meeting the owner's wife come under that heading, too?"

There was a sharpness to her tone Trevison did not miss. He waited a moment then said: "About yesterday . . ."

She interrupted: "Yesterday was your business. It is nothing to me."

Trevison had a brief wish that it was, that she cared about his being with Roxie, and was looking to him for an explanation. A moment later he put aside the hope but he felt inclined to say: "I knew her back in Dodge City."

Halla moved her shoulders, a small motion meaning much, meaning little. "She apparently believes in renewing such old friendships. In a grand way."

"Not necessarily my wish," Trevison said.

"That was apparent," she murmured. Some of the cool briskness had left her and she was now friendlier. "Troy read one thing in the scene. I read another. All a matter of viewpoint, I guess."

"Thanks. Now, I'll be moving on."

She stopped him. "It's noon. You might just as well drop by the house and eat with us."

It was common courtesy of the range country. He said: "Thanks, but another time. There's a few calls I will make before sundown. I hope the invitation will stand."

"Any time you are passing," Halla said smilingly.

Trevison swung away, and headed for the McMahon place. There were no steers there. He drifted for a good hour searching for the herd. He found it, and all bore McMahon's Double M brand.

Pewter Quinn was standing and waiting for him on his porch when he rode into the man's yard.

"Step down," the rancher greeted him.

Trevison shook his head. "Obliged, but I'm looking for some cattle. Thought they might have come by here."

Quinn said: "They did . . . or at least some did. About four o'clock this mornin'. Why?"

Trevison started to say *rustled,* but changed his mind. Keeping the lifting temper from his tone, he said: "Any thought as to where they were headed?"

Pewter Quinn rubbed the back of his neck. "There was a big trail herd movin' north. From Matamoras, somebody said. Likely they threw in with them."

"Didn't see who was driving the herd?"

"No," Quinn said. "Too dark. Anyway, no business of mine. They your steers?"

"Looks that way. How far ahead you think that trail herd is?"

"Not far. Ten, twelve miles maybe."

Trevison nodded his thanks and swung the buckskin east. He was debating with himself the value of running down the Matamoras herd and checking it for Triangle W beef. Very likely Quinn was right; that's where the stock would be, but by this time it would be so thoroughly integrated with the main herd, that a day would be required to cut them out. And that was something the trail driver would not be in favor of.

He rode slowly on, pondering the problem. If he was figuring right, Troy and Steeg met the big herd, sold them the beef they had driven off the range, collected the money, and were now in town enjoying themselves. They would think the steers they had driven into the breaks would cover their trail sufficiently to throw off all pursuit. Rolling this over in his mind, Trevison came to a conclusion. He cut the buckskin about and drove hard for the road, anger pushing hotly through him. The stock might be gone—but Troy would not enjoy the money for long!

He entered Canaan at a fast trot and bore straight for the Longhorn Saloon. Three horses stood at the rail, none of them familiar. He tied the buckskin alongside them.

Touching the butt of his gun with his fingertips, he pushed through the swinging doors of the saloon into the shadowy interior and halted, allowing his eyes to adjust themselves. Except for three riders sitting at a back table playing a desultory game of cards, the place was empty.

He walked to the bar, watching the alarm rise in the barman's round eyes. He said: "You remember me, friend? I'm the man you steered into Jeff Steeg's arms the other night."

Trevison's tone laid its chill upon the man. He looked down, nervously wiping at the shelf behind the bar. "I don't reckon I . . ."

"I was going to drop back and take you apart then. But I figured it wasn't worth the effort . . . until now."

The card game stalled. The three cowboys were watching Trevison. He swung his gaze to them, hard and arrogant. One by one they looked away. The bartender said in a breathless way: "What do you mean by that?"

"Where's Troy Washburn? Where's Jeff Steeg?"

The barkeeper shook his head. "Ain't here."

"I can see that," Trevison gritted. "Where can I find them?"

"I don't know . . . ," the man whined.

Trevison reached over the bar and grabbed the man by the front of his shirt and jerked him forward. His eyes popped wide with fear and his mouth fell open.

"Where are they? You've got five seconds before I crease your skull with my gun barrel."

"Abilene," the man gasped. "They said Abilene . . . they was goin' there."

Trevison pulled harder, dragging the bartender higher up on to the bar. "Where in Abilene?"

"I don't know, mister! Honest I don't! Maybe the Silver Dollar. I've heard Jeff talk about that place."

Trevison pushed the man away. He slammed hard against the backbar. Bottles clattered and some fell.

Trevison said coldly: "Now, we're even for the other night. Next time you head a man into trouble think about it first. It could get you killed later."

He pivoted on his heel, covering the card players with a sliding glance, and walked to the doorway. Abilene. That was the answer and it figured right. Troy and Steeg with money to throw around, would be in one of two places, either the Longhorn or in Abilene. And they were not at the former.

He mounted the buckskin and rode him to the livery stable. The horse was tough but he would not be able to stand up under a fast run to Abilene and back. Leaving him there, he rented a stalwart gray and within a half hour was heading south. The afternoon was fading, but not Wayne Trevison's anger. Indeed, when he rode into Abilene, his temper had built itself into a hard, reasonless fury against Troy Washburn.

XIV

He made his way along the street, squirming with the night's traffic until he located the Silver Dollar Saloon. It was a two-storied, sprawling affair. He circled it to its side door. Dismounting there, he tied the gray to a cottonwood growing in the yard. Pausing for a minute to be certain he had not been followed, he climbed the short landing and let himself inside.

He halted again, letting the shadows drain from his eyes and accept this new and sudden change. He was in a short hallway that came out at the end of the bar, and after a moment he followed it down.

The place was packed and no one saw him arrive. The line at the long mahogany bar was shoulder to shoulder and three bartenders worked pouring drinks and keeping the counter clean. A barkeeper paused in front of Trevison. "Yours, friend?"

"Beer," Trevison said, and watched the man glide smoothly away. The beer came sliding back to him, and he laid his coin on the counter.

Over the rim of his glass he studied the crowd, ticking it off as best he could. But it was a shifting, buoyant mass and he had difficulty. He found Jeff Steeg first. The big cowpuncher was at the far end of the bar, his back half turned, one elbow hooked on the counter, talking with a woman.

Trevison swung his attention then to the tables, to the card games in progress. There he would most likely find Troy Washburn. One by one he checked them, and, when he was done, he had not located the man. The bartender came up again.

Trevison laid his hand across his glass. "Where's the big game tonight?"

The barkeep ducked his head to the left, to the doors past the end of the bar behind Steeg. "Back rooms." He cast a doubtful look at Trevison. "High stakes for a 'puncher. You figure to set in?"

Trevison shook his head. "Might," he murmured, and pushed out into the milling crowd.

He circled widely around Jeff Steeg, wanting no trouble from that point at this particular moment. There were two doors behind the bar. He opened the first quietly and saw three men at a round table, their guns lying in sight as they played silently. A fourth man, sitting astride a chair and leaning on its back, watched with close interest. He did not look up as Trevison made his examination. Troy was not in there.

He moved to the next door and pushed it open. Smoke hung about an overhead lamp, and the sharp *click* of chips was the lone sound that greeted him. Five men were at the table and one of those was Troy. He sat with his back to the door. Trevison slid softly into the room and one of the players, a man with thin, sallow features and smoking a black cheroot, flicked him with only casual interest, then went back to his game.

Trevison drifted quietly up to a point just behind Washburn. He was carefully probing the faces of the others in the small box-like room, assessing their possible reaction to the move he would soon make. He noted then there was no other door besides the one he had come through and the single window was high and small, of no use as an exit.

Trevison's gaze came back to the game. The pot was a heavy one, coins and currency piled high in the center of the table. It was the final round of cards. The man with the cheroot drew one. Next man dropped out; Washburn called for two. The fourth player drew a single, and the last stood pat. Washburn checked the bet and the player who had stood pat tossed a gold eagle into the wager. All players called, and, on the lay down, Washburn was high man.

Trevison watched him drag the bills and coins in. When he reached into his shirt pocket for his roll and had folded the addition to it, Trevison leaned over his shoulder and plucked it from his fingers. Washburn yelled his surprise. One of the players exclaimed: "What the hell?"

Trevison, hand resting suggestively on the butt of his gun, back-stepped to the door. Placing his shoulder against it, he thrust the money into his pocket. Washburn had scrambled to his feet, eyes wild, mouth working convulsively.

"Just all of you stay seated and nobody will get hurt," Trevison said coolly. "Make no sudden moves. This is no hold-up, otherwise I'd be taking all of your cash. I just came after the money this man forgot to turn in after he sold some cattle of mine."

"Why, you . . . !" Washburn began hotly.

"Go ahead," Trevison invited coldly. "Let's hear it."

But Washburn had no more to say. He watched Trevison with a hard and narrow gaze, white with anger.

Trevison said: "I want no trouble from any of you. But follow me through this door and you've got it."

He reached for the knob, pressing into his hip, and turned it. He pulled back the door, eyes drilling into Washburn. "Don't come after me, Troy," he warned softly, and stepped into the main part of the saloon.

There were the immediate sounds of hurried confusion beyond the door, but it did not open. His threat was holding good—at least for a time. He ducked away into the jamming crowd, endeavoring to move fast but unobtrusively for the batwings, clear across the room. He was halfway there when Troy Washburn's voice yelled: "Jeff! Trevison's out there somewhere! Hey, Steeg!"

Trevison worked his way through the closely packed shapes. He kept his head down, moving steadily. He would like to stop and locate Steeg and Washburn, and thus get a better idea of his chances, but common sense told him it was wiser to keep his face hidden and press on.

Grim humor was moving through him as he recalled the shocked amazement in Troy Washburn's eyes when he had taken the money from his fingers.

"Steeg!" Washburn's voice again lifted above the din. "You see him yet? Jeff! Where are you?"

The big cowpuncher made no audible answer and this disturbed Trevison. If the man had replied, he might have been able to pinpoint his position in the crowd.

"Over there! Over there by the doorway!" Washburn sang out suddenly.

A man next to Trevison wheeled and stared. He said—"This one?"—and grabbed at Trevison's arm. Trevison, seeing the swinging doors only a half dozen steps away, struck out viciously, driving a solid fist into the man's belly. The grip on his arm relaxed at once. He pushed for the doorway, hearing Troy's insistent yells grow behind him, and the clamor of the crowd lift with them. Another man loomed dead ahead and then faded quickly aside as Trevison bore straight on. The doors, at last, were close. Another yard and he shouldered through them and cut sharply left—coming hard into Jeff Steeg.

Trevison had the advantage of the moment. Surprise was with him. He had a fragment of time in which to set himself and swing. The blow caught Steeg on the side of the head, too high to be decisive, but its tremendous force rocked the big man to his heels and off balance and sent him staggering away and off the porch.

The crowd was boiling through the doorway and out into the street. Shouts, laughter, the shrill cry of a woman as unwelcome hands took advantage of the situation. Trevison crowded Steeg, driving him back before he could get squared away. There was no time to fight now.

Grim and silent, he drove his fists into Steeg, the man's grunts plain in his ears. A gun crashed through the night, coming from somewhere in the jostling crowd. Trevison thought—*Here comes the law now!*—and lashed out savagely. He had to break clear of Steeg and get away, at any cost. But Steeg was fighting back. Trevison rushed the cowpuncher, striking with all he had. Time had again run out. He had to get away; he could not afford to let any law officer arrest him, regardless of the charge. Steeg's face was suddenly close before him, his eyes alight with hatred and fury. Blood smeared his features, trickling from his flattened nose and crushed lips.

"Got you, Trevison!"

"Not yet, Jeff," Trevison murmured. He drove his left wrist deeply into the man's mid-section. Breath exploded from Steeg's mouth in a whistling gasp. He buckled forward. Trevison, timing it perfectly, caught him with an upswinging uppercut that connected squarely. Pain shot through Trevison's arm all the way to his shoulder and he had a moment's fear that he had broken his hand. Steeg reeled away drunkenly into the murky darkness, falling sideways like a hewn tree. Trevison, dragging deep for wind, dodged off to his right, toward the protective blackness of a building hard by. The mouth of an adjoining byway opened up, and, seeing starlight at the far end, he started down it at a hard run. Back of him in the street the shouts increased. A man, nearer than the others called—"Halt! I'll shoot!"—in a sharp, commanding voice.

The end of the alley was near. Trevison ducked and ran on. The bullet cracked in the narrow cañon between the two buildings, the sound a deafening, shattering wallop in his ears. He reached the end and swung right, going toward the gray horse waiting for him near the Silver Dollar Saloon. Boots were rapping along the hard-packed ground of the byway, and drawing closer. An open doorway of the building he had just rounded showed darkly in the pale shine. He swerved toward it, grabbed the knob, and the door came shut with a slam. Another two strides and he had reached the far corner of the structure and was around it and heading back for the street.

"In that old store!" a voice yelled behind him. He grinned mirthlessly. They had taken the bait. "I heard the door slam shut!"

"Get around front, somebody!"

Trevison entered the street, walking swiftly to where several horses waited at a tie rail. Men were pounding up the length of the vacant building. The crowd had mostly trailed through the byway, and now were gathering at that opposite end. Standing there with the horses, like a rider who apparently had just arrived, or was leaving, Trevison called to the nearest man: "What's going on around here?"

"Got a jasper holed up in there," the man replied breathlessly. He swung his sweaty face toward the back. "We got him blocked here, Marshal!"

"What'd he do?" Trevison asked, pulling the reins of a little buckskin free.

"Hanged if I know," the fellow answered. "Everybody's just tryin' to catch him. Somethin' he did back there in the saloon, I reckon."

Trevison swung up into the saddle. If his luck would only hold for another few seconds, just until he could reach the darkness beyond the street he would have done it.

"Come out of there!" A man was yelling into the empty building as he crossed the street. "We got you covered!"

Trevison reached the opposite side and rode into

the deep shadows of an alleyway. Following this path eventually brought him to a point opposite the Silver Dollar. For a long minute he watched that structure, seeing the gray waiting patiently for him at the side tie rail. There were few people in the saloon, none on the porch or in the yard. The majority of Abilene was down the street where the demands for him to leave the empty storehouse were growing more insistent.

"Smoke him out!" a voice yelled. "Throw a little fire in there, Marshal. That'll bring him out!"

Trevison grinned in the darkness. He cut the buckskin back and traveled another 100 yards north along the street. There, well beyond the flare of light, he crossed over, doubled back, and came into the yard behind the saloon. He exchanged the buckskin for the gray and swung quietly out of the town for Canaan.

A mile away he paused to study the lurid glow hanging over Abilene. Apparently they had gone ahead with the idea of smoking him out, but somehow the fire must have gotten out of hand.

Around eleven o'clock that next morning Trevison rode into Canaan. He was weary and hungry. He pulled up at the stable, dismounted, and walked thc tired gray inside. The hostler came from the rear to meet him, took the gray, and moved to exchange the gear to the buckskin, now rested after a night's sojourn in the barn. When he was back, Trevison paid the toll and returned to the street. He headed first for the bank.

Frank Gringras came to the door to meet him, watching him silently as he looped the leathers over the bar. When Trevison wheeled toward him, he said: "Man, you look beat. Anything wrong?"

Trevison dug into his pocket. "No, just collecting for some cattle." He handed the roll of bills to the banker. "Add this to the Washburn account. Troy sold some steers."

Gringras looked closely at him but Trevison's face was closed, showing nothing. Gringras shrugged and turned about. "Wait until I make a receipt."

Trevison leaned against the door frame, letting his glance travel the town. Halla Greer came into view, straight and tall on her little pinto horse, and pulled up at the general store. Trevison watched her with interest.

"Better get yourself some sleep," Gringras advised, thrusting the slip of paper into his hand. "Things all right at Washburn's? You going to start the drive soon?"

"Soon," Trevison murmured, and walked away.

He slanted across the street to a small shop where the barber plied his trade. Trevison sank into the hard, straight-backed chair and, as the man drew a checked apron tight around his neck, said: "Haircut. Shave. And don't wake me up if I fall asleep."

Only moments later, it seemed, the barber was gently shaking his shoulder. “Finished. I let you alone for an hour, long as I could. Now I got another customer.”

Trevison felt much better. The few minutes’ sleep had taken the edge off his weariness. He paid his bill and went back into the street. Halla Greer’s pony was now in front of the bank, and, as his glance came to rest upon it, the girl came from the building and mounted up. She swung back up the street and Trevison sauntered out to meet her.

She pulled up before him, watching him with her serious, half-smiling eyes. “Find your rustlers, Mister Trevison?”

He said: “I did.”

“Just now get back?”

He nodded. “Rode in an hour ago.”

“Must have been a long ride,” she observed thoughtfully.

“It was that,” he agreed, “and a hungry one. Would you allow me to turn your invitation around and ask you to have dinner with me? Here at the café.”

Halla smiled quickly. “Of course. I had planned to eat in town today.”

She dismounted, and he led the pinto back to where the buckskin waited. Trevison’s towering shape made the girl’s slight figure seem small, almost child-like against it.

They reached the restaurant and Trevison held

back the door for her to enter, following himself. Inside, he pulled up short, the sparse form of Sheriff George Bradford blocking his way.

Bradford was an old man, of Tom Washburn's generation. He had a seamed, deeply grooved face only partially hidden by a goatee-style beard and full flowing mustache. His hair was almost snow-white and it hung long, shoulder-length, beneath a black, flat-crowned hat.

He said unsmilingly: "Been expecting you, Crewes."

Trevison settled himself gently, all the old mistrust of men wearing stars coming to the fore. He was worried about this totally unexpected encounter with the law. It disturbed him, thinking of what Halla Greer might hear and see, and the possibility of her getting hurt. He threw a quick, sideways glance at her, seeing the frown the name, Crewes, which Bradford had used, brought to her eyes.

He said coolly: "Little pressed for time, Sheriff. Anyway, why should I drop by to see you?"

"Rule of mine," Bradford mumbled. "Always like to know who's in my town. Understand that's your name . . . Crewes. Jim Crewes."

In the hush of the room, tight with tension, Trevison said: "They call me that."

"Your real name?"

Trevison waited out a full minute, calculating the pressures. Under the direct, probing gaze of the sheriff he said: "There anything wrong with it?"

Bradford eyed him in a dissatisfied way. "You look a little familiar. We ever met before?"

Trevison shook his head. "Don't think so."

He brushed by the man then, cutting him out. Taking Halla by the arm, he guided her to a back table and seated her. Pulling out a chair for himself, he settled down, tension drawing his nerves taut. He lifted his glance to Bradford, who stood there watching him with crimped eyes, while he sought to justify the suspicion that flowed through him. A minute later he shrugged, drew back the door, and walked into the street.

Trevison, only then, turned his attention to Halla. Her face was a study and he knew she was experiencing deep wonderment about him, about the name Bradford had used. He said: "I'm sorry about it. About the sheriff."

The waitress came up and they ordered, Trevison asking for coffee to be served at once. When they each had their cups, Halla said: "Which is your name, Crewes or Trevison?"

He said: "Trevison."

"Are you wanted by the law?"

He said —"Yes."—and watched something move into her gray eyes, a dullness that told of her dismay.

The waitress returned with their plates and no more was said of it. For a few minutes they ate in silence, and, when they were ready for pie and a final cup of coffee, she lifted her gaze to him.

"You said you found the rustlers. Does that mean Troy?"

Trevison smiled. "Not hardly right to call a man who takes some of his own cattle a rustler, I reckon."

"But he had taken some and sold them, and was going to keep the money. Like those he sold my father."

"Yes," Trevison said. He dug the makings out of his pocket and rolled a smoke.

She watched him light it. Then: "That's where you've been, getting the money from Troy?"

Trevison slanted a sharp glance at her. He said: "Gringras talks too much."

She laughed lightly. "Don't blame him too much. I wormed it out of him."

She was silent after that and he knew she was wondering about him. There were things she knew, others she assumed; now she was having a hard time putting them together and making them join in the nice, perfect way women like to have such things fit. She had talked with Gringras, therefore she knew he had followed Troy and collected money from him. And then turned it in to the banker. Yet, he was a man under an assumed name, a man wanted by the law for some crime or another. It simply was not compatible. A criminal riding all night to turn back money he could have easily gone on with.

"Don't let any of this disturb you," he said with a grin. "There's an answer to it all."

She started at the sound of his voice. She said: "I'm sure of that." A moment later she added: "You should smile like that more often. You always look so grim! Smiling does something for you . . . breaks those bitter lines around your mouth."

Trevison shrugged. "Man needs something to smile about, or for, these days. Maybe you're that something."

She viewed him archly, words forming upon her lips. But she passed them by, giving him instead her serious smile. She rose, and he got quickly to his feet.

"Time I was leaving. Are you riding back to Triangle W now?"

"With you, I hope," he said.

He dropped two silver dollars onto the table, and they walked out into the strong, warm sunlight. They turned toward their horses and Trevison saw, in that instant, the shape of Bradford come from his office and slant toward them. At once anger stirred through him, building its strong, pushing impatience. He halted, saying softly: "Go ahead, Halla. This may be trouble." But she refused. She stopped, as did he. Bradford strolled up, and came to a halt in the center of the street, his gaze on Trevison.

"Just thought I'd ask again. You sure we never met before?"

Temper plucking at his self-control, Trevison held a tight rein on his words. From the corner of his eye he could see Halla, watching him with anxious interest. He said: "I still doubt it, Sheriff. Never been in this country."

"Where you from then if this ain't your country?"

Trevison waited out a long moment, letting the man know he did not appreciate the question that, by right, he could let pass. He said: "Lots of places."

"Any place special?"

Anger snapped in Trevison. He laid a cold glance on Bradford. "Sheriff," he said in deliberate calmness, "you don't know me. You never met me before. You can believe that. Now, let's get something understood. You got some charge you want to trump up against me, bring it out and let's hear it . . . otherwise stay away from me."

Bradford stared at Trevison, his faded old eyes level and undisturbed. He shook his head. "Sure, son, sure," he murmured, and moved away.

Trevison watched him leave, heat running slowly from him. A warning began to lift; Bradford was suspicious. He knew something, probably that Crewes was not his real name. And maybe, stored back there in his memory, was the recollection of a face on a Reward dodger. Likely that was what he had been doing after he left the restaurant, checking through his stack of posters at his office. Apparently he had not found it, or he would not still be uncertain of his ground.

He was aware then of Halla, waiting there beside him. She said: "We'd better start . . ."

He nodded. "Of course. I'll say again I'm sorry. The sheriff seems to have something on his mind."

She turned to him, her face still. "Are you worried about it?"

"I never worry"—he smiled—"only try to be careful."

XV

The first miles were quiet ones. Halla was wrapped in her thoughts and Trevison, not wanting to disturb her, let her have her way. He confined himself to considering Sheriff Bradford and the possible danger that might lie at that point.

They left the loose, powdery dust of the road and struck out across the grass of the prairie. Off to the right, a bright splash of lighter green marked the location of a spring, with its inevitable stand of cottonwood trees. Halla turned to him. "It's hot. Shall we rest a bit in the shade?"

Trevison nodded his agreement, and they swung toward the trees. Reaching there, they stepped down, and he led the horses to water. Halla found a seat on a rotting log, and, when he came back, she did not face him.

Trevison held his peace. She was, he realized, having her own deep and fierce struggle over him, trying to place him in his proper niche in her mind, and decide her feelings for him. Women were like that; a man was good or he was bad—and there was little compromising middle ground. Thus Trevison kept silent, allowing her to come to her own conclusions.

He could not keep his steady glance from her, and the thought of her passing from his life was an unwelcome one. There was something about this woman that reached out and took firm hold upon his consciousness. He loved her. He stirred suddenly, catching himself at his own thoughts. The slightest groan escaped his lips. *What a fool I am to think of things like that! Me . . . a man with no future, no home, no place to go . . . nothing!*

"You said they wanted you. Is . . . is it for something bad? Something really serious?" she asked.

He said: "Murder. I killed a sheriff."

"Murder?" she echoed faintly. "Just like that . . . murder? No reason? No cause?"

He said: "That's what they called it. It's what the Reward dodgers with my picture on them say . . . 'Wanted for Murder.' "

"But was it?"

He shook his head. “No.”

A small whisper of relief slipped through her lips.

He said: “I told this story once, back in Montana. Nobody believed it except one man, and he couldn’t help.”

“Go on, Wayne. I want to hear it.”

He dropped his glance to his hands, fisted into hard knots across his knees. Slowly he released them, spreading his fingers widely as the tenseness decreased. “I had a brother, four years younger than myself. My folks were killed by Indians when I was ten years old. A rancher by the name of Goodman took us in and we grew up there. That’s where I met Tom Washburn. He was the foreman for the outfit . . . and the only father I can remember. After Tom left Montana, we stayed on at Goodman’s. But my brother got mixed up with a couple of ’punchers. There was some trouble. A man was killed in a hold-up. My brother came and told me all about it. While he was guilty of being with the two men, he was not there at the time of the killing. I sent him to stay with a friend of ours, until I could get things straightened out with the sheriff.

“I went to see the sheriff, a friend of mine, I thought. I told him the story. He said, if I would persuade my brother to give himself up, he would see he got a fair deal. They already had the actual killers. Maybe he would get a short time in jail for being a part of the gang, but not for any murder charge. I talked my brother into it because I was convinced it was the right thing to do. I didn't want him dodging around the rest of his life with a price tag on his head. He came in with me to the sheriff and turned himself in. Next day he was dead."

"Dead?" Halla echoed. "Dead?"

Trevison nodded slowly. "The sheriff told me he had tried to escape. His deputy backed him up. They were moving him to another jail in the next town. For safe-keeping, they said. I got there only a few minutes after it happened. He still had the handcuffs around his wrists. And his feet were roped under his horse. The bullet was in his back."

There was horror in Halla's voice. "But if he was handcuffed and tied to his horse, how could he . . . ?"

Trevison said: "Same thing I asked the sheriff. He said he guessed I was a little too smart and went for his gun. I shot him before he could draw."

Halla considered this for a time, then: "How did you get away, with the deputy there?"

"He was on my side. I went back to the town with him, thinking he would back up my story of what happened. Instead, he said I had tried to spring my brother free, and in the shooting the sheriff had killed my brother, and I had then put a bullet into the sheriff. It was a fine, old double-cross . . . and it branded me an outlaw."

"You were able to break jail later?"

"This friend of mine, the only one who believed my story, smuggled me a gun. I managed the rest."

Halla said nothing for a time, thinking over what he had said. Then: "Of course it was no more than self-defense. Did you ever think of going back and trying to clear your name? There must be some way it can be done."

"How? Every lawman between here and Miles City is just looking for the chance to collect rewards like the one on my head. Not to mention the bounty men and plain cowboys. I'm worth a thousand dollars, dead or alive, to any of them."

She shuddered. "But you can't go on forever like this, looking over your shoulder, wondering if there's somebody on your trail. Like there in town today. I could see the change come over you when Bradford stopped you. You were different, a man I'd never before seen. You make me think of a wolf backed into a corner, ready to fight it out to a finish."

He grinned. "That's a good way to put it . . . a wolf at bay." The smile faded. "One they'll never collect bounty on," he added grimly.

"But you can't . . . ," she began, lifting her hands in a palm upward gesture. "There must be some way to change it."

Trevison shook his head. "I've thought about them all. Even tried for a while to do it, but it's my word against the deputy's, and they listen to him.

Only answer I've ever found is to keep moving. Maybe Mexico one of these days."

"It wouldn't end there. Somebody would recognize you eventually and bring you out. Maybe dead, across the back of a horse."

He shrugged. "Something I would have a little say-so about. Man doesn't follow this trail for as long as I have without learning to look out for himself."

"But you can't do that forever."

Trevison said—"I've managed so far."—and got to his feet. He stood there, tall, wide-shouldered in the sunlight, looking off into the far reaches of the prairie. He half turned and found her close beside him, looking up into his face. His arms went around her at once, drawing her into their strong circle, pressing her against him. His mouth found her lips, the solid pressure of it bringing a faint gasp from her.

"We . . . had better go," she managed after a moment.

He released her at once, moving away wordlessly. There was no apology in him, no regret, and he made no comment. He merely walked to where the horses waited, gathered up the trailing reins, and led them to where she stood. He helped her mount, and then swung onto the buckskin.

They had covered a mile when he broke his silence. Drawing in close beside her, he laid a hand upon hers. "We will forget what happened back there. It's not in the cards much as I would like to think so. I can't drag you into my troubles."

"Two people often do better solving a problem than one," she murmured.

He shook his head. "Not this kind of problem. My mistakes are my own. I'll not have you or anybody else paying for them. Now, we'll talk of other things."

She started to raise some protest, make some objection to his strong words, but thought better of it. After a time she said: "How are things at the Washburn place? Will you soon be ready for the drive to Dodge City?"

"Shouldn't be too long," he replied. It was idle talk, both of them skirting the subject of his past, his future. "Farr thinks we should be ready in a week or two."

"What about Troy? I know he has given you a lot of trouble. Will he ever change, you think?"

Trevison said: "Probably. He's wild and spoiled. Give him a little more time, maybe he will come out of it."

She looked at him sharply. "You are saying that for my benefit! I doubt if you believe it. Don't spare him because of me. It has always been a fond dream of my father's that someday Troy and I would marry. But it's no desire of mine and I think now he has changed his mind about it."

"A thing I'm pleased to hear," Trevison stated.

Halla said—"Oh?"—in a wondering sort of way. When he said no more, she added: "You don't think much of Virgil, either, I guess."

"He's different. That I will say."

"And his wife . . . ?" Halla remarked with a teasing laugh. Immediately she sobered, seeing he did not consider it so lightly.

"I'm sorry for her," Trevison said. "What lies ahead for her as his wife can be nothing short of hell and misery."

They were climbing the last rise, reaching the crest. Triangle W's scatter of buildings lay before them in the afternoon sunlight.

Trevison said: "We'll stop for a cool drink, and then I'll see you home."

"See me home?" she repeated with a laugh. "Why, nobody's done that for me since I was a child. But I like it."

They rode down the gentle slope at a leisurely pace. As they drew closer and things began to grow more distinct and take shape, Trevison saw several of the men in the yard, one of them Jay Farr. They were standing a few yards from the main house, halfway to the corral. The cook was on the kitchen step, leaning against the door frame, his attention, too, focused on the house. As they rode in, Trevison heard the shrill voice of Roxie and the stronger, demanding tones of Virgil Washburn.

Trevison pulled up, Halla close to his side. Farr

came over to meet them, his long face sober. Roxie's scream lifted in volume. And there was the dull *thud* of a striking object.

"What's going on in there?" Trevison asked.

Farr touched the brim of his hat to Halla and nodded. Then: "Been that way for more'n an hour. Her yellin' like that and him a-cussin' and a-hittin' her with something. Started in there myself a half dozen times, but then allowed as how I got no call to interfere in a family squabble."

Trevison glanced back to the house. Farr was right, of course, but he did not know how much of Roxie's crying he could stand before he would be compelled to take a hand.

Halla said: "I think I'd better ride on. Don't bother to come along."

The sudden flat crash of a gunshot rocked the yard.

Trevison came off his horse in one long leap. He sprinted for the side door. It burst wide and Virgil Washburn, blood streaming down his shirt front, staggered into the open. He fell almost at once, his fingers clutching a riding crop tightly.

A moment later Roxie appeared. Her hair was down about her waist, her upper clothing in shreds. Her face and bare shoulders were covered by livid, red welts. She looked dazedly about the yard and, seeing Trevison standing there, gave a little cry. Dropping the gun from her fingers, she ran sobbing to him.

Roxie threw herself into Trevison's arms.

"I didn't want to do it . . . but I couldn't stand any more of his beatings."

From his knees alongside Virgil Washburn's body, Farr said: "He's dead."

Halla Greer dismounted and moved quickly to where Trevison was holding Roxie loosely against his chest. She laid her hand on the girl's shoulder.

"Why not come home with me, Missus Washburn?"

Roxie half turned and faced her. She shook Halla's hand away. "No! No! I'll stay here . . . with Wayne."

Farr had swung to one of the men standing nearby. "Ride into town and get Bradford. Get the coroner, too." The cowboy wheeled to comply, and Farr motioned to another rider. "Get a blanket out of the bunkhouse and throw it over him. Don't go meddlin' with nothin' now, especially that whip. That shows it was self-defense."

Roxie had quieted some. The hysterical crying had diminished and now she stood almost silent. Halla had not gone yet. Trevison pushed Roxie away gently. She reached into a pocket and produced a wisp of white and dabbed at her swollen eyes.

"Hadn't you better go with Halla?" Trevison suggested. "I'll have the boys hitch up the buggy. You will be better off with her."

Roxie stared at the blanket-shrouded form on the ground. "Is he dead?"

"He's dead," Trevison answered soberly.

The girl shuddered. "I'll never forget the look on his face when I pulled the trigger. Never . . . not if I live to be a hundred years old!"

"Don't think about it now," Trevison said softly. "Go with Halla."

Roxie swung then to Halla Greer. She said: "Why? I'm all right. I don't need her help. Nor anybody else's. I want to stay here where I belong . . . and with you, Wayne."

Trevison saw the stillness move into Halla's eyes. Without speaking, she turned and walked away. Trevison started to follow, to go after her. Roxie threw her arms around him, holding him back.

"Wayne! Stay with me . . . don't leave me now."

He watched in silence as Halla swung to her saddle. When she rode by, not a half dozen yards distant, she held her gaze straight ahead, and he could see her face was devoid of expression. Trevison felt a heaviness settle within him then, a great hopelessness that knew no end. He followed the spotted pony as it climbed the far slope, Roxie babbling at his side about the two of them, how they could now be together and own this ranch and times would be for them as they once had been, long ago. But he was only half listening. Finally he said: "Hush, Roxie."

He reached down and picked her up, and carried her into the house. Looking back over his shoulder as he passed through the doorway, he had a last glimpse of Halla just topping the ridge and going out of sight.

Sheriff Bradford arrived accompanied by Dr. Skillings who also served as town coroner. As Farr predicted, Bradford and the physician declared it to be a matter of self-defense and Roxie was exonerated of any willful blame.

Bradford said then: "You want us to take him into town?"

Farr spoke up. "Reckon not, George. We'll bury our own dead. Tom would've wanted him put right alongside himself and the missus, there in the family plot back of the ranch. Obliged to you, though, if you'll pass the word around and tell the preacher to come out."

"All right," the sheriff answered. "What about Troy? He know about this yet?"

Farr shook his head. "He ain't been around for several days. Thought maybe he was in town and you'd tell him."

Bradford looked thoughtful. "I don't think he's in town, Jay. Leastwise, I sure haven't seen him lately."

Trevison, keeping out of the conversation up to this point, said: "Try Abilene. The Silver Dollar Saloon."

Bradford swung a quick, enquiring glance at Trevison but he made no comment. Farr broke in: "I'll send a man over there right away. Tell the folks the service'll be about dark. That'll give Troy time enough to get here."

Bradford nodded and climbed into his buggy. Dr. Skillings came out of the house where he had been attending to Roxie.

"Gave her a little something to make her rest. And I put some ointment on those bruises. Virgil must have been out of his mind, doing a thing like that."

"Never know what's inside a man," Bradford observed as they pulled away.

Troy was not in Abilene. The cowpuncher Jay Farr had sent for him returned the next day and said he had tried not only the Silver Dollar, but every other gambling house in town as well, and in addition he and the marshal had checked at the hotels and livery barns. One man said Troy had left town after some sort of ruckus a few nights before. He did not know where he was headed.

The service was conducted by the minister just as the sun was dropping over the rim of the range. There were a few people from town, and Halla Greer and her father. None had come for Virgil's sake; he had no friends. All were there out of respect for Tom Washburn and his wife. Virgil was buried in the small, fenced-in plot of ground reserved for such purposes on a slight knoll behind the ranch buildings.

Trevison stood near Roxie through it all, there being no one else for her to lean upon. Twice he glanced at Halla but she kept her eyes down, and, when it was all over, she paused to murmur her condolences to Roxie, and then left without looking at him.

After supper that night, which he ate with Roxie in the dining room of the main house, she said: "I'm going away, Wayne. Leaving for a while. Will you come with me?"

Impatiently he said: "Of course not. You know I have this job to do. I can't stop until it's finished."

"You mean the trail drive to Dodge? That's the end of your job. All right, I'll meet you there."

He shook his head. "No point in that either, Roxie."

"No point," she echoed. "Wayne, it is everything! Now we can have all the things we both wanted . . . and together. Don't you realize half this ranch is mine, maybe all of it."

"I understand it," Trevison replied heavily.

"Then why won't you meet me in Dodge?"

Trevison rose, and walked slowly across the room to the stone-faced fireplace breaking the wall's center. He rolled himself a cigarette, lit it, and flicked the match into the gray ashes. He was a silent, brooding figure standing there in the shadowy room, trouble creasing his brow and deepening the lines around his wide mouth.

"I said this once, Roxie. I'll say it once more and ask you not to force me to do so again. There's nothing for us. Not here, not there, not anywhere. It's all gone and forgotten. It ended there in Dodge and it will never come back again, no matter what the circumstances."

Roxie listened to his words. She was utterly still, only her fingers moving as they traced out a seam in the lap of her dark traveling suit. After a long time she said: "It's Halla Greer, isn't it, Wayne?"

He shrugged. "If such a thing was possible, yes, I suppose it would be Halla."

Roxie said—"I see."—in a low voice. "And you're no man to settle for second best."

He shook his head. "There's no such thing, Roxie. You know that. Either it's all or it's nothing."

"I'm going on to Dodge tomorrow. I'll be there when you arrive with the herd. If you have come to your senses, you'll find me at the hotel. Good bye, Wayne."

She swirled abruptly away from him and crossed the room. She paused in the doorway leading into the rest of the house, her fingers resting lightly on the knob. In a kinder voice she said—"I'll be waiting for you."—and then she was gone.

• • •

A week or so later Jay Farr came off the range. He corralled his horse and stomped across the hard pack to where Trevison and Frank Gringras were talking. Roxie had gone on to Dodge City. Troy Washburn had not been found, and Trevison had not seen Halla since the afternoon of the funeral.

"Reckon we're ready to move," Farr announced. "Pull away in the mornin' if you say the word."

"You figure plenty of extra horses? At least five for every rider?"

"Plenty of horses," Farr replied patiently.

"How about Indian Creek?"

"Water in it all right. Not much, accordin' to Jesse, but enough."

"Cook and chuck wagon ready to go?"

Farr said: "Everything's ready to go, Mister Trevison."

"We'll pull away at daylight then. Pass the word along."

Farr said: "You still figure on takin' that short cut? Instead of the regular way?"

Trevison said: "I am. Long as there's water, we can handle the rest."

"You're the ramrod," the old cowpuncher said, and turned away.

Gringras spoke then. "Sounds mighty fine. You sure got that herd ready to go in short order."

"Still a long way to Dodge City," Trevison reminded him.

"Expect you'll make it," the banker replied. "I've got no doubts about that part. However . . ."

Trevison swung his hard, driving glance at the man. "However what? Something on your mind?"

Gringras moved his shoulders nervously. "Nothing, much. Well, I was just wondering about the money end of it. You plan to draw cash or take a draft?"

Trevison's face was humorless. "You've been talking to Bradford, I see. Well, don't worry about it. You'll get your money. I'll bring it to you and personally lay it in your hand."

"Of course," Gringras said quickly. "I know that. Forget I mentioned it." He offered his hand.

Trevison accepted it, shaking it briefly. "See you in a month or so," he said, and turned to his bunk.

XVI

The drive started out well. Triangle W riders had combed the range and every piece of marketable beef had been rounded up. Nearly 2,800 head, Farr told Trevison as they rode to the crest of the knoll beyond the water hole, and watched the herd get under way.

Trevison had called all his riders together and outlined his plan. They would head north for Indian Creek. There they would water the stock and then swing east, keeping slightly north. This should bring them in a short distance below the usual Red River crossing. It would be a hard drive; they could not afford to lose a single head, and the fewer days they were on the trail, the better it would be.

"Anybody back out?"

Farr said: "One. Ranny called Lillard that came over from Abilene. Said it looked like too much hard work to him, but I figure he was a bit shy when it come to trouble."

"Trouble? What trouble?"

"Trouble we'll prob'ly get from raiders. Goin' this route, we're bound to have it."

Trevison looked closely at the old cowpuncher. Driving the cattle over this new and uncharted trail was the one single thing they had not agreed upon. He said: "Don't worry, Jay. We'll make it through."

Farr shook his head. "I'm hopin' so. We lose this herd, the Washburn place is ruint for sure."

That first day they covered almost twenty miles, bedding the herd down at sunset in a wide, shallow valley. The cook set up camp on a short hill overlooking the swale, and the meal was ready when they had settled the herd. The wrangler strung his rope corral for the horses and turned it over to the night hawk. The night guards rode off into the darkness and the day crew came in.

The herd was quiet. They had trailed well and the riders were all in good spirits, lying sprawled around the campfire, drinking coffee, smoking, telling their tales, and making their jokes. Somewhere off in the night, one of the cowpunchers crooned softly of a girl in San Antone waiting for her cowboy to return, and Wayne Trevison had his thoughts of Halla Greer. But they were momentary thoughts. He brushed them away with a quick impatience. There was no use in thinking of Halla, of what might have been for she was now a part of the past. And Roxie. She would be in Dodge City now. Waiting for him, she had said. Maybe Roxie had the right idea, after all. Grab what life offered and make the best of it.

The next day was much like the first. Grass was fair and the herd showed little signs of thirst, mostly because it stayed cool and partly cloudy. By the middle of the following morning, however, it was a different matter. The clouds had blown away and the sun poured down from an empty sky. The steers turned contrary and restless. Trevison was glad they were not far from Indian Creek.

They reached it just after midday, halting the main body of stock a short mile back. Trevison and Farr rode on ahead to look the situation over. They decided the best plan was to water the herd in small bunches, then move them on to a higher plateau a few miles farther for the night. This they did, and it was fully dark when the job was over.

It was an easy camp. The herd was satisfied,

filled with good feed and plenty of water, and the going had been smooth.

"Come tomorrow, it won't be no lark like this," Farr said that night as they rolled into their blankets. "Country's fair rough from here east."

Scouting ahead, Trevison found the old cowpuncher to be right. The prairie descended into low, broken hills with many rocky arroyos and sharp draws and red-fronted bluffs. He had the herd swerved slightly northward to miss the worst of it, but this slowed them down considerably. When darkness caught up, they had lost their good average.

Near noon the next day, hot and dusty, they came up hard against a steep-walled slash cañon that offered no safe crossing for the herd. Trevison and Farr rode along its rough and ragged edge for a long five miles, before they located a break-off sufficiently wide and gentle to allow the cattle to cross over. It was sunset by the time the herd had reached that point. Trevison, taking no chances on a night stampede so close to the cañon, had the crew drive them back a good two miles to bed them down.

They lost two steers crossing the ravine the next morning, but Trevison considered himself lucky. The crossing was narrow and the animals behaved surprisingly well. There was just that one bad minute when a small bunch broke and ran. That was when the two longhorns were killed, piling up at the bottom with broken necks.

"Some good in that killin' after all," Farr said when they were again on the move. "That one old mossyhorn was a looney, anyhow. Always tryin' to break and run. Kept the others all fired up half the time."

It was the same rough, rock-strewn country all that day. They made a poor camp, to the bawling of the restless herd, and the night guards were busy. The stock was on the move, almost of their own accord, well before daylight, seeming to sense the smoother prairie land that lay ahead. Their need for water was again making itself felt. But there was little to be done about that. The river was a long day away.

The day crew rode in and turned their horses over to the wrangler. Erickson, drawing water from the barrel on the side of the chuck wagon, turned to Trevison.

"Saw riders up ahead today."

Farr heard that and moved to Trevison's side. He said: "How many?"

"Four," the cowpuncher replied. "Settin' there on top a hill, watchin' us move up."

"Look like Indians or white men?" Trevison asked.

Erickson shook his head. "Not Indians. They was all wearin' big hats."

"Any idea who they were?"

Erickson shook his head. "Too far off for that."

Trevison turned away, his face knitted into a study. Farr followed him. "Could be riders driftin' along. Don't have to be raiders."

Trevison shrugged. "That's sure, but this is a long way off the main trail for men changing towns. Better double the night guard."

Farr said—"Sure."—and wheeled away. Then he checked to say: "It occur to you there might be a couple o' people just hopin' you wouldn't get this herd through? Like maybe Troy and Jeff Steeg?"

"Troy's got everything to lose, if I don't," Trevison said. "Steeg I could understand trying to stop us, but not Troy. We fail to get this beef to market and turn the money over to Gringras at the bank . . . it's the end of Triangle W."

"You think that means anything to Troy? No matter what kind of man Virgil was, he kept thinkin' about the ranch. Troy's not that way. He thinks about Troy, nothin' and nobody else."

"Tom was half in each of them," Trevison said thoughtfully. "Too bad the two of them couldn't have been one man. Maybe he would have been more like Tom."

Farr considered this. "Reckon that's about right."

Trevison listened to him clomp away in the dark, and then swung to the corral. He picked up his horse and rode off into the night, striking due east. He rode for the better part of four hours, climbing the low hills, throwing his search in all directions for the glow of fire, the sound of a camp—for anything that would reveal the location of the riders Erickson had seen. But if they were still in the country, they kept well hidden. Trevison returned to his own camp, heartened by the thought it was the last they would spend off the main trail.

There were no signs of the mysterious riders on the following day. The herd reached the smooth country and, sensing the river, moved fast. Around the late part of the afternoon the broad, silver band of the Red came into view, and the crew let the herd have its head. It broke and ran, stringing out across the grassland like a brown, gray, and white flood, not stopping until it had merged with the river, until the cattle were standing belly deep in the water. When they had slaked their thirst, they began to drift for the opposite shore, to collect there in small bunches.

That was when the raiders struck.

They came from the screening border of trees beyond. A dozen riders or more. Trevison, riding near the back of the herd, caught the crackling splatter of their gunshots, and had sporadic glimpses of them through the dust being churned up on the far bank by the cattle. He yelled at Farr 100 yards away and dug spurs into his horse's flanks.

Several hundred steers were across, on the firm

ground at the opposite side of the river. At the first crash of gunfire they veered madly away, running northward parallel to the river. Water sheeted out in arcing, red-tinged spray as Trevison drove recklessly off the bank. The shots had started the main body of the herd to milling, and now they were attempting to wheel in midstream and go back. There was that immediate danger of disaster in the river.

"Keep them coming across!" Trevison yelled to Farr.

The old cowpuncher, driving hard behind him, ducked his head in understanding and spun away, boring straight into the wildly struggling longhorns. A rider came off the bank in front of Trevison, following Farr. Trevison reached the far side coming up onto the rocky ground. A large herd of steers was stampeding upriver, a half dozen men in their wake, hazing them with gunshots and shouts.

At that moment Trevison caught sight of the chuck wagon up ahead. The cook had pulled to a stop and was out of the wagon and down on one knee firing at the raiders with a rifle. He buckled suddenly and fell forward as the raiders swept by.

Jesse Shelton rode up, his face dust-caked and strained. He had his revolver in his hand. He said—"They got Tim!"—and fought to keep his nervous, wild-eyed horse still.

Grim-faced, Trevison flung a glance at the herd. Farr and the others were getting it under control. He said—"Let's go after them, Jesse!"—and sent his horse plunging ahead. Shelton came closely behind. The stampeding steers were now far ahead, almost lost in the lifting pall of dust and rapidly falling darkness.

Another Triangle W rider swung in beside Trevison. Over in the river the main herd was still threshing around in the water. Several steers were down, being trampled and drowned as other fear-struck animals struggled to reach solid ground. A gun cracked somewhere ahead and Trevison heard the moan of a bullet over his head.

Three of the raiders were cutting away, coming back and firing as they rode. A fourth was bearing straight for the chuck wagon. Trevison snapped a quick shot at the nearest rider. It was a clean miss and this brought a low curse to his lips. He fired again and this time the man jolted in the saddle, clutched at his leg, and veered off. Jesse Shelton and the other cowpuncher were off to his left, shooting steadily. The remaining two raiders began to swing away.

"Chuck wagon!" Shelton yelled.

Trevison swiveled his attention to that. It was a rising mass of flames, the horses fighting wildly in their harness to escape the fire. Trevison raced toward it. Jesse Shelton said—"I'll fuller them hounds!"—and stopped abruptly. A bullet had caught him. He folded silently and tumbled from the saddle.

Trevison drove hard for the chuck wagon, a blazing torch pulled madly in a wide circle by the crazed horses. It capsized suddenly, throwing a dozen smaller torches, from its interior, up and out into the night as bedrolls, groceries, and miscellaneous equipment were flung free. The horses broke loose and went screaming away across the prairie.

The two remaining raiders were lining it for the stampeded stock, now out of sight in a band of trees far on ahead. Trevison, furious at the loss of Shelton, of Tim the cook, as well as the stock, jerked his horse to a halt. Steadying his gun with a crossed forearm, he took deliberate aim and fired. One of the escaping raiders stiffened and fell heavily. His companion ducked lower over his mount's neck and spurred on. Trevison again took careful bead. But his bullet was low. It struck the man's horse instead. It staggered in flight and went to its knees. Trevison fired again quickly, and missed. The raider, luck favoring him, ran a dozen yards and caught up his fallen buddy's horse, vaulted into the saddle, and was again running hard. Trevison threw another shot at him, but by then he was too distant and the darkness made him a difficult target.

The rider who had sided him with Shelton came

up, his face flushed with the excitement. “Jesse’s dead. We go after them?”

Trevison shook his head. “Better go back and help Jay and the boys. Don’t want to lose any more stock. I’ll see about the cook.”

The cowboy spun away, and Trevison rode on to where the cook lay. He was dead, shot through the chest. Trevison walked to where the wagon still glowed in the darkness. Provisions lay scattered about, along with pots and pans, some of it ruined and beyond use, some of it fairly intact. The water barrel was smashed. Blankets and bedrolls were smoldering lumps. Trevison stood silently in the center of it all, anger not yet gone from his tall frame. It had been a neat, well-planned attack. It had caught them when they were least able to defend the herd. And two men were dead. Jesse Shelton and the cook.

He strode back to the buckskin and stepped to the saddle. A mile away he could hear the bawling of the herd, but he did not immediately turn to them. He went, instead, to where the dead raider lay. Perhaps it would be a face he would recognize, and thereby verify a dull suspicion that was glowing within him. He dismounted and rolled the man to his back. Striking a match, he looked closely at the stiff drawn features. It was a stranger.

Farr rode up to meet him when he returned. What was left of the herd was finally across, drifting slowly away from the river. They were tired, nervous, and the crew was holding them in a tight circle.

Farr said: "Lost a man there in the river. Horse fell and he drowned 'fore we could get him out from under them critters. Lost about seventy head of stock, too."

Trevison said: "They got Jesse and the cook."

Farr swore softly. "Mighty hard to take. We goin' after them?"

Trevison shook his head. "Probably the worst thing we could do. They'd sure be back soon as we got out of sight. I think we all better sit tight with the herd until daylight. Then I'll do a little looking around."

"Reckon you're right. Hate losin' all them steers, though. How many you figure they got?"

"Good three hundred head."

"How about the chuck wagon? I saw it burnin', seems like."

"They set it afire. Most of the grub is lost. And the water. Guess we can make out until we reach the next town, but you better name somebody to cook so he can get a meal started. We'll night camp about a mile ahead."

Farr cut around and disappeared into the darkness. Trevison rode to where Shelton lay. Dismounting, he shouldered the man's body to his saddle and led the horse to the edge of the trees. Here he laid the man down beyond the reach of the herd. He brought up the cook and then the raider and placed them beside the cowpuncher. The cowboy who had drowned in the river was brought in by Erickson.

Later, with Erickson, he set about collecting the food and other items that were usable. When Farr and the herd moved into the swale for the stop, they had a camp of sorts established. The men were sobered by the deaths of Shelton and the others. They wordlessly assisted the new cook in getting the fire going, and performed the many chores attendant to getting the meal ready without being asked. When they had finished with their light rations, they exchanged guard duty with the other riders, so they might eat.

They buried the four men there off the trail, piling rocks over the graves and marking them with crude crosses. In the flickering torchlight they had laid them side-by-side, the raider with them, for even a man such as he deserved a decent burial.

The night hawk had his rope corral up and, when Trevison, far from sleep, went there for a mount that he could use in looking over the herd, he found the wrangler standing near Shelton's sorrel pony, rubbing him affectionately along the nose.

"Reckon this old hoss'll miss Jesse," the man said as Trevison came up. "Jesse had him learned to nuzzle for sugar." He paused. "Was you near Jesse when he got his, Mister Trevison?"

Trevison said: "Yes. It was quick."

The wrangler looked off, his gaze on the faint, distant shine of the river. "Lot of men layin' under the ground on this old trail. Good ones and bad ones both. You reckon it'll always be like that? Shoutin' and killin' and raidin' a man's cattle like they done? Why can't they get some law up here?"

"They'll have it someday, Dobie," Trevison said. "Thing like this can't go on forever."

"Sure like to lay my sights on the ranny what shot old Jess. And Tim, too."

"The one that got Jesse is dead. We buried him back there in the trees."

"But he's dead too late for Jesse. You need a horse, Mister Trevison? How about takin' Jesse's sorrel? I think he'd like for you to be ridin' him out there tonight."

Trevison nodded, and swung to the horse's back. The saddle was not large enough for his liking, and he knew the sorrel was tired, but he would not ride long. Just a short run to look at the cattle. By then he would be sleepy. He smiled to the wrangler and moved off into the darkness. Anyway, why argue with a sentimental cowboy?

They replenished their food stores at a small town in the Indian Territory, obtaining also a wagon that would serve their purpose. The herd moved along at a good average speed, feeding well. Being one of the first drives, the grass was yet in fine condition.

They lost twenty more head near the Canadian River when a crashing thunderstorm struck and set the herd to running. Trevison and Farr kept them stampeding in the right direction, however, and, when the race was over, they had gained a few miles despite the loss of steers.

After that, days were much the same, starting early, ending late, with always a sharp look-out for raiders. That particular night, as they made camp a few miles from the North Fork of the Canadian, Farr asked: "You think we'll run into that stock of ours in Dodge? Doubt if they're far ahead of us."

Trevison said: "Don't think it's likely. They'll never go to Dodge. They'll swing wide, missing the town and head on for Montana or the Dakotas."

"Not much of a herd to drive that far," one of the riders commented.

"The steers they got from us are just a part of their herd, if it's one of the usual raider bunch. They get together and hit the trails for a month or so, collecting all the beef they can get, and hiding it somewhere off the main run. Then they blot the brands and put on their own. When they got a fair-sized herd, they drive it to a railhead some place and sell it."

"Why you figure they won't get to Dodge?"

"Most drives on the trail end there. Less chance of them getting spotted at some other railhead."

"Sure like to set my eyes on one of them critters with a Triangle W brand on it," the cowpuncher said. "Have me some fun makin' the jasper with it explain where he got it."

"Don't worry," Farr said, pouring himself another cup of coffee, "we'll never set our peepers on them steers again . . . and know it. They'll be wearin' somebody else's mark by then."

They crossed the sluggish Cimarron and were in Kansas, four days out of Dodge City. Trevison did not ride on ahead, as many a trail boss did. For one thing, he still searched for the raiders and the missing steers, making wide forays each night and working far ahead of the herd during the daylight hours, hoping to pick up their trail. But it would seem they had disappeared from the face of the earth. He found no trace of them.

XVII

They bedded the herd down about three miles south of town. It was cool and cloudy and it had showered briefly that morning. The cattle were quiet and willing to stop to graze on the sparse prairie. Leaving Jay Farr in charge, Trevison rode into Dodge City.

It was shortly before noon and the streets were teeming with traffic. He traveled the length of

Front Street and two others, hauling up finally at the railroad office. Tying up at the rail, he entered the small quarters where a man with sharp eyes and quick, bird-like movements sat behind a scarred desk. He glanced up at Trevison, smiling.

"What can I do for you, cowboy?"

"Looking for Phillips, the agent."

"That's me," the man said heartily. He came out of his chair, surveying Trevison's trail-stained shape. "You the man bringing in that herd from Texas?"

Trevison said: "My name's Crewes. I brought in a herd. Whether it's the one you heard about I wouldn't know. I've got them bedded down a little ways below town. Thought maybe you could put me in touch with some buyers."

"Sure," Phillips said. He reached into his inside pocket. "Got a letter here for you."

Trevison took the note, sealed in a railroad company envelope, and ripped it open. It was a receipt for 326 steers. It was made out to Troy Washburn, who was signing, it noted, for James Crewes.

"Washburn said you'd be along later with the rest of the cattle. I was to hold these in the pens until you arrived."

Trevison turned the envelope over in his hands. It was addressed to James Crewes—not Trevison. Trevison's mind raced ahead to an understanding; Troy had executed the raid, and then repented his actions. In that there was some sort of victory; Troy, at last, had come of age, had accepted his responsibilities and become a man. Too, he had labeled the note for Crewes, not Trevison, indicating he was respecting the big man's desire to remain unknown.

Anger lifted in Trevison then. Maybe Troy was sorry for what he had done, but forgetting was not that easy—or so simple. Three good men, not to mention the raider, were dead beneath the dust along the trail, all because of him. And that was hard to overlook.

Phillips said: "Washburn went on. Said he'd see you at the ranch."

"When was he here?"

"Day before yesterday. What happened anyway? You get separated somehow?"

Trevison said: "Yes, that's the way of it. Now, where's those buyers? Like to get that herd off my hands before the day's over."

Phillips lifted a flat-crowned hat from a hall tree and moved to the doorway. "Only one man in town now but prices are good. He'll pay you top."

They walked to the Dodge House and found the buyer, a man named Gunderson. They had a drink together, and then all three, with a tally man, returned to where Farr held the herd. Gunderson spent an hour working through the herd, checking it critically, and, when he was satisfied, came back to where Trevison and Farr waited with Phillips.

"Pretty good shape," he commented. "Always like these early drives. Beef's good. I'll give fourteen dollars."

Trevison considered for a moment. "Make it fifteen and you've got a deal."

Gunderson thought that out, plucking at the loose skin under his chin. "Sold," he said finally. "Move 'em to the loading pens. My man here will do the tallying . . . with one of yours, of course."

Trevison ducked his head at Farr. "He will look after our end of it."

Farr swung away to get the herd moving. Gunderson settled himself back into Phillips's buggy. "How do you want your money?"

"Twenty-five hundred in cash, so I can pay off the men. A draft on the rest. Make it payable to Frank Gringras, West Texas Bank. It's at Canaan."

Gunderson wrote it all down in a small, folding notebook. "Meet you in Phillips's office, ten o'clock tomorrow morning. So long."

The buggy sliced away and started for town. Trevison stepped to the saddle and followed Farr, already getting the herd into motion. After it was under way, he rode up beside the old cowpuncher and told him about Troy and the steers waiting in the loading pens. When he was finished, Farr wagged his head.

"Sure took an almighty long time, but I guess that boy's finally growed up."

"Only one thing wrong with it," Trevison said.

"Yeah? Now, what's that?"

"There's four men dead back there on the trail. Troy's growing up came a little late for them."

The tally man was waiting when they moved the herd in toward the pens. Trevison showed him the receipt for the 300-odd head Troy had left, and the man took up the count from there. Trevison helped for the better part of the afternoon, and then went on into town after telling Farr to bring the crew to the Dodge House for the night.

The release from the long drive and its weighty responsibilities was beginning to make itself felt, as he rode into a livery barn and stabled his horse. It was difficult to believe the job was almost over, that the endless hours of worry, and tension, and everlasting vigilance against the many dangers were done. It was like coming alive again. Like a condemned man receiving a last minute, unexpected reprieve. That thought sobered him.

The stableman came up, taking the leathers from his hand. Trevison said: "You the owner here?"

The man said: "Sure. Name's Jensen. Something I can do for you?"

"Got about fifty head of horses I'd like to sell. They're out near the loading pens. You interested?"

The stableman looked thoughtful. "Well," he said cautiously, "might be. Horses not worth much around here. Every trail herd comes up dumps their nags here in Dodge. Keeps prices beat down pretty low."

Trevison said: "Take a look at them anyway. Triangle W brand. I'll be at the Dodge House if you want to make me an offer. Name's Crewes."

Trevison strolled along the street, having his look at the old and familiar places, remembering the good things that were in his mind. He registered at the hotel, informing the clerk that his crew of eleven men would arrive later, and to have quarters ready for them.

At the old Long Branch saloon he had a drink, and from there went to the barbershop. He waited his turn for a hot bath in the tin tub in the back room. Afterward, he had a shave and a haircut, preserving most of the beard acquired on the trail. He made that one concession to caution. He doubted anyone in Dodge would recognize him, but he was so near the finish line now he was taking no chances.

He bought himself some new clothes: Levi's, a couple of shirts, a new pair of boots, underwear, and a jumper at Zimmerman's place. He wound up the shopping spree with a steak and potato meal at the Bon Ton Café. When Farr and the crew came into the Dodge House at full dark, he was sprawled contentedly in one of the deep chairs in the lobby.

"That's for me." Farr grinned, and went to his room.

Trevison advanced the crew money from the amount he had drawn in Canaan for expenses at the beginning of the drive, advising them to meet him the following day at the railroad offices when he would pay off in full. They went their ways, some to follow much the same pattern he had just concluded, others to celebrate the end of the trail in typical manner.

The stableman came in soon after that, bringing with him a man he introduced as his partner. Trevison accepted their offer, reserving enough mounts and pack animals for the return trip. Thus, it was all done; nothing remained now except the meeting with Gunderson and the payoff. Then it was back to Canaan.

He had considered the possibility of sending the remaining money and the draft back with Jay Farr, knowing it would be in safe, honest hands. But he had told Gringras he would finish the job and lay the money in his hands personally, and, until that was done, his obligation to Tom Washburn was incomplete. Farr would do this for him, but he would not have it that way.

He walked out into the street. Dodge City was in full night bloom, lights from the stores and saloons bringing all things alive. He started along the dusty way, thinking again of Canaan, of Halla Greer. Like a picture, he could remember the way she looked at him, the deep, mysterious seriousness of her, the cool grayness of her eyes that looked upon him with such calm reserve and remoteness. But Halla, however indelibly she was stamped upon him, was not for him. He kept telling himself that, knowing it to be utter fact. A door had closed that day Virgil Washburn had died and Roxie had turned to him for solace. And it was a door he dared not reopen for it could lead to nothing but emptiness.

He thought then of Roxie. She was here in Dodge, waiting for him. Then he thought of Halla Greer—the woman he loved. Roxie would have to forget him—he could never go to her.

He stood for a minute, there at the edge of the street, while people pushed by him and the dust hung like a thin, silver fog in the cañon between the buildings. Talk, shouts, laughter, and the hammering of pianos floated lightly through the warm night. Somewhere, over near the Long Branch, an exuberant cowboy emptied his revolver, the shots hollow and flat.

XVIII

He rode into Canaan on a bright June day with the sun streaming out of a cloudless sky. Jay Farr and the five men who had elected to return to the ranch had cut off back up the trail and likely now were making themselves at home in the Washburn bunkhouse. Three horses stood hipshot in front of the Longhorn, and farther along he noted Noble Greer's yellow-wheeled buggy at the general store; the rancher was probably taking on some supplies. Trevison headed for the bank.

Frank Gringras sat at his desk and the clerk behind his wire cage thumbed through a stack of papers as Trevison entered. The banker came out of his chair hurriedly, a broad smile wreathing his face.

"Trevison! Sure good to see you! You made a right fast trip."

Trevison nodded his greeting. "A thing I wanted to get done in a hurry," he said dryly. He withdrew the letter from his pocket, the same envelope Troy Washburn had left for him with the railroad agent. "Everything's in here. The draft, and what money I had left from the cash after paying off the crew. Look it over and see if it tallies."

Gringras laid it aside. "Later be all right? Or are you in a hurry?"

"Figure to ride on tonight if everything's settled up. Appreciate you checking it right now."

The banker emptied the envelope on his desk. He counted the money and figured for a minute with his pencil. Then he said: "Right to the penny. Except, you didn't draw your own wages."

"None necessary," Trevison answered with a shake of his head.

"But Tom said you were to be paid. Hundred dollars a month. Only right you should take it."

"Maybe," Trevison said, "but I don't need it and I don't want it. I will keep the bay horse I'm riding, if that's all right with you."

Gringras said: "Well, if that's the way you want it. The horse is yours, of course." He paused. "Troy says he was there in Dodge."

"Ahead of me," Trevison said non-committally. "I didn't see him."

"Mighty fine thing, way that boy's changed. He'll do all right now. Tom can thank you for that, too."

Trevison gave him a bitter smile. "Doubt if it's any of my fault. Everybody grows up someday."

"I suppose," Gringras said absently. "Sorry you want to push on. Country's wide open for good cattle growers. You could do right well around here on a ranch of your own. I expect you could stay on and run the Washburn place, if you took your mind to."

"Guess I'm not the settling-down kind," he said, and offered his hand. "Thanks for the help."

Gringras smiled. "It's my thanks to you."

He stepped outside and walked a half dozen feet into the street, throwing his glance again toward the general store. Greer's buggy was still there, and now Halla sat in the seat while her father loaded a box in the rear. As he looked, Halla turned and saw him standing there. She started, a smile breaking across her lips.

In that same instant Jeff Steeg's coarse voice came reaching across from the Longhorn, shattering the quiet.

"Hello, Trevison! Been waitin' around for you!"

Trevison wheeled slowly about, the impact of the man's tone conveying its message of danger.

"Went and done me a mite of checkin' while you was gone. Over in Abilene, at the marshal's office. They got a real nice picture of you there, Trevison."

So time had finally run out, after all. Trevison settled gently in his tracks, squaring himself away. The old coolness sifted through him; the danger-ridden moments of the long trail were once again with him. It turned him grim and nerveless, once more the lone wolf with the instinct to live, to kill to live. He watched Steeg narrowly, seeing him move deeper into the street. He came to a spraddle-legged halt thirty feet away.

"Best thing about that picture, Trevison, was what it said. One thousand dollars reward! Dead or alive!" Steeg's face was a leering, grinning mask.

The street had become a breathless, silent cañon of trapped heat. Behind him Trevison could hear Gringras and his clerk, the scraping of their boots plain as they moved to a window to watch. Halla and her father, he knew without looking, were still there. But nobody else. Only the empty, twisted street.

Trevison said: "All right, Steeg. It's up to you."

"That the way you want it?"

"You'll have to take me."

From the corner of his eye Trevison saw the

figure of Sheriff Bradford come out of his office and halt suddenly. A moment later the man's voice called out: "Hold up there, Jeff! Wait a minute!"

Steeg laughed, a harsh and grating sound. "Stand back, Sheriff. He's my pigeon. Worth a thousand dollars in gold to me up in Montana, dead or alive. And he wants it dead!"

"Wait . . . !" Bradford's voice sang out again.

Trevison saw the break in Steeg's expression as he went for his gun. His own hand flashed down. It came up, his gun firing twice. Steeg caught both bullets. He stiffened, fell, dead before he struck the ground.

Trevison remained in that pose, half crouched. He swung slowly to Bradford, eyes dark, glittering slits.

"All right, Sheriff. Let's finish it now. What I said goes for you, too. You'll have to take me."

Bradford hauled up short. "Put up that gun, Trevison! That's what I was trying to tell Jeff."

Trevison was conscious of Gringras, coming up from behind, of Bradford's rattle of words. He turned slightly and saw Halla. She was staring at him, her face a mirror of horror, her eyes filled with fear.

"You're not wanted in Montana. Done a little checking with the deputy U.S. marshal in Miles City . . . telegraphed him about a dodger I saw in Abilene. That sheriff and the deputy you shot were both crooked as a dog's hind leg. They'd been in on a bank robbery in Cheyenne. Law was getting close. Seen a chance to hang it on you . . . and tried. The deputy was caught red-handed, shot it out, and confessed it all before he died. Seems you done the law a favor shooting that sheriff."

Not wanted for murder! Not an outlaw! He half turned about. Halla was getting down from the buggy. He watched her reach the ground and start toward him.

"You've been worrying about your back trail all this time for nothing."

Trevison heard the words in a maze of confused clamor within his own mind. It was coming hard to him, this realization he was at last a free man, that he no longer need fear the shadows and closed doors, and that which lay around a corner. He opened his arms and Halla came rushing into them. He drew her closely.

"Oh, Wayne!" she sobbed. "I didn't know how much you meant to me until I saw you there . . . standing facing him with a gun!" She trembled violently.

Trevison pressed her to him, the last vestige of reluctance flowing from him. He said softly: "Never mind. It's all finished now. Over for good."

"I don't care about anything, about anybody! I'll go with you anywhere, do what you have to do. . . ."

She had not heard Bradford's words. She still did not understand what had happened. He felt humble there with her in his arms, hearing her declare her love for him—regardless of who he was—and what lay before him.

He said: “There’s no cause for any of that now. I’ve been cleared in Miles City. There’s no longer any price on my head.”

It took a long moment for the meaning of that to break through her anxiety, to reach her. And then a long sigh escaped her lips. “Then you can stay? You don’t have to go?”

“Not unless you want me to, Halla.”

“Nothing matters,” she said. “Nothing, as long as we’re together.”

From his shoulder he heard Gringras say: “Come in when you got time and we’ll talk about that spread for you. What I said back there in the bank still goes.”

Noble Greer chuckled. “You’re wasting your time, Frank. Looks like Trevison’s already got himself a place to look after . . . mine.”

About the Author

Ray Hogan was an author who inspired a loyal following over the years since he published his first Western novel, *Ex-Marshal*, in 1956. Hogan was born in Willow Springs, Missouri, where his father was town marshal. At five the Hogan family moved to Albuquerque where they lived in the foothills of the Sandia and Manzano mountains. His father was on the Albuquerque police force and, in later years, owned the Overland Hotel. It was while listening to his father and other old-timers tell tales from the past that Ray was inspired to recast these tales in fiction. From the beginning he did exhaustive research into the history and the people of the Old West, and the walls of his study were lined with various firearms, spurs, pictures, books, and memorabilia, about all of which he could talk in dramatic detail. "I've attempted to capture the courage and bravery of those men and women that lived out West and the dangers and problems they had to overcome," Hogan once remarked. If his lawmen protagonists seem sometimes larger than life, it is because they are men of integrity, heroes who through grit of character and common sense are able to overcome the obstacles they encounter despite often overwhelming odds. This same grit of character can also be found in Hogan's heroines, and in *The Vengeance of Fortuna West* (1983) Hogan wrote a gripping and totally believable account of a woman who takes up the badge and tracks the men who killed her lawman husband by ambush. No less intriguing in her way is Nellie Dupray, convicted of rustling in *The Glory Trail* (1978). One of his most popular books, dealing with an earlier period in the West with Kit Carson as its protagonist, is *Soldier in Buckskin* (Five Star Westerns, 1996). Above all, what is most impressive about Hogan's Western novels is the consistent quality with which each is crafted, the compelling depth of his characters, and his ability to juxtapose the complexities of human conflict into narratives always as intensely interesting as they are emotionally involving.

Center Point Publishing
600 Brooks Road • PO Box 1
Thorndike ME 04986-0001 USA

(207) 568-3717

US & Canada:
1 800 929-9108
www.centerpointlargeprint.com